CARLI'S KILLS

Kyle Michel Sullivan

Published 2022 by
KMSCB, Buffalo NY

For adults only

Font cover photo courtesy Shutterstock
Back cover photo by JamTheCat
Cover design by JamTheCat
Copyright 2022 by Kyle Michel Sullivan, DBA: KMSCB
ISBN 978-1-7376331-3-6

Acknowledgements

Thanks to Vicki Johnson Howard and Sue Bowdley for their help in editing and keeping the book on the right track

CARLI'S KILLS

Table of Contents

You Gotta Start Somewhere

Well...the one thing Carli Vincenzo did *not* expect, this evening, was live porn. Granted, she wasn't exactly supposed to be where she was — hidden in the massive walk-in closet of a massive master bedroom of a massive condo on the twenty-fifth floor, on a Saturday night. Okay, early Sunday morning. But since the woman inhabiting that condo had been out with her latest boyfriend for a late dinner, she really should not have been surprised when they wound up in bed, having very involved sex. The only surprise was how she seemed to enjoy him just as much as he was enjoying her, if you went by her groans, gasps, sighs, snarls, groping hands and kicking legs, and those perfectly manicured fingernails digging into his totally naked ass.

He was Michael Avery Malsby, but he was immaterial to the task at hand. Carli's focus was one Anastasia Florencia Deveaux, known as Stasi to her minions. Her, Carli hated with every fiber of her being.

To start with, she was twenty-three years old, ten years Carli's junior and fifteen years younger than pretty-boy Mikey. Height? Five-seven. Weight? A hundred and ten pounds. Body by personal trainer, which meant strength was less important than looking good. What threw it all off was her breasts, which were definitely enhanced by some upscale cretin in Beverly Hills. There was also the rather obvious nose job, which did rather help the symmetry of her face while mitigating the cold hint of cruelty in her big, bad, baby-blue eyes but failed to mitigate the fact that her head was probably a size too large for the rest of her.

All of which disgusted Carli.

Seriously, how could any man be attracted to a plastic, entitled bitch, like her? Was it the challenge of being the one guy who could handle *Little Miss I Count And You Don't* when no one else could? Talk about dumb; all he would find was he had greatly overestimated his prowess in that department.

And yet, here was Mikey, the latest in what Carli knew was a long line of idiots. Apparently, Stasi showing a willingness to get as down and dirty and hard at fucking as any of her lads meant they thought they were important to her.

God, why are men so stupid?

Of course, consciously ticking off Stasi's so-called *attributes* meant subconsciously comparing them to her own, whether she intended to or not. Yes, she was twenty-five pounds heavier than this wisp of nothingness, but she was also three inches taller, with natural curves and un-enhanced breasts that looked damn good. And she was strong, thanks to fourteen years in the army. She also had brown hair, dark eyes and lips that were the most kissable ever, according to the men *she* had known, so she had confidence enough in herself and her abilities to not let sluts like Stasi wear her down.

Another thing that helped her self-confidence was watching Mikey think what he was giving her really good sex, with his humpity-humpity-bunny-fuckity-fuckity ways. She halfway wondered if she should take him on just to show him the true path to nirvana. The way to so many serious, solid, screaming sensations, you wind up blind, for an instant, at the moment of climax. The kind that lifts you into the clouds and dances with you amongst the stars. He looked enough like Chris Evans for her to want to, and she knew that if she did, he would never cast a glance at a superficial Barbi-bitch like Stasi, again.

Seriously, everything about her was so surface level, from her too-tight designer outfits to her B-Hills coiffed hair to her silver manicure. Hell, silver everything! As in the molding atop the polished white walls and even the floorboards. As in silver lamé drapes flanking sliding glass doors that opened to the silver railing on the balcony. As in even the fucking sheets, comforter and duvet. Add to that the six-inch deep carpet in black and white waves with a faux polar bear rug atop it, Carli's sense of taste was hideously offended. What made it worse was the massive shell-like headboard done in chrome and so perfectly polished, it looked like a *Debbie Does Dallas* version of the mirror scene in *The Lady From Shanghai*. Especially as it reflected Mikey's ass moving up and down in a half-dozen angles while Stasi's legs wiggled beside it like a crab grabbing at the air.

Talk about creepy.

Fortunately, the room faced south, to overlook the LA basin. Much better than east or west, where the morning or evening sun could blast in against that headboard and shoot out a beam so hot it could whip up a fire as far away as Malibu.

Or Silver Lake.

Of course, the whole condo had the same emphasis. Dozens of photos of Stasi on the walls, in silver frames. No plants to cut through the knife-like decor. The only books were on coffee and end tables, all of them wrapped in polished silver bindings.

A peasant's version of nouveau-riche.

But what could one expect? Daddy had built his multi-millions in real estate back in Phoenix, straight out of a double-wide mobile home for the first ten years, so she was not born into a taste-oriented family. Nothing wrong with how daddy got started; it's how he wound up wearing ten-thousand dollar bespoke suits with ostrich cowboy boots that cost two-thousand dollars. And having a twenty-six year-old trophy wife ensconced in a penthouse on Phoenix's North Central. And actually thought buying himself a seat in the Legislature was the same as buying some class.

As for Stasi's mom, she now played drunk golf in cotton, khaki and turquoise ensembles outside a faux-Pueblo condo that fronted an evergreen course that cost more to keep watered than interest payments on the national debt. Pathetic people who thought wasting money showed how important they were, and who stupidly thought that also bought love. It was so steeped in desperation, she might have felt sorry for Stasi had the little bitch not caused the death of someone Carli loved.

So Carli had cringed her way through the rooms, after sneaking in, looking for the best spot to sit and wait for her prey to come home. Her baby-bro, TF, a massive computer maven, had sussed out Mikey was escorting Stasi to *Rudolpho's Bistro*, one of those fine dining establishments where they charge to breathe the air and *recommend* at least two hours to truly enjoy your repast.

Carli didn't ask how he had sourced this info, mainly because he was so secretive about it, he wouldn't have told her, anyway. As he had once said in response to a question, "Better not to know and be able to go than not."

It seemed to make sense, at the time.

Anyway, despite the building's vaunted security system, TF had wormed a way in so Carli would not be seen, heard, noticed, or recorded, he was such a whiz.

If that description's still used, today, Carli thought.

"The residents have key fobs to get in and out," he had told her. "If that's lost, they have passcodes to override it."

"Even the garage?" she had asked.

"That's a micro-bug fixed on the car. It's automatic and the code is noted in their system. Too fuckin' easy."

"And you've got the override?"

He had cast her a withering glance that all but screamed, *Carls, c'mon.*

So in through the garage she had gone. In fact, the one negative aspect was how she had to race up twenty-five flights of stairs within a certain timeframe to get to Stasi's floor. TF had set their cameras to loop for a certain amount of time, and while she was in good shape, that was still more Stairmaster than she'd done in the last six months.

"Damn me for slacking off," she'd grumbled at level fifteen.

But they had timed it so she could pop into the condo before the loop ended. Then she had time enough to find the spare keys to Stasi's big, bad, silver Mercedes, and take a moment to Zen.

Until an hour later.

When Carli had heard Mikey softly purr, "Y'know, Stasi, I don't need another drink...not right now..."

"Oh, are we in a horny hurry? Or about to fall flat?"

God, even the tone of her voice was grating.

Both had sounded a bit drunk with wine and lust, if one went by the giggling and growling between them. So into the closet Carli had slipped, leaving the door open just enough to peek out and watch. Not because she wanted to see Stasi strip down; it was big, bad Mikey she was curious about. Visually. The photo TF had pulled up provided promise.

Which was fulfilled when they stumbled into the bedroom and he doffed his shirt to reveal a well-pumped back. Then shifted his pants down to expose tight, dove-gray boxer-briefs covering a nice round butt. Then he yanked the briefs off to verify he was definitely concu-boy material.

Oh, and could I handle that, Carli giggled to herself.

Finally, he and Stasi had fallen on the bed, and he had started his bunny-humping against her. Normally, that would be a demerit, in Carli's book, but some good clenching action by his rear cheeks mitigated the notion. As did the strong legs and fine hands, and how he'd focused his lips on her breasts and neck and kisses at the same time he was bopping in and out and up and down.

Carli had a good idea he was not like this with his lady, by marriage. The wife was probably there to make a home and care for the kids and present a nice patriarchal front to the world. True of too damn many men, still. Which was why Carli had sworn never to get married. She had long seen the institution as a means for males to own females and was nowhere near about being equals. To those men, the home-bound-female was in one cubicle of their tiny brains, the world of available women in another, and thanks to their sense of self-importance, everything was wired to the head of their dick instead of the one on their shoulders.

Carli's own research had proven Stasi loved to use that to her advantage. Not for money. No, it seemed more like the power trip of fucking with another woman's life so she could have fun with any man she wanted. Which would last until the guy started getting too close; then he'd get kicked to the curb.

So that made Mikey another himbo thinking he was Einstein.

Which is what made her decide to let him live. She hated to hurt pretty things, and there was no sense in wasting someone who might be fun to use, later. Especially if he wasn't really involved in the issue at hand. Might even arrange to *meet cute,* so as to draw him into her sphere, since there was no question he would soon be an *un*-married man. And horn dogs who get dumped by their wives are easy pickin's.

And there are lots of you I wouldn't mind picking at, she told herself. *But first things first. Get it done, folks.*

As in, finish up.

Today, okay?

Damn...another merit for Mikey was his staying power. Very few men lasted more than five minutes pumping in and out like he was, and they'd been at it for a good twelve.

Not that Carli was keeping time.

It's just, watching this nonstop live porn was starting to affect her...oh, let's just say, *equilibrium.* Which could detract from her plan.

Not good...but, again, she could handle it.

It's just that Mikey's ass. Mikey's legs. Mikey's back. Shifting and moving in the slashing shadows. Even the nape of his neck, so recently barbered and clean. Drifting into his shoulders. It was all so fucking hot. If Stasi had been a guy, too, that would have made it impossible to keep control.

Nothing like some gay porn to take a girl over the line.

At least he was starting to go faster.

And faster.

And Stasi was close to screaming.

Getting close, they were.

That's when a neighbor pounded on the wall, next door, and howled, "Keep it down in there!" Barely audible but still heard. As expensive as this damn place was, they could have added a tad more insulation during construction.

Good walls make good neighbors, don't ya know, to pervert a phrase.

In response, Stasi got louder. Screamed. Laughed. Dug her nails into Mikey's lovely ass, making him howl.

Waves of desire crashed through Carli and she crushed her legs together. Almost sighed herself into an orgasm.

Faster he went, and faster and faster...until he gulped and jolted and grunted and slammed hard into her.

Once.

Twice.

Oh, yes, so very good, Carli thought. *And here comes a third one. All puns intended. That is a most excellent sign.*

And what was better? Stasi was all but purring. Apparently, Mikey had taken care of her, too.

Oh, he was definitely boy-toy material. Maybe carry him off, afterwards?

*Down all them flights of stairs? Fireman style? Forget it Carli.
File him away, for later.*

Still, she drew in a long, soft, deep breath, letting the sensual
nature of the moment envelop her. Wondered how difficult it would
be to work Mikey up, again, tonight? She knew she looked good, even
under the black, full-body leotard she was wearing. Granted, her lips
were hidden behind a balaclava, but it might be fun to see what she
could get away with, once she was done.

When Mikey finally rolled off Stasi, his front turned out to be
almost as nice as his rear. A good face with features that would do
well in an aftershave commercial. Smooth skin. And a nice-sized
erection that was in the process of dwindling.

But no condom? Oh, that's a demerit, you bad boy.

He lay flat on his back, still breathless and exhausted. Light trails
of sweat whispered off his face and torso as he said, "Oh, shit, Stasi.
I never met a girl could do what you do. Son-of-a-bitch."

Meaning you've never had many girls.

Stasi ran her hands up and down her body, stroking breasts that
were...that were still pointed straight at the ceiling?!

*Did men really think that's how they were supposed to be?
Seriously? God, they really were born stupid.*

Then Stasi sighed, "You were...good."

He laughed. "Comin' from you, that's a real compliment. Never
had a girl rate me as hard as you."

Wait till you hear my rating, hot stuff, Carli smirked.

Stasi looked at him. "How many other girls have you been
with?"

"None, since you."

Her nails toyed with his left nipple, but they were not really
playing, considering how he inadvertently cringed as she said, "Not
even your wife?"

He rose to lean on one arm and look at her. Kiss her. More sweat
trailing down his torso in ways that were elegant and erotic. "That was
never sex. Just another form of masturbation."

Okay, Mikey, never diss the soon-to-be-ex.

Stasi giggled. "You're a sick fuck."

"I try." He kissed her, again. "Would you marry me if I was
free?"

Oh, no, big mistake. Huge. Massive!

Stasi jolted upright, sharp and sudden, startling him. "What the
fuck're you talkin' about?"

"I — uh — it's just — well, Melinda and me, we don't love each
other, anymore. I don't think we ever did, really. It was more like her

dad and my dad wanting to merge families, merge companies, some shit like that, so we got talked into it. Then we had the twins. Now they're off to college. She's goin' nuts trying to make herself look like she's twenty, again, and it...it's scary."

Oh, shit, what'd your parents do? Sell you into marriage straight out of high school? No wonder you're so randy and inexperienced. Take away a demerit.

Stasi jumped from the bed and went to the balcony, saying, "Fuck, Mikey, why you gotta bring that shit up now? We were havin' fun."

"I am," he said, rolling up to his feet like a cat rolls out of bed. He took a long stretch then joined her outside.

Nice shifting motion in the bod, buddy. Oh...and the sheets are wet. Another good sign.

Now they were both out of sight.

It was time.

Carli slipped a police baton from a belt around her waist and gripped it tight in her right hand, then slowly, carefully, quietly opened the closet door.

She stepped out, moving soft enough to be totally silent, to find...

Stasi and Mikey standing on the balcony, their backs to her, looking out over the ocean of shimmering gold lights laid on miles and miles of black velvet, far below. A vague breeze whispered against the silver lamé drapes, catching the warm reflection from below. It was oh-so romantic, just like a Woody Allen movie.

Mikey embraced Stasi around the waist, from behind. "But wouldn't it still be fun if...y'know...if you and me — ?"

"Don't you dare say that fuckin' word, again," she snapped.

He caressed her shoulders. "But I thought — "

She shrugged him off. "No, Mikey, you didn't think. Men like you never do. Well, not with the head on your shoulders."

True, that.

Carli drew closer, silent as death.

The club at the ready.

The two of them stood there, bathed in the glow of a nearly full moon in a clear sky, above.

"Stasi," he said, "I want to be with you."

She turned to him. "Mikey, I like you. I like fuckin' with you. But that's it. And if you're gonna get all possessive and demanding, then that is...it...and..."

Her voice trailed into silence as she looked straight at Carli. Her expression became confused and her mouth opened. Obviously, seeing a black-clad figure approaching you from within your own bedroom just did *not* make sense.

Mikey noticed her gaze and started to turn, asking, "What?"

BAM!

Carli slammed the baton down on his head, sending him to the floor, unconscious.

Before Stasi could even think to scream, Carli jammed the baton between her plastic breasts to shove her over the balcony's railing.

She screamed, then.

All the way down.

Twenty-five floors.

Until she slammed against the tiles next to the pool. The walls and the oh-so-perfectly chlorinated water were stained with her blood and brains.

And that, as they say, was that. Regarding Stasi.

Carli sent a text to TF. *Done*. Then she looked down at Mikey. Still considered sending him after her, on behalf of his wife. But he did make such a lovely picture, lying in the soft moonlight, naked. And the truth was he hadn't actually done anything to die for.

Not like that little bitch had.

She crouched down and brushed a bit of hair from his forehead. It felt nice. Clean. Even being wet with sweat. Then she fondled him, and she had the feeling his balls could have used another milking.

But no time for that.

She tossed the baton out over the balcony, checked her phone then dug Mikey's wallet from his pants for the address on his driver's license. She found some business cards next to it, so removed a glove and, using a fingernail dipped in his blood, wrote it on one of them. Finally she slipped the wallet back in his pants.

She finally got a text that said, *Ready*, so slipped out of the condo and back down the stairs to the garage.

She used the car alarm to find Stasi's Mercedes convertible, quickly screwed a dealer tag over the license plate, pulled off the balaclava, put on a sun hat to hide her face, fired the car up and drove out of the garage without the least bit of trouble.

She was curling off Wilshire onto The 405 when she saw TF's response, on her phone.

Done.

Meaning, he had now erased any trace of him hacking their system. Perfect.

Moments later, she was driving east, along The 10.

* * * * *

Mikey was still unconscious when the building's security crew found him. Blood from the injury to his head stained the polar bear rug. Paramedics were called in and he was rushed to a nearby trauma center, where it was determined he had been struck with something hard and blunt, and he had suffered a severe concussion. He remained unconscious for twenty-nine hours and woke with no memory of what had happened.

They found the baton rolling in Stasi's blood, next to the pool. Careful analysis showed it also had some of Mikey's DNA on it. The blood had ruined any chance of lifting fingerprints, but they didn't really need them. Security cameras showed no unknown person entering the premises. No one snuck down the hall to Stasi's condo. The door showed no sign of forced entry. The only person who could possibly have wielded the club was Stasi.

They did find a hint of unusual activity immediately after she jumped. A silver and chrome Mercedes C Class convertible, with its top up, left the parking garage. A woman in a hat that covered her head was driving, and it had no license plate on the front, just an unreadable dealer tag on the trunk lid. That raised some questions, because none of the guests had a car without regular license plates. A survey of the residents brought no information to clarify that, but the car could not have entered or departed without the proper codes or entry fobs, so it was shrugged off.

The only scenario the police could come up with regarding the death of Anastasia Florencia Deveaux was that in some fit of jealous rage, she had clubbed Mikey, thought she killed him and jumped to her death. Neither her mother nor her father believed it, but search as they might, they could find no indication of anyone else in the condo. No fingerprints or DNA other than hers and Mikey's. Nothing. So Stasi was consigned to that world of crazy females who freak out when a married boyfriend won't divorce his wife. Open and shut case.

At first.

Cantina Nights Ain't Right For Fightin'

To call Cantina Madriza a run-down, low-rent biker bar in the middle of the nothing of Eastern Arizona would actually be a compliment. Surrounded by desert, boulders and rock formations backed by distant mountains? Check. Scrub, cactus, dust storms, tumbleweed stampedes and dirt devils sharing habitation with coyotes, lizards, vultures, prairie dogs and a host of other critters? Check. Are there wide gullies everywhere awash with flood waters from rains in the mountains...for about ten minutes a year? Check. The usual crap.

The building started life as a gas station backed up to a ragged set of foothills. It was fronted by a two-lane blacktop called The 14, that started in a town named Cabrillo and ran due west through the middle of all that nothing straight to The 191. The only spot along that desolate road that wasn't abandoned, long ago.

As for Cabrillo , it was one of those towns that only exist because of an extension campus off a large college established in a larger city — Nathan Cruz University, where the main focus was geology, of course, though studies in antiquities, photography, historical artifacts, and technical-slash-science writing were also offered. Oh, and was there a lot of geology in these hills, flat desert and low plateaus. All stretching back millions of years. All very brown and bleak, except to the Rock-Jocks, as geology majors were referred to by the locals, be they male, female or non-binary.

The Cantina was mostly fake adobe with wooden, shack-like extensions built out in two directions to add interior space. The earth around the eastern side was hard-packed for parking, the western side was chaotic brush and bramble, and between it and the foothill was a long narrow mobile home from the 60s that sported a porch at the front door and was dirty enough to qualify as part of the land.

Inside the Cantina were a medium-length bar, booths lining two walls, tables and chairs scattered about, and a couple of pool tables that had seen better days many, many, many days ago. The floor was slats of wood that creaked, the faux wood-panel walls were lined with neon signs for various breweries, only half of which still glowed bright, and Christmas lights from the 50s covered the ceiling to provide a soft but acceptable level of illumination and faux warmth.

Adding to the general ambience were two large dirty multi-pane windows that almost offered the ability to look out on the nothing that was outside.

The bar had the usual drafts on tap — Coors, Coors, Coors and Michelob — with a selection of bottled brews lined up against the requisite mirror behind it, most of them Mexican. Wine was available if you really-*really* wanted it, and while the selection of quality hard liquor was promising, in truth it was just some cheap crap decanted into a name brand's bottle then sold at premium prices to those who didn't know what good liquor should taste like.

Meaning, the Rock-Jocks.

Ah, yes. The boys and girls of University life. Being in the middle of nowhere and with minimal adult supervision, it made sense that Cantina Madriza attracted hoards of the entitled progeny, for a bit of slumming. Granted, it was more than twenty miles from campus, but that made the place seem even more foreign and exotic. They would zip up in their cute little Beemers and Audis and Jaguar SUVs, and jostle for space in the not so large parking area, laughing loud, as they were wont to do. Scream-talk if they were a pack of Mildreds, which is what the tech-writers were called, since they were usually girls or gay. None would show till after they'd fed at the refectory, since you had to hit Tucson to find a Denny's. Unless you loved things like Mickey-D's, Taco Hell or felt brave enough to trust your insides to Bellamere's, the town's one and only truck stop.

All would sport designer-stressed jeans and jackets that fooled no one; hair coiffed just right, shining and squeaky clean; desperately trying to hide how innocent they really were while not really understanding what easy pickings they were for the biker crowd, even as they were overly sure that daddy could protect them from any-and-everything and make certain they receive the proper genuflections from *their lessers*.

AKA: anyone who was *not* a Rock-Jock or a Mildred.

The only one outside their realm who was held apart from all that condescending rigamarole was Zeke Lindstrom. The bartender. Because he was the epitome of dark-eyed, dark-haired handsomeness. Just shy of thirty, with a neat goatee framing a quiet smile, he was charmingly buffed into fine proportion. Granted, he always wore rather clichéd cargo shorts and a simple dress shirt with sleeves rolled up, as well as Doc Martens, but his perfection was cemented by the tattoos up his left arm, neck and throat in elegant designs that covered sharp, angry scars.

As well as a one-time tracheotomy.

Oh, and that his left leg was bionic; that was the epitome of cool.

How he lost it, no one had the indecency to ask. Instead, many stories were woven to explain it, from a bomb in one of the wars to a nasty motorcycle wreck to falling while rock climbing to a shark attack, all made even more romantic by his refusal to discuss it. Consensus was, any man who looked like that and dressed that simple, and who had obviously been damaged so horribly yet still had a strength and tenderness about him, belonged in nothing less than the latest *Hallmark Movie*, as the hero.

Which is probably why he was nicknamed *Prince Hot Tatts*. Deliberately spelled with two *T*s to make him even more special.

Of course, it didn't hurt that he was also seen as fair, because he carding everybody — old, young, male, female, all IDs were input into the computer, and no ID meant coke or juice, only; no exceptions. The very epitome of even-handedness.

No one ever made a fuss about it, because reality was, if some underage twerp was really serious about getting drunk, there was always a guy playing pool or just sitting in a booth who would sneak a shot of whiskey in that coke or juice for a couple bucks. Sometimes they would even offer something...oh, let's just say *a little extra* to go with it.

Which Zeke was willing to ignore, making him seem even cooler. They didn't know it wasn't because he didn't care but because Dax Castor, leader of a local biker gang, owned the bar, and it was usually guys from his pack who were doing the *offering*. So Zeke would make like the three monkeys and let it be.

So long as the innocents weren't impaired when they ready to leave. Should that happen, they'd get a nice Uber ride for sixty bucks, tip included, on daddy's credit card. Whether they wanted it or not. How they got back to pick up daddy's car was their own problem. More than once a Mercedes had sat in the lot for a couple days before its owner remembered where they'd left it.

Of course, no real biker worth his Hog would show up before ten, by which time most of the kids were gone or Uber'd off to their dorms and condos. Any strays left behind were considered fair game. On more than one occasion, Zeke had gently stepped in to protect the virtue of a college girl...or boy, since even biker chicks were not known for their gentle manner when they were in the mood. Fortunately, the bikers respected him enough to stand down.

The college crew never came on Sundays. It was like an unwritten law that only Hogs and Triumphs were allowed in the parking lot, that night. Then the place was closed Mondays and Tuesdays, to give it time to be cleaned and fixed and restocked and everything. All nice and easy, almost to the point of monotonous.

Just the way Zeke liked it.

But then came the Wednesday after Stasi died.

That night started out quiet. Mid-terms at the university meant the entitled ones were in self-imposed lock-down till Friday, and next week was Spring Break, so it would be completely dead. Still her suicide was the talk of the bar with the bikers who came in, because she was infamous in the area. Once a student at Nathan Cruz, her far too notorious life had long been a topic of gossip and innuendo. They chatted with Zeke for a bit, and he even joined them in a beer, but there was a carefulness to him that refused to draw any information from him, about her, so the conversations had not lasted long.

Causing some to say they *just knew* he'd had a thing for the crazy little bitch and that was why he was so stand-offish: he was sad. Others laughed it off, insisting Zeke would never fall for someone like her. It made for some spirited discussions, which he just smiled over. People could be so silly.

But then a woman showed up. Tall and curvaceous, wearing tight, black flared jeans, a black quilted jacket from some designer, and a black shirt unbuttoned just far enough to reveal a nice set of breasts. She had a tiny waist cinched tight by a thick belt and massive silver buckle, straight black hair cascading down her back, and a black baseball cap atop it. High-end cowboy boots finished off the ensemble and her face was carefully made up in a haute-couture style. The name on her Nevada Driver's License? Orneta Hughes.

For some reason, Zeke doubted that was true, but obviously she was of age to drink so he let it slide. Sometimes it's best to follow the letter of the law, nothing more.

She got a Dos Equis then sauntered over to the pool table and began to play. Setting everything up like a pro. Stretching over the table for a shot. Squatting down to eye the balls. Chalking her cue incessantly. All done in a way that managed to show off every aspect of her hourglass figure.

She caught Zeke's attention because eight years at this bar had given him a sixth sense for picking up on trouble, and she radiated it. Even Rhonda, the Cantina's one and only waitress, kept a wary eye on her.

Poor Rhonda. Last name, Felmer. Plain hair, plain face, probably twenty pounds underweight to pull off the canvas-mini-skirt, tie-dyed t-shirt cut at the waist to give her a midriff, and doll-like boots on her feet. She was somewhat underdone in the makeup department, and the emphasis on turquoise jewelry on her wrists and around her neck just made her seem thinner and more desperate. She could also be kind of pissy when a solo woman came in; she would have to be all but forced to serve them.

"They don't tip," she'd snarled once, to Zeke, "and they look around at the boys to see if there's anyone they wanna get fucked by."

Zeke had never made an issue about it. If he had to drop off a drink because Rhonda was sulking in the ladies room, no big deal. It made for more *personalized service*, and he used his heartbreaking smile to smooth over any ruffled feathers.

Well...it looked like it would be that way, tonight.

Except the black-haired woman kept nursing her beer as she played game after game. By herself. Any biker who came over to offer a match was politely brushed off with a simple, "I just want to be alone." Spoken with a deep huskiness that hinted at a disinterest in the male gender. But somehow Zeke got the feeling she was waiting for someone. Who? Guess he'd find out, eventually, but he doubted they would be female. If that's the company she was looking for, Selena's, a bar south of town, would have been a better fit.

Then about nine pm, Grady Cannon showed up, followed by Spit Rodriguez and Katty Black, Spit's current, and probably only-ever, female squeeze. They were all part of Dax's pack, and were the only three who'd made it a habit of appearing before the Rock-Jocks and Mildreds left, mainly because Spit and Grady were known to offer that *little something extra* to the entitled ones.

As they sauntered past the bar, Zeke cast a quick look at the woman, wondering if what she was after was some pot or pills. But she just lined up her next shot, not even glancing at the trio.

Except for some reason Zeke was certain she was aware of them. He began to wonder if she could be a state cop. If so, Eldora Parridge, the local sheriff, would not be happy. But the kids weren't around to sniff up some fun stuff, tonight, so it should be okay. Still, Zeke felt more than a little on edge.

Especially when he caught the woman casting a sharp glance at Grady.

Mr. Cannon was a pug Irish linebacker type, closing in on forty, who used to be in top shape but had gone to seed. Unlike Zeke's close-cropped hair, his head was shaved, showing off a fleur-de-lis tattoo over each ear. He was never outside without his sunglasses, even at night, and seemed to have nothing but ragged t-shirts, ratty Wranglers and a rough pair of dirty Dingo boots to wear. It was only his bushy eyebrows that gave away the fact that he was red-haired, and he wore neither cap nor helmet, even on his Hog.

An ex-marine, like Zeke, he was also a long-term friend. They had met in that rehabilitation department too many soldiers had wound up at. His issue was his arms and hands; they had been burned in a chopper crash. Thanks to the Army's surgeons, he could use them, but with limited success. Elaborate tattoos of lions and tigers and bears, oh my, covered that scarring, right down to and including his fingers.

"Those hurt and bled like a motherfucker," he'd told Zeke.

"Why'd you get them?" Zeke had asked, eyeing the tats.

"For the fuck of it," Grady had sighed. He'd flexed his fingers as much as he could. "Remind me there's still so much fuckin' pain in the world."

"As if we need reminding."

They were both at Beaumont, on Fort Bliss, undergoing hard-assed physical therapy. Because Zeke's left calf had been blown off by an IED, in Afghanistan, he was learning how to walk on a bionic one...and not doing well. In fact, his attitude had been way below the line. Grady had connected with him, smacked him around, some, then dragged him across the border to watch more detail get added to a flying eagle on his chest. It was during their second trip over, and they were sitting in a sad cantina on Avenue Lerdo listening to guitar music, downing Dos Equis and munching on scary tacos, when Zeke had asked him about the tattoos on his fingers.

"What about you?" Grady had shot at him, after taking another swallow of beer. "Think you might?"

Zeke had held out his left arm. Eyed the scarring on it. "We'll see."

"Ones doesn't wanna get hurteds, too much?" Grady had said in a baby tone.

Zeke had just chuckled. "I had a tatt. On my calf. Left one."

Grady had stiffened. "Oh. Shit."

"Yeah. It was a nice one. So I know what it means. Just get into Zen mode."

Grady had forced a chuckle. "You're a good kid."

"Cut it out. You ain't that much older'n me."

"Ten years, motherfucker." He had leaned back to gaze at the slow-moving ceiling fan. "Ten years an' two fuckin' lifetimes."

They had watched out for each other, ever since.

When Grady was discharged, he joined up with Dax, since he knew him from Iraq, and it was him who got Zeke the job at Cantina Madriza. Even got him set him up in the trailer out back, as part of his salary, as well as use of Dax's old Harley in place of his own *little Honda*.

"This is Hog country, son," he had told Zeke. "You can get by with this little beastie, okay, but not that baby bike."

Zeke had caressed the Harley, almost lovingly, as he'd said, "It's beautiful. But can I work it with my leg?"

Grady had smacked him on the back and said, "I'll help you figure that out." And he had.

Eight years later, they were like brothers.

Now Grady wasn't perfect. He could have serious moments of paranoia and could even curl into a ball on Zeke's couch, some nights, unwilling to even move. When he got like that, Zeke's spotty dog, Loki, would lie next to him, offering comfort; he was the only other person the little mutt would do that for. Grady would just hold him and stroke him and say nothing, and Zeke would leave him be.

Now Spit, he's the kind of guy who might turn out to be attractive if he'd just lose half the weight he was carrying. And not carrying well. Mid-thirties. Ragged beard. Clothes a size too small. Black hair long and always looking like it needed to be washed. Tattoos on his arms but nowhere else. That anyone knew of or even wanted to know about.

Well, anyone but his Rubenesque biker girlfriend, Katty, whose patchy jeans outfit was always a size too small, who had piercings in her piercings, whose pastel tats were in confused opposition to the rest of her attitude, and whose hair was so bleached, you could be sure it was sterilized till the dawn of time.

Zeke knew little about those two, and he liked to keep it that way. Spit was the bullying type who'd make obnoxious comments and get people riled up then look around as if to say, *I's just jokin'*.

Katty was pretty much his twin, in that way, and in the time since those two had connected, just under a year ago, more than once Zeke had been forced to step in to keep one from killing the other over some idiotic slight...till they had calmed down and were back to saying *Baby this* and *Baby that*.

Like they were still in high school.

All three rode Choppers, sported leather wrist bands and jackets, and wore fat belts with buckles the size of Texas on them. Zeke figured eventually Spit's would pop him, like a balloon, the way his gut hung over it. Then there'd be Spit everywhere.

And just the thought usually made him cringe.

Grady, Spit and Katty stripped off their jackets and took up residence in their usual booth, close to the pool table. The moment he'd heard their Hogs approaching, Zeke had started pulling their usual order, so Rhonda was already bringing it to them — Coors for Katty, Michelob for Spit and a bottle of Dos Equis for Grady. All nice and normal.

Except this time, Spit snuck into the side of the booth that gave him a glorious view of the black-haired woman's rear as she did her thing around the table, and he began to chuckle like a growly hyena at her every move.

Katty noticed and it did not lead her anywhere near a good mood.

Another red flag to Zeke. He had a feeling her black nails were about to have some of Spit's red blood on them. But nobody was actually doing anything wrong, yet, so he kept back.

And kept wary.

Until the woman came around to the end of the table near the booth, dipped down to eye the lineup, for a long moment, then rose and stretched over the edge to set up her shot.

That's when Spit got up, chuckling, "Gonna take a piss." And as he walked past the woman, he grabbed her ass and chuckled, "Sweet cheeks."

And got the woman's pool cue whipped up between his legs.

He yelped, grabbed his balls and fell over...then *really* howled, "Aw, fuck. Fuck. My back. Fuck."

Which startled the few bikers in the Cantina into laughter.

"Oh, shit," sighed Zeke.

Grady huffed, got up and helped Spit slowly rise to his feet, hunched over like a little old man. Zeke threw a heating pad into a microwave that was behind the register.

Katty just sat there, glaring at Spit and snarling, "Serves you fuckin' right, asshole."

Grady guided Spit back into the booth. Let him settle into the seat and press his back against the boards.

"How bad?" Grady asked.

"You don't wanna know," Spit growled.

Katty dug her nails into Spit's arm, angry.

"Ow!" he yelped. "Baby, my back."

"You're lucky," she snapped. "I'd of poked out an eye."

Rhonda held back a laugh and got the heating pad, for him.

Grady noticed the woman was just standing there, watching them, impassive, cue held in a way that she could use as a weapon, if need be. He shook his head, saying, "Now you hurt Spit's back, and him havin' to work, tomorrow."

"His name fits," the woman said, her voice low and growly.

Grady looked her over. Lovely and round, like an hourglass. Nice tits. Then he saw dark eyes gazing back at him and painted lips caught in a half-smile, which brought *What're you up to?* and *You lookin' at me; you really lookin' at me?* to mind. It had been a long time since he'd had a woman gaze at him, *that way*, especially one who was nice to look at, so he wasn't sure which way it could be.

"Now you know his name," Grady said. "What name fits you?"

She just chalked her cue, her eyes locked on his.

"O-kay," Grady chuckled. "What name fits me?"

She examined him like a jackal might contemplate its next meal, and kept chalking her cue. But in an almost erotic way.

"How 'bout a game?" she finally asked. "Winner names names."

Holy shit, she IS lookin' at me, Grady thought.

He held up his hands and wiggled his fingers as best he could, which wasn't much. "Ain't so good with pool."

She took a hand to look closer, as if she had just noticed the scarring under the tattoos. She seemed amused. "Let's say I spot you a couple balls." Then she leaned back and blew chalk dust off the cue.

O-KAY. This was going too good to pass up, even if he was shitty at the game. He grabbed a cue. Set his beer beside hers. Fired up a joint and offered her a drag, which she took and drew in like a pro. She held it for a nice long moment before letting the smoke drift through her pursed lips in a way that was so sensual, Grady's dick was suddenly filled with great expectations.

"Stripes or solids?" he managed to ask.

She shrugged.

He looked the table over. She had already dropped two of each, so he leaned across, struggled to set up his cue, shook a little but then smacked the cue ball...

And dropped a solid! That was a first.

He looked over to ask if Zeke had seen it, but the guy was busy prepping an order for Rhonda. In direct violation of what was anticipated for the evening, a pair of Rock-Jocks in designer slum-wear had come in, set themselves at a table, and now were focused on their phones.

Grady felt a twinge of envy at how easily they dealt with the tiny keyboards. Texting twerps. More smarts in their fingers than in their brains.

But then he noticed Laila, a biker chick with boobs, curves and attitude, in black leather everything, hair the color of cotton candy and lips vampire red, was circling in on them. He chuckled. Those boys were about to find themselves on the ride of their lives, and their daddies' credit cards would soon be maxed out. He hoped Laila would take pictures; he loved sharing her misuse and abuse of the little shits.

He turned back to the woman, saw she was eyeing him, waiting, her mouth slightly open, her tongue poised just under her upper lip.

He gulped. Felt more of that expectation in his dick. Suddenly more awkward than usual, he lined up too fast and shot.

And missed.

Dammit. He was getting flustered.

She let out a sigh, casually leaned over the table and dropped one. Then she rounded it, completely, eyeing the balls as she chalked her cue, her every step screaming of sex. She stopped next to Grady, nodding. Gave him a smiling side glance. Grabbed hold of his beer and took a nice, long swallow. Again, her eyes never left his.

"Mexican beer," she said.

"Like yours," he said.

"Good taste."

Needless to say, subtlety was not on the agenda.

Then she leaned over the table, her amazing hips nudging him aside. He had to hold his breath in fear he'd scare her off with his giggles, and...

She missed her next shot.

It almost looked deliberate.

She rose, gave a little girl pout and said, "Oopsie."

That, Zeke did notice. To him, it looked like she was playing Grady, and not a game of pool.

He was about to say something when Rhonda came up, sighing, "The boys're buying Laila a Mimosa."

Zeke shot an even warier glance at Laila, saw she was seated next to the buffer of the two lads, and turned back to Rhonda. "A Mimosa?" he muttered. "Since when?"

"Since those two're drinking them."

Zeke rolled his eyes. "You had your smoke break, yet?"

She nodded.

"What kind of car they in?"

"An HRV."

That brought a smile to Zeke's face. "Better let Laila know."

Meaning she'd go relatively easy on the lads, since the folks were obviously not of great wealth. Then he turned to open another split of cheap champagne.

At the pool table, Grady dropped two more. Damn, his luck was killer, tonight! That left a pair of stripes and the eight. It was not an easy shot, so he missed it. But then the cue ball rolled back into a perfect set-up to drop the eight in a side pocket. Grady grunted in irritation.

Until the woman said, "Go again."

Grady looked at her, confused. "Huh?"

"It's a perfect lie. Shame to waste it."

Grady had to let out that giggle, it was too great.

"First time a woman ever said that to me. Shit, anyone ever said that."

"You can tell a lot about a man by how he handles what's on the table." Then she licked her lips.

O-KAY!

Despite being hard as a rock, in one area, which canceled out any and all potential paranoia and worry, Grady managed to line up his cue, take a couple of fake jabs...

Then sank the eight.

He also pushed the side of the table while doing it, in order to, oh, *arrange himself* inside his jeans, hoping to offer a better indication of what he had available. When he rose, he knew he was showing off a nice, solid piece of piping.

"I win," he said. And he noticed the woman actually *was* staring straight at his crotch. Wow!

"So what's *my* name?" she asked, her voice playful.

Oh. Shit. He hadn't thought about that. He fumbled his words a bit, then said, "How 'bout *My Girl?*"

She gave him a smiling shrug of agreement, then all but cooed at him, "But only for tonight."

She finished her beer, put away the cue, and strutted to the main entrance, her every move like a panther prowling her domain. She cast a glance back at Grady as she exited.

Zeke was setting Laila's Mimosa on Rhonda's tray, so saw her leave. Then he saw Grady grab his jacket and scurry after her.

"Grady," he said, wary.

The guy spun around and cast him two quick thumbs-up, with a grin that was ear to ear.

Zeke motioned to him. "Grady, wait, what about...?"

But Grady had already waved him off and hopped outside.

Zeke frowned. Something about this did not sit right. Grady probably had a fair amount of cash on him and should have left it with Zeke. But he had lock boxes on his hog's tail, and he was smart enough to know not to let that into the conversation. Then was one of the unwritten understandings between all men — if a woman seemed willing to go as far as that one seemed ready to, do *NOT* get in the way.

So Zeke sighed and turned to watch Rhonda set the drinks down, and *mention she just happened to be in the market for a Honda HRV and could the boys tell her something about them?* Then listen in rapt attention as the less buff one did. Seeing Laila go from *Little Kitten* to *What The Fuck?* was almost worth it.

Back in their booth, Katty was giving Spit the *you-son-of-a-bitch* silent treatment as he sat flat against the back of his seat, heating pad almost ready for another nuking. At least she had pulled a bottle of Advil from her purse; it sat before him, its top off. But he was still in pain, and now he was glaring at the entrance.

He snarled a soft, "Fuckin' cunt."

He'd make damn sure he got the details of Grady's night, in the morning. That might make up for having to strap his back brace on, again. Then maybe he'd pay the bitch a call, himself.

Once his back was okay, of course.

He'd have chuckled over the thought but Katty was reading his mind, and suddenly her black nails were drawing some of his red blood from a forearm.

"Shit, baby," he growled. "What the fuck?"

"You go near that bitch," she snarled, "I'll cut your balls off."

"Shit, I can't even move an' you're at me 'bout that?"

A truly wicked grin crossed Katty's face. "Then let's go home. An' you're goin' straight to bed."

He nodded. "Set my heatin' pad goin' and..."

"An' you'll take care of me, right?"

"C'mon, baby, you know I can't move when I'm like this."

"You can move your tongue, well enough."

He looked at her, irritated. "An' what's in that for me?"

"Makin' me happy, again." Then she dug her nails into his thigh, very nearly cutting through the jeans.

He grimaced and nodded and said, "I can live with that."

She patted his cheek and sat back to finish her beer as Rhonda brought over Spit's second one. "We'll have one more, each," she said. "Loverboy's payin'."

Which he whined about...but did.

The midnight black sky was well-pitted with stars, thanks to the moon not yet having risen. Free and open and clear. Dark empty landscapes in the distance, no hint of life to them. No traffic, either, just the straight, gray ribbon of The 14 slicing through it all. A new silver Mercedes C class convertible whispered down it, as sharp and silent as death.

Well, silent in comparison to Grady's Chopper, an older one but in top condition, with black fiberglass lock-boxes over its rear wheels. Goggles covered his eyes while his leather jacket offered the barest minimum of protection against the chilly wind. A joint barely held in his lips. None of that kept him from *thrumming* and *drumming* and having all sorts of fun playing tag with the car. Rushing ahead to pull in front. Slowing down to let it pass. Laughing smoke drifted behind him, like exhaust fumes.

The top of the convertible was down. The cold wind whipped at the woman's hair, but she seemed to thrill in it. Seemed to enjoy parroting his little dance. She even laughed as Grady slowed down, yet again, to let her zip past, then flipped him off before letting him catch up for another pass. But this time, when he drew parallel to the driver's door, she beckoned him closer, smiling.

He edged to within a couple inches of the speeding car; he didn't want to scratch it and piss her off. Not yet. She reached up with her left hand, motioning to the joint. He handed it to her, she took a long drag, then handed it back before letting the backs of her fingers drift down his jacket to tickle his crotch.

He gasped from the joyous explosions firing through him and almost lost control of his bike. Hot DAMN! He shot ahead, damn near popping a wheelie, from excitement.

She laughed, smoke whispering from her, then she hit her brakes, did a sliding turn to the right to rush through a gate, gave him a *honk*, and raced down a gravel road.

Grady heard, saw, slammed the Hog into a skid, spun around and roared back to the gate, snarling, "Shit," at least a dozen times. Maybe two-dozen as he chased after her.

He couldn't run too fast over the dirt and rocks because the billowing dust and lack of light kept him from seeing very far ahead. No matter how much he wanted — hell, *needed* to fuck that woman, his chopper was too valuable to wreck. Especially since he didn't have insurance.

He finally managed to see a vague red glow through the muck, which went bright and stopped and vanished.

He slowed down as he neared an isolated house that looked as if it were hiding from the world. Half-rock, half-wood, all beat-up, dark, surrounded by nothing but scrub, even in the shadows you could tell it hadn't been painted in thirty years.

The Mercedes was by the front door, the woman leaning against it, watching him glide up. He pulled to a halt behind the car and got off the bike. Dust now layered his front, from head to toe. He beat most of it away and removed his goggles to look around, not at all impressed.

"Didn't know anybody lived in this shack," he said.

"It's an Air B&B," the woman said as she pushed away from the car and started for a side door. "Convenient. Nicer inside."

"Oh, then should I hose-off, first?"

She looked at him, seeming to chuckle. Even in the pale starlight her smile was lovely. "A wet tee-shirt contest. I could live with that."

Which brought a giggle from him.

"Why not just wash your face? Use some mouthwash, too. Or would you prefer another Dos Equis?"

"Shit. You gotta ask?"

She simply reached over, linked a finger in a belt loop and pulled him in through the door.

He giggled.

They entered the kitchen and she left the lights off. He grabbed at her, as best he could. Tried to pull her close for a kiss.

She twisted away, saying. "Let me get those beers. You can use the kitchen sink, for your face. Wash your hands, too."

"What for? I wore gloves."

"Even more reason. Oh, and check your teeth for bugs."

"Need a light for that."

She chuckled then turned on a battery-powered one over the sink. It cast a cold, eerie glow.

He giggled and glanced around. And blinked. The appliances were ancient. Very Forties and Fifties. Even in half-darkness it looked sad and just make-do. And dirty. People rented this place?

For some reason, he thought of his grandmother's place, outside San Antonio, which had always been about to crumble into dust. He shrugged, yanked off his jacket, dropped it and turned on the faucet. It grumbled and groaned but clean water soon poured out.

She pulled a couple of Dos Equis from the ancient fridge.

He grinned. "How'd you know?"

"Told you, Mexican beer's good."

"What's your real name?" Grady asked as he ran soap up his arms.

Her voice went sing-song as she said, "Call me Stasi."

"Hmph. Knew another chick by that name. Bitch was fuckin' crazy."

The woman looked at him, over her shoulder. It was dark so he couldn't see her expression, but she was very still. "Are you one of those types? Thinks all women are insane?"

Oops, wrong thing to say, Grady. Backtrack. Quick.

"No," he shot out. "Shit, no. *She* really was. Something lost in her brain. Some cog or shit like that. What'd Zeke call it? Slapsis? Sleezis?"

"Synapses?"

"Yeah, that's it. I think," he said as he wiped his hands on his shirt. "She killed herself, she's so out of it."

She gave a soft laugh then offered him an open beer. He grabbed it and almost dropped it, thanks to his scarred fingers and it being wet. Coming out of a fridge? That was weird. Still, he gave her an embarrassed shrug then guzzled some.

"So what do I call you?" she asked, batting her eyes. "Asshole? Motherfucker?"

He chuckled and backed her against the counter to press against her, one hand caressing a breast, saying, "I'm Grady. Mm. Nice. Like 'em real."

"Do you?" She gave a deep, throaty chuckle.

"Yeah, feels right," he murmured as he leaned in to kiss one.

She chuckled. "Oooooh, Grady's hungry."

He nuzzled her breasts. "Been a long time since I ain't had to pay for it."

She moved back, a little. "You screw working girls?"

"Now an' then, this joint up in Scottsdale," he said. Then realized what he was saying. "Oh, but...but not in a while. An' I'm clean. I...I even got a condom."

"That's good." She ran a finger over his lips. "So what's it like, being with a whore?"

"Shit, I don't do it so much. Just when the boss fronts me a little extra." He drank more of the beer, but did not see rejection in her eyes so added, "Okay, it ain't the same. I get just as much out of it as jackin' off. Bein' with a woman who wants to be with you? Who ain't doin' it for the money? I dunno, it's all different. Better."

"You mentioned it's been a while since..."

"Aw, c'mon, I don't exactly look like *Captain America.*"

"Oh, poor Grady."

She ran her fingers along his chin. He tried to kiss her, but she put her own bottle to her lips, teasing him.

"Well, it *is* going to cost you," she murmured. "Just not in money."

Then she set her beer down, reached around and grabbed his ass, making him yelp. Then she purred, "Oh. Nice. Big. Round. Something to grab hold of."

He giggled and almost got a kiss in before she leaned back, ran her hands up his sides and grabbed the throat of his shirt.

Now he gasped. "Careful, this is my saint shirt."

"Saint shirt?"

He giggled as he said, "All holey."

She laughed and tore it open and he gasped, "Aw, fuck!"

"Soon enough," she said as she looked at the tattoo of that elaborate eagle in flight, head on, its wings unfurled, its outer feathers curling around his nipples. Both of which were pierced with adorable gold rings.

"Oh, yes," she whispered. She traced her fingers over the eagle's wings before flipping at both rings.

He really got caught in the giggles, now. "Oh, shit, shit, girls do that to guys?"

"Depends on the guy." Her smile widened. "Have you had a dude do this to you?"

"Shit, I ain't gay."

"But haven't you ever gotten drunk? Let a guy play around?" She gave the rings gentle tugs. "Get you ready? Go down on you?"

"Yeah, fuck, a mouth's a mouth," he said, breathless. But then he jolted and added, "I mean, I was at this dyke bar and kind of drunk and..."

"You were at a lesbian bar? Trolling girls who don't like boys?"

"Naw. I know the owner. She gives me a place to crash, now an' then, an' there's this older guy an' he...well, I let him...well..."

"You let him do this?" She twisted his nipples, soft. Erotic. Ran the tips of her fingers over them, barely touching.

Every sensation he could think of rammed through every part of his body. He could barely speak. Barely nod. "Fuck. Better. When it's you."

"Love your tatt. Any more to play with?"

He pulled her close, almost breathless. "Stasi see, real soon."

She licked her lips and dribbled beer down her front.

He whimpered and dove down to lick it up. Which, of course, led to him nuzzling her breasts, again, this time dipping his tongue into her cleavage and crushing his crotch against hers.

"Oh, fuck," was all he seemed able to say, till he stopped at finally realizing, "You're in a girdle?"

"A bustier. Adds to the moment, don't you think?" Then her voice went way down low and growly as she added, "I've also got boots with six-inch-heels. Up to my knees. And a whip, if you're interested in that." She ran a hand up the inside of his thigh then groped him, in full. Massaging his balls and dick.

Oh, was he ever! He leaned back, a little, and let out a long slow sigh of the deepest pleasure before guzzling more beer.

She unbuckled his belt. Undid the buttons on his jeans. Shifted them to his hips before kneading his ass. He did not dare move for fear he might fire his load, right then, as she ran her fingers back up his sides, under the torn shirt, and tickled his tits, again. Toyed with the hair on his chest. On his poochie little tummy. Into his belly-button. Up his arms.

Holeeeeeeeee shit, was this perfect.

He pulled her tight and ground against her, about ready to pop out of his FTLs and...

The room shifted.

He grunted, confused. Leaned on her, trying to keep his balance. Suddenly, his heart pounded a mile a minute and his head spun and nothing made sense.

She pulled away from him, fake concern on face.

"Too much too soon? Grady can't handle a woman he doesn't have to pay?"

"Just feel weird," he muttered, "and...and..." His voice trailed off.

"Grady, have roofies been used on you, before? Like maybe by that gay guy who pinched your tits?" She really pinched them, again. Hard. The sharp, sudden pain jolted him back into focus, for a moment. "You so sure he didn't go any farther than a blow job?"

He stumbled back. Only barely beginning to understand. "Ruh...roofies? Me? That beer..." He was able to make out she was grinning at him, standing there, waiting. He grabbed the kitchen counter and tried to move to the door. "Fuckin' bitch. What you...what you doin'?"

What she did was trip him.

He dropped to the dirty, cracked linoleum. Smacked his head, hard. Tried to talk but his words dribbled into nothingness. He rolled onto his back to see...

Her smiling down at him, the light over the sink illuminating half her face, the other half in shadow. But even seeing just half her smile showed it was one of the scariest he had ever seen. As he drifted closer and closer to some weird unfocused darkness, he heard her growl, "Now I'm naming names, you son-of-a-bitch," before he passed out.

*****

It was still dark when Grady woke. And it was fucking cold. His head pounded. He couldn't focus his eyes. His mouth was brittle and tongue felt swollen, and he was sure he'd been run over by a truck. Shit, how much had he drunk, last night? A breeze whispered over him, making him even colder, and...and...

Holy shit, am I outside?

Well, that made absolutely no sense because Grady did *not* sleep outside. Ever. He needed a ceiling above him with his back firmly against one of the four walls around him. But that was not happening, right now, was it?

Because there he was, face down in grit and sand and stones. Did he pass out? Did he have a wreck on his chopper? Was he crashed on the side of the road?

Aw man, everything that happened with Stasi — was it just a dream?

He tried to roll over but couldn't move. He flexed his arms. They were frozen behind him, and his legs would barely move. He tried to speak but his mouth wouldn't let him. Some kind of crap was shoved in it and he couldn't spit it out. That's when he finally realized...

He was gagged, his hands were bound, behind him, and his legs were bound at the ankles and knees. And he was on his belly in the dirt.

Which made no sense!

Then he felt someone pulling at — pulling at his jeans!? Forcing them down his legs to his knees! Sitting on him as stones and rocks and grit dug into his chin and pecs and stomach

Shit, am I being stripped?! Oh, no fucking way.

He struggled and pushed, but all that brought about was a sharp, sudden smack to his ass.

"Oooohhhh," said a low growly voice that sounded familiar. "Grady's wakey."

He tried to raise his head to look over his shoulder but couldn't turn far enough to see anything. So he began to grunt and howl.

Whoever was yanking at his jeans stopped and pulled at the waistband of his FTLs. Which weren't the cleanest he'd ever worn.

Dammit.

Hadn't his mother always yelled at him to always wear clean underwear, in case of moments like this? Always? Shit.

The waistband snapped back against his skin, then he heard a cold, hard voice snarl, "Yell all you want. Won't do any good."

Stasi! Shit! She's doing this to me? But her voice is different. What the fuck's going on?

He starting to breathe heavy, and the thing in his mouth wouldn't let him speak. He still managed to grunt, "What the fuck, bitch? You into some kinky kind of shit? Lemme go! This ain't fun!"

She chuckled. He felt her tear open a leg of his FTLs then slap his semi-naked butt, a couple of times, not at all playful.

"Kind of hairy," she said, "but not bad. You ever do nudes, Grady? Show it off for the boys?"

Shit, this had to be a dream. Some bitch had kidnapped hum, tied him up and was stripping him? Was she about to ravage him? All the times he'd imagined it and now it was really happening? Really?

"What the fuck, Stasi? What you gonna do?" He talked slower, trying to enunciate. He was pretty sure she understood him, but all she did was grab his cheeks and spread them apart, then begin rubbing what felt like a bat between them.

Oh, she's not gonna do that. She wouldn't. She couldn't!

All she said was, "Oh, I guess it's only polite to let you know, I'm not Stasi; she's dead."

Dead?!? She's using the name of that crazy bitch who smashed her boyfriend and killed herself?

"What the fuck?" Grady managed to growl, despite the gag. "What's this all about? What's fuckin' goin' on?" He kept on and on with questions of the same basic nature as he felt that club press against his asshole...

And push against it!

All coherent thought vanished as he bucked and fought to shift away, but she rode him like you would ride a bronco, laughing. Suddenly, the damn thing was vibrating and he felt...oh, no, he felt...

HOLY SHIT, IT WAS SLIDING UP INTO HIS ASS!

He bucked at her, even more, but all that did was help her push it even deeper. She was splitting him in half, he just knew it. The soft humming and shivering of it tore into his very being as he screamed and struggled, but he could not stop her. All she did was use his twisting and fighting to turn him onto his back, pushing that thing deeper inside him, massaging him in places only shit had ever gone.

He was gasping and grunting and his eyes were jammed shut in pain, so he only barely felt her tear his FTLs open at the slit to reveal his pride and joy, but he sure heard her sigh. "Oh, Grady, you're not circumcised."

What? What the fuck? Who cares? She's fucking raping me and so fucking what if I ain't cut?

He opened his eyes and finally saw the woman...but she didn't look the same. He hair was brown, not black, short with no bangs, and she was completely naked. Well, except for latex gloves on her hands.

"I don't understand why all men don't have this thing cut off," she sighed, pinching at the foreskin.

He grimaced and tried to shift away from her as the vibrations inside him kept shattering him to the core.

She continued with, "Ruins the look. Gives them the appearance of a garden hose or an anteater. Gets dirty. Jews and Muslims have the right idea; just get rid of it."

He squirmed more as she pulled the foreskin back, making him moan, "Leave me alone. Leave me alone! Leavemealone!" And not in ecstasy.

"At least you're clean," she continued. "That's a positive. My mother's big on cleanliness. This being dirty causes cervical cancer, you know. That's why all of my brothers are cut."

And suddenly, she was stroking him! And she was rolling his balls with her other hand!

What the actual fuck? Is she jacking me off?

She kept on with, "But that's my mother. Very heavy into the old testament, where they were obsessed with foreskins. Trust me, I know. I read the whole book. Had to." She chuckled, then began to pull at him, hard.

"Momma didn't expect me to notice was how stupid and male-centric it was. I mean, seriously. Making faith all about men getting cut then spending a chapter in Galatians saying, *Never-mind.* Do you know why they changed their opinion? Peter was requiring men to be circumcised in order to convert to Christianity, but they wouldn't so all the religion was getting was women. What a horrifying thought — a religion made up of nothing but females. Small wonder there's no peace, with it."

She kept running her hand up and down his dick. Rolling his balls with her other hand. Pulling at them. Soft and easy but insistent. As for that thing up his ass, still shivering and humming, now he was aware enough to figure it was a vibrator. And to his horror, it was making him feel jolts of pleasure, something he didn't think a guy should feel, in a situation like this.

"Momma wasn't happy with me when I pointed that out," she continued. "But she wasn't happy with me, a lot. I wasn't exactly a nun, growing up. And now?"

Well, now, as much as he hated to admit it, the vibrator was feeling good. Especially when she toyed with the ring in his left tit. The fire that shot through him made him clench his ass, intensifying the vibrations inside him, causing him to push harder against her hand.

He was now fully erect.

Nobody's gonna believe a naked woman did this to me.

She stopped stroking him. He groaned and shifted as his dick bounced back on his belly. Then the woman entered his field of vision. He was pretty sure this was the same face, but no makeup made it seem different. Plus, her eyes were cold and cruel. She held up a gray backpack, that had been in one of his Harley's side boxes. It had the money he'd collected, that day, from Dax's dealers. But it had been locked!

Dax is gonna fucking kill me. Why didn't I hand it off to Zeke?!

"You think this is all I'm after, don't you?" she said.

He tried to spit out a flurry of curses along the lines of, "You fuckin' bitch, don't you dare fuckin' do this to me, you fucking cunt, I'll cut your fuckin' tits off," and on and on as he struggled to free himself while dealing with that thing up his rear. Wasn't doing any good. He now see ropes were also wrapped around his chest holding his arms in place. Dammit.

"The cash is nice, but it's not why you're here." She dropped the backpack and squatted down to flick at his penis, saying, "Humph, that erection didn't last long. Doesn't Grady have any staying power? Let's see what we can do about that."

She shoved a hand between his legs, found the base of the vibrator was still just outside his asshole, and flicked a switch. It began to work harder and louder.

Grady tried to scream. He strained at the ropes, but all he succeeded in doing was crushing his hands and arms against the hard rocky ground. He cursed and howled and screamed and struggled.

She began stroking him, again, and toying with his balls as she said, "Y'know, men always have been pussies. I figured that out when Moses was too weak-assed to circumcise his son, even to save his life. His wife had to do it. Proved to me that women are stronger."

The vibrator kept humming on and on. Worked faster and almost angrier. Rubbed inside him in ways that sent shivers through his dick and balls...and to his shock, he found he was getting off on this.

She pinched his foreskin, again. Hard.

He yelped, then he started to whimper.

Still stroking him, she tickled the fingers of her other hand up through his pubes to his now-heaving little belly. She caressed the eagle on his chest and toyed with the rings in his tits and pulled at the hairs on his pecs and tummy. He squirmed and tried to shift away but could not. Just grew harder.

"What do you think?" she finally asked. "If I was a man doing this to you, would you be able to keep from getting an erection? I doubt it. As you mentioned, little horn-doggies like you can find satisfaction with either women or other men, in the right place at the right time."

She kept working his dick, gentle but insistent. His ass clenched. He pushed against her. That fucking vibrator was feeling better and better. He was close...so close...

"You fuckin' rapin' me," he choked.

"Oh, Grady, can a woman rape a man? Many say no, that men can only rape women. I think this proves otherwise."

He grimaced, the sensations crashing through him far too demanding to ignore or fight or even try to discuss.

She chuckled. "Maybe you're just like this Marine Captain I knew. Built like a brick shithouse, with a voice you could hear clear to the South Pole. Had a wife and five daughters, back home, and loved a big black dick up his ass when he was fucking me. Is that you, Grady? Should I phone a friend?"

She sat up, still stroking his dick. Up and down and up and down.

"He and I had lots of fun with this gorgeous lad named Kareem. Sarge loved being the meat in our sandwich."

She sighed and continued, "It's funny, but just thinking about Kareem. His smooth skin. No tats. Hair in just the right places. A smile that could shame the sun and an ass that would turn any man gay, just picturing him gets me going."

She caressed the eagle on Grady's chest then pinched a nip, again.

"And needy. You're not as taut as him, or big as him, but would you still like me to ride you? I'm already undressed."

Grady was beyond rational thought, by this point. Just breathing heavy, half from fear and half from mere horniness. He managed to growl, "You're fuckin' rippin' me off and you wanna fuck, too? That's fuckin' crazy. Get this thing outta my ass! This is fuckin' rape, you fuckin' cunt! I'll get your ass in jail and fucked every night, bitch!"

She chuckled, shifted back and pulled harder on his dick.

He grunted.

"So you don't like it when you don't get to consent? You get to do what you want, but if anyone does it to you, oh, *not nice*."

She stroked faster. He groaned.

Then he felt a surge explode in his groin and fire up from his balls to the base of his dick and he jolted and gasped and clenched and tensed and...and...oh shit, he ejaculated. His cum splashed back onto his belly and dripped into his pubes as he cried out like a dog finishing inside his chosen bitch.

No, no, no, it ain't possible. She's got me tied down in the middle of the desert and she still got me to cum? How the fuck could that be?

Then she pinched and twisted the ring in his left tit and he fired, again. Clenched his ass and shoved his hips into her hand and whimpered and gasped. His breath was sharp and ragged.

Oh, but the pleasure washing over him — it was way beyond belief. Like the first time he'd jacked off. Sensations danced through every cell in his body, from his groin to his toes and even his ears. He had never experienced an orgasm like this, before. He nearly blacked out from its his force. From its near perfection.

Except that damn thing was still vibrating inside him!

"Was that good for you?" she asked, as she wiped his cum on his face. "Did you enjoy it, you little cunt?" She straddled his body, her eyes filled with hate. "I'm not here for money," She said. "I'm here for this."

She held up her iPhone and started a video playing.

Of a college-age girl held down on a pool table.

In the Cantina.

By Spit and another man as Grady fucked her.

She was whimpering and vaguely struggling, her bra and blouse shoved up to reveal her breasts, her jeans down on one leg, her short black hair tangled, as he slobbered all over her, giggling.

Grady took a moment to focus.

Her voice was ice. "This girl was Lara Vincenzo. You and your buddies raped her. Anastasia Deveaux recorded it. Did she give you a copy to jack off to?"

He looked from her to the video, shaking his head, trying to say, "No...she was...was a whore we bought...from Nogales..."

"She was from San Diego, you son-of-a-bitch. A student at Nathan Cruz University."

She closed the video, set the phone aside.

And held up a short, sharp, wicked knife.

It reflected happily in the moonlight, looking as evil as anything ever had. She caressed his chest with it. Around his nipples, one after the other. Trailed it down the treasure trail over his belly. "She was my daughter. She killed herself, almost a year ago."

He whimpered, confused. He was soft, again, so she pinched his foreskin. He tried to squirm away but she had too good of a hold.

"I'm here to give you pain, Grady," she growled, "like you gave to her. And to me."

Then she pulled his penis out as far out as she could.

Cast him a smile of the purest delight.

Then calmly cut it off.

Blood spewed and, despite the gag, Grady's choking shrieks of pain filled the empty, endless desert night. But it was no longer silent.

A number of coyotes were now howling in empathy

A Shift in the Supposéd Meaning of the World

County Sheriff Eldora Parridge loved the desert, no matter what time of year it was. The endless vistas lined by distant mountains in a hundred shades of brown. Chameleons and road runners and coyotes and hawks managing their co-existence despite blistering summers that were dry enough to wither you to nothing within a day, if you didn't keep hydrated. Or not use plenty of sunblock. SPF100. At a minimum. Cacti blooming in the occasional rains of winter. Freezing nights followed by brilliant days that could turn hot or chilly, usually in direct opposition to what the weather report said. The desert was a beast of its own, going its own way, beholden to no one and with its own form of beauty, and that was why she felt kin to it.

Eldora also carried her own form of beauty. Not like you would find in the pages of *Vogue* or *Mademoiselle*, but strong-featured and striking in a way that was impossible to forget. Taut eyes. Firm mouth. Nose neither long nor short. Solid body in the appropriate form. She had reached her full height of six-foot-one by ninth grade, and the taunts and catcalls of her being a dyke and ugly bitch and horse-faced cunt during her years of high school had built her into someone who not only had a hide as tough as asphalt, but was unwilling to put up with shit from anybody. Didn't hurt her daddy had taught her a good smack just above the right eye or straight into the right side of the mouth of any tormenter was the fastest way to draw blood. Then came the nose. As more than one girl or boy learned the hard way, via trips to the emergency room with mommy to be patched up. After which she would dare the principal to punish her for standing up for herself, thus cementing the knowledge in one and all that she was to be left the hell alone.

Of course, daddy being both a drinker and a long-haul trucker, he had casually forgotten he was married and had a daughter by not returning from transporting a load of used cars up to Denver, one day. After that, her mother had started having lots of fun with lots of other truckers. Leaving Sung Eldora to fend for herself, much of the time.

Not that she cared. Isolation from them both, coupled with her being completely self-sufficient by the age of eight, made her ready to face the world head on and join with her chosen profession — that of the sheriff's department. Straight out of high school.

Of course, there were also the childish taunts from fellow deputies, but she had also decided long ago that men with fragile egos were unworthy of her attention. Instead, she took joy in damaging the poor little things by showing all she needed to break up a fight was the bite in her voice and an occasional punch. There was also her way of cutting off a robbery by just letting the idiot criminal see she had arrived, had her pistol out, and was eyeing him like a wolf eyes its dinner. Even drunks got sober faster when faced with her displeasure.

That's not to say that she couldn't be open and understanding. Like on the occasions where she stopped a cute young man for a traffic violation. Sometimes, she would offer the lad tips on how to beat the ticket, in a softly purring voice...

Though she never did *not* write it.

All of this had proven she was on top of things, and was probably why she'd wound up elected to the office, three times. She might not be loved, but she sure as hell was considered fair.

Of course, the rumors about her being a lesbian continued, which she found funny. The fools of the world seemed locked in the idea that a woman in control of herself must be a dyke or a cunt. Typical idiotic nonsense.

Still, she kept her hair cropped close, never wore makeup, and the last time she was seen in a dress was her Senior Prom. Which she attended with an amazingly handsome young man of the Apache tribe who was as tall as she, had gleaming black hair, cheekbones that could cut a steak, piercing eyes and profile, and a willingness to eviscerate anyone who dared vote against her for prom queen.

Which she won.

Of course, he also got king.

And in the truest of clichés, she lost her virginity to him, that night, every minute of which, she had loved.

In a less common cliché, she enjoyed repeating that loss, with him. A lot. Even when he wasn't there. It didn't take much to recall the smooth strength of his muscles. The tenderness and need of his kisses. His hands so gentle and yet so strong. The beauty of him entering her. Combining these memories as she lay in a tub of hot water, candles burning around, a glass of bourbon on table next to her, with a lovely phallus to assist, she could easily bring that cascade of sensations to fruition. Didn't even need a romance novel.

They had been inseparable until he joined the marines. Neither of them cared to wait for the other, but in another cliché, they still swapped Christmas cards and fruit cakes, every year.

Eldora had enjoyed the last piece of his most recent one, the night before. Heated with butter and a nice pot of Earl Grey. Made her feel so domestic. For about five minutes. Followed by an hour in the tub.

What added to her reputation for strength was that she had a cast-iron stomach when it came to violent car wrecks, messy domestic disputes and bodies found in the desert after having been feasted upon by buzzards and scorpions and flies and such. So when the call about a body in the desert came in, just before five, she ordered her usual cheeseburger, fries and strawberry shake from a burger joint, grabbed it five minutes later, and had her dinner on the way; this one sounded like a long-haul and she was a bear when she was hungry.

Thus, her tummy was nicely satiated and she was halfway through her fifth cigarette of the day when GPS finally took her off The 14 onto a rutted dirt road. It ran through the middle of an area where the lovely brown became an ugly shade of shit, and the surrounding country was flat enough so that, even from more than a mile away, she could see where she needed to be.

Helped that the buzzards were still circling.

She drove her heavy-duty SUV across an arroyo that was still a bit damp from a recent rain in the foothills and aimed for a low plateau. As she approached, the forms of two Bureau of Land Management mini-SUVs took shape, both neatly parked next to one from the Sheriff's Department. All well and good except for one thing.

Atop the plateau sat a silver Mercedes C class convertible. Top down.

Now that you don't see every day, she told herself.

Two BLM Agents stood next to the SUVs, talking to a bright, buff, young deputy — Reymon Cardenas. He was one of those happy, eager types, like a rambunctious puppy, and maybe just a bit too honest to make it up through the ranks, but Eldora did like his smile and dark brown eyes.

And the way his butt and legs filled his uniform.

Of course, no way she could do anything about it without trouble from those who loved to make trouble. She accepted just being happy he'd joined the force, and that she could enjoy the picture he made.

He was facing away from her so she got a nice look at the part she most appreciated before one of the agents saw her coming. That made him to turn and wave at her. He wasn't smiling like he usually did. Verification this was not good.

She pulled up behind his SUV to call, "Reymon!"

"Hey, Eldora," he called back. She let all of her deputies call her by her first name. Built a stronger bond.

She got out and asked, "Anybody touch anything?"

An older, more officious BLM agent approached her, saying, "My guy didn't even go all the way up on the plateau. Second he saw what was there, he come down and called it in. On the radio. No cell phone out here."

She looked at his associate, and could now tell he was greener than anything ever could be, in the area. "That him?"

The first agent nodded.

"Why's he here lookin'?" she continued. "Federal boundary's a couple miles west."

"Drivin' on The 14. Saw the buzzards, this mornin'. Still at it, en route back, so came to see about it and found the car. How'd they get that flash ride up there?"

"Always ways to do somethin' stupid. Reymon, you got the license plate?"

"Just got down from there," he said. "Funeral home's en route to collect, too. Tucson's sending a couple guys down from the coroner's office."

She nodded. He was always right on the ball. Even with his honesty, he might wind up in her job, someday, if she wasn't careful. He needed to get married; pull some of his focus to something else. Maybe she could play matchmaker.

"See if we can connect it to a name," she said.

Reymon dipped into his SUV.

Eldora climbed up the plateau's crumbling sides onto the flat top to find...

A lump of a half-naked body lying next to the car, bound and gagged. Crawling with ants. Flies everywhere. Large pieces of flesh torn away. Clothes torn open and bloody. Blood soaked into the dirt. She got the impression the body was male, but there was so much damage, there was no telling, yet. The only part at all recognizable was what looked like red eyebrows poking through the mess.

She almost recognized them, but then her attention was caught by an empty honey bear, which was also crawling with ants and flies, inside and out.

Oh, the implications of that were not at all conducive to pleasant dreams.

"Ain't been here long," she murmured, "but we sure ain't gettin' no prints worth shit off him."

She stayed at the edge of the plateau, away from the body and car, and looked up at the buzzards; they would not be happy at being deprived of the rest of their meal. She also figured she saw at least two coyotes waiting in the nothingness, hoping for a quick snack. If they hadn't already helped themselves, the sneaky little bastards, because if this body did turn out to be male, it looked like they'd already made off with the equivalent of a hot dog and prairie oysters. She sighed. The desert wasn't wasting any time trying to take this over.

She carefully walked the periphery of the plateau. It was obvious the car had been washed after it was up here, thanks to how little dust was on it and the crustiness of the earth around it. But no footprints that she could see. Anywhere.

On the side facing the distant foothills, she noticed a vague road ran from them to the plateau. Also, this side's angle wasn't as steep. Maybe thirty, thirty-five degrees? A sharp grade but not impossible, and boards had been put down over the deeper ruts in it. Those might offer some usable information.

Thing was, she could not see any fresh tire tracks leading along that trail. Or up the side or around the plateau. That strongly suggested whoever did this was — oh, dare she think it? *Covering their tracks?*

The thought made her snort with derision.

She turned to look the car over, more carefully. Why drive it up here and *then* wash it? Just to remove fingerprints? DNA? Possibly, but it was still weird.

She continued around the periphery of the plateau, glancing between the edge and the car, finding nothing.

Until she reached the Mercedes' tail.

And got a good look at the license plate.

From California.

ZtaziBB.

Eldora sagged and a long, weary sigh whispered from her.

Bushy red eyebrows.

Grady Cannon.

Oh, no, no, no, no, no, no, no, no. Those implications were not acceptable. Not in my territory, dammit.

"Hey, Reymon," she called down. "Got ID on this car yet?"

It couldn't be. It couldn't be. Tell me it's not. Tell me it's not.

He stepped out of his SUV to call back, "Yeah. Belongs to Anastasia Deveaux. Got an address on Wilshire, in LA."

Oh, shit, shit, shit, shit, shit. It was.

But just to be safe — "You sure 'bout that?"

"That's who comes up. But that's a guy up there, isn't it? And that name? I heard that name, somewhere — oh-oh-oh! She was in the middle of that drug shit, back when I was in training."

Eldora stormed back down from the plateau, snarling, "Pipe it down, Raymon! We don't know what's goin' on, yet. Seal off the area, best you can. Call in some of the boys. We're doin' a full search, five-hundred feet out before sundown."

He held up a roll of Police Tape. "Already on it." He tied one end of the roll to his SUV then unwound it to mingle in some scrub, the other side of the road.

The first BLM Agent met her at the base of the hill. "I know that name. She was on the news, night before last."

Three nights ago, idiot, Eldora thought. Why were BLM guys always so limited in their intellectual capacities and not cute enough to make up for it?

He continued with, "Tried to kill her married boyfriend then killed herself. In LA."

Which was the official word, but nothing had been mentioned about her car missing. And no way in hell had it been parked here since before her death; it was too damn clean.

"Careful what you say, son," she said to him. "Her father's Winston Deveaux. A state rep. He gets pissy 'bout gossip."

"Ain't gossip; it's news."

"Fine, you can tell him that. Or you can be smart and shut the fuck up." She looked around, and frowned. Down the trail she saw dust from an approaching vehicle.

"Raymon, you got a statement from these boys, yet?"

"Yeah. Recorded on my phone."

She nodded and turned back to the BLM Agent. "Okay, you and your partner ought to head back to federal property. Keep it low till we got an idea what happened. Deveaux is not a happy man, right now, and he already hates Bureau people; no need to give him any targets. You got me?"

The BLM Agent nodded and called to his associate, "George, let's head home."

The green BLM Agent nodded and wandered back to his SUV. The first guy got in his own and they started to turn around for the road, but Eldora stopped them. She pointed across the flatland to the arroyo and said, "Go back that way; it runs around under The 14, just a ways down. I didn't see any tire tracks when I crossed it, and I don't want any extra tire tracks 'round here." Then she smiled. "'Course, it's a little muddy. Think these sweet little baby trucks'll make it?"

The man snorted, relayed the directions to George and in moments, they were gone.

The funeral home's van pulled up, just then, and she walked over to meet it.

It would be an understatement to say she was not happy.

*****

She would have been even less happy if she had known that, just over a mile away, up in the rocks of the foothills, Carli was watching her through the sniper scope of a NEMO Omen .300 Rifle. A tan tarp stretched between two boulders protected her from the sun's glare, and the rifle was propped on its stand, as steady as it could be. Next to it was her phone, and next to that, a radio receiver attached to her laptop.

Recording from a small, high-powered microphone she had taped to the bottom of the Mercedes' exhaust pipe.

She chuckled at how confused they'd be, when they found it.

She shifted to watch Raymon unfurl the roll of tape. Which made for very pleasant viewing; she did love a man who fit his uniform so nicely. Points for that. And for his big brown eyes and open smile. He was on the young side, but since when did that matter?

And what was even better?

Her research had found he was still in training when Lara was raped. The so-called *investigation* and aftermath was all the Sheriff's and county DA's, so he could be kept out of the mess.

Which made Carli happy. She hated to hurt pretty things. She just hoped he would stay out of the way.

She shifted the scope to watch Eldora approach him.

"You okay, son?" the sheriff asked, her voice barely crackling through the receiver. They were at the edge of its range.

"That guy," Raymon said. "You think he was dead 'fore the ants and...and...everything got to him?"

It took Eldora a moment to say, "Hope so."

Carli chuckled and quietly snarled, "How kind of you to concern yourselves."

She drank some water and watched two men get out of the gleaming white funeral van. Her hope was they wouldn't take very long; she didn't have anything to eat, up here. But she could handle it. She had once gone without food for two days, in the 'Stan, thanks to a dumb Second Lieutenant who waited till the last minute to send off an order for provisions, the logistics office taking their sweet time sending them out, and the supply convoy being attacked. It took that to convince them that *just in time* shipping simply did not work in a war zone.

But watching Eldora and Reymon climb back up onto the plateau then take photos with their phones, she got the feeling they'd be done and gone around dusk. Then she could slip back to her campsite, have a can of beans and a beer, boil some water for a nice hot shower and get ready for stage three in her war plan.

A lovely young man named Zeke.

Word Spreads Like Buttah

Cantina Madriza's first hour was going to be quiet, again, so Rhonda made sure all the tables and booths were clean and the pool equipment in place while Zeke checked stock and went online to put in orders for whatever was getting low. Big, bad, boss Dax was insistent about maintaining a certain level of supply, especially as regards the beer. Which always made Zeke huffy. They had almost enough for a brewery in the cooler by the back door. There was also an apartment refrigerator under the cash register to keep the mixers, and a small ice maker next to it, though ice was not much in demand since the brews were the big draw.

The good thing was, the Cantina had kick-ass WiFi, thanks to a satellite dish. On a dead night, or a sleepless one, Zeke could fire up video games on his cell phone or the bar's computer. His laptop was also patched into it, giving him access to loads of streaming channels.

Dax let kids from an Apache community down the road come in to use it for their homework. Oren, the scroungy old desert rat who did the Monday-Tuesday cleaning, would let them in those days; Zeke did the rest of the week. Tables in one extension were set up specifically as their space, so long as they were done by seven; that was when things would normally pick up.

Zeke enjoyed seeing them working at their tables. Ranging in age from six to sixteen, they murmured encouragement to each other, tossed suggestions about and tracked along on shared laptops and tablets till the Cantina's witching hour was close at hand. Then they would scurry to get done and out the door so one of their parents would ferry them home in a passenger van/school bus. It was all so domestic.

Zeke had never known his parents. Orphaned at five months of age, he had been adopted by the Reverend and Mrs. Lindstrom in Chapel Hill, Minnesota. At least, he assumed he was orphaned. He had no idea who his mother or father were, if he had brothers and sisters, or what his real family line was. The Lindstroms had always refused to discuss it. The closest he got was when he was ten and, in a rare moment of sharing, Mrs. Lindstrom had told him, "Me, I was born in Stockholm but the mister was in St. Paul. It was his parents born in Upsala, both."

"So where was I born?" he'd asked.

"Close here," was all she said.

Then not another word. So he decided if the Lindstroms were going to be his full-fledged parents, then he was going to be a Viking, like Thor.

Oh, they had not liked that, at all. They considered Vikings to be vicious beasts, thieves who ransacked monasteries and poor little villages and on and on, and had tried for years to crush the idea. Finally, after the umpteenth lecture on the evil of his chosen lineage, he had responded with, "I gotta be something, and you won't tell me who I am, so I'm them."

Which had brought him a night without supper and a week of holy silence from them both. Then came the lectures turned to how he was an ungrateful child. How he'd been brought away from an orphanage — which one they never would say — and how they had given him a warm home, food, clothing and a chance at a good life.

Zeke wasn't ungrateful; he knew the Lindstroms had provided him with a finer existence than he probably would have had, anywhere else. Even though they were strict Lutherans, he was treated well-enough. So he had done well throughout school, and played football, basketball, baseball, and ice hockey. Treated the Lindstroms with respect. Helped around the house. Had friends they actually approved of. Dated girls they liked. Even attended Sunday services at the Reverend's church.

In a suit and tie.

From the age of four.

But never were they *mom* and *dad*; always *Reverend and Missus Lindstrom*. Like how you'd address a babysitter or friends of your grandparents. Never one word of praise or affection, just expectations met or not. A rather cold and austere existence, both physically and emotionally. It took him years to recognize this was not really normal.

Once he did begin to wonder, he found he had no friends he felt were close enough to discuss it. They all seemed too happy at home.

No Ingmar Bergman introspection, please; we're Nordic, not chatty-cathys.

Still, one girl he liked, Katherine Holstrom, who was blond and round and easy to kiss and fool around with, did once say, "Sometimes I wonder if you're their kid or their pet."

"What you mean?" he'd asked.

"You never do anything they don't want you to. Like you've been to obedience school. None of the other boys're like that."

Fortunately, by that point he was smart enough to keep her comments to himself. But the vague understanding that his existence was not like that of others began to dig at him. He paid more attention to the kids around him and saw Katherine was right; they had built a sense of independence and self-assurance that he did not have, and it built in him a growing confusion and sense of worthlessness that finally exploded when he was seventeen.

One form of the Lindstrom's tight control had been to never allow him much spending money. Nor was he allowed to work after school. Instead, he had to focus on his studies when not at practice or church. Well, there had to be some way around that, so Zeke began scoping out ways to bring some cash in, surreptitiously, of course. Being an observant lad, he had finally noticed one way of doing it was by offering *recreational chemicals* to the kids, at school.

A senior linebacker was the main source for that sort of fun, so Zeke had seen to it they became buddies. The Lindstroms approved of this because, even though he was Catholic, he was on the football team. That excused a great many sins. Then when he graduated on to Notre Dame, Zeke happily took over his source, clients and stash.

His first real act of rebellion...well, second, if you included the Viking aspect of his life.

His third was using his initial profits to pay for an elegant tattoo of a Viking face and helmet on his left calf. The Reverend and Mrs had long insisted ink on the skin was a sign of the devil. So he'd worn nothing but long pants and jeans for months after. But eventually the Mrs. did catch a glimpse of it and informed the Mister, and he'd demanded Zeke have it removed.

Which was met with a blank refusal. Zeke had just turned eighteen and knew he was under no legal obligation to do what the man said.

His fourth act of rebellion.

To say things had deteriorated rapidly, from there, was like saying America's Civil War was a family disagreement. The lectures became rants. Zeke was used as an example of the evils of recalcitrant children, in his sermons. The self-adulation by the Lindstroms continued, with them openly providing him with all he needed until he graduated high school, despite his turn to the devil, because they *had promised God to so do*.

Then not a week after he crossed the stage to accept his diploma, Zeke had been busted for dealing. The cops had coerced a semi-friend into buying some pot from him, and after the merest of trials he had been sentenced to ten years in prison. That is when the Lindstroms had washed their hands of him. In fact, he was fairly certain it was Mr. Lindstrom who had narc'd on him. It wouldn't have taken much talk in his congregation to work out how Zeke was making his money. Fortunately, the judge had given him the option to join the marines, to get out of it; once he got an idea of what prison would be like, he had jumped at the chance.

He had neither seen nor spoken with the Lindstroms, since.

For which he kept telling himself he was not the least bit sorry.

But now that ink was gone, along with his calf. He'd been riding in a Hummer when the bomb went off. Two other grunts had died, and they damn near lost him, twice before they got him to the medical unit. Then came waking to find he was no longer whole, after which was months and months of surgery and painful physical therapy...and deep, dark despair.

Every moment of it scarred into his psyche.

He had an idea that if the Lindstroms had been informed of this, they probably felt more than a bit of self-satisfaction at how their claim the tattoo was the mark of Satan had been proven true. Zeke, however, felt it had protected him by sacrificing itself. Which served to intensify his connection to the idea of being a Viking. A man unto himself and beholden to no one...

Well, no one but Grady and Loki. Both of whom had helped him through his darkest times. They were his family, now.

Loki, his blue-speckled Cattle dog. Who was more protective of Zeke than anyone had ever been. He would always let him know when someone uncertain was approaching. Not by barking, but by putting himself between him and them, standing very still and growling.

So Zeke pretty much liked his life, right now. Liked being alone, miles from anyone. Untroubled by the snarling world of civilization. He could play his guitar until six or seven in the morning, which was when he usually started getting sleepy. Or he could punch at a heavy bag hanging from a post by the front porch. He had even set up a make-shift target range behind the trailer, to practice shooting. He could also just get drunk and howl at the moon all night. With Loki joining in. Then would come a shower, to where he would be relaxed enough to sleep the day through.

With the AC on full blast, of course, even in winter. He still had the Minnesota climate in his blood and just could not rest when it was too hot, and never mind that bullshit about it being a dry heat.

What made it all even better was, he had a special place to go to, every Friday night. He'd hop on that old Harley, Loki in a cozy dog-seat and on his best behavior, and ride to a road twenty-odd miles down The 14 that provided a straight line to a multi-level group of rocks. Up on them, he could just sit and watch the sun rise, slow and elegant. Remind himself of the beauty of the world.

On the occasions he did need someone to be with? Well, Grady had introduced him to Loretta's, a nice, big, rambling ranch house in Scottsdale, where the girls took care of him in every way. Especially one named Candy, with wild, woolly hair and ebony skin. She loved Loki almost as much as he did, and truly did seem to enjoy just being with them both. And never a comment about his missing leg.

Just release.

Comfort.

Non-important companionship.

Amidst some of the ugliest green furniture, ever.

The situation last night had unsettled Zeke enough that he felt it was about time for another visit, come Monday. Not so much for the sex but the moments of just lying next to Candy and talking about nothing. He had more than enough cash put aside, thanks to tips, and the next ten days were shaping up to be quiet as hell, at the Cantina. Not just due to Spring Break but apparently there was some big biker gathering up in one of the Dakotas, so most of the locals were heading out. He could use a moment or two of female companionship, and Loki wouldn't mind being pampered.

He was about to call Loretta's for an appointment when he heard a pair of choppers roar up and Loki start barking in fury. Zeke knew exactly who was about to enter and called to Rhonda, "Guess who."

Rhonda rose from her table and snuck the book she was reading behind the bar, saying, "Now? He never shows till after midnight."

She put two glasses and a fifth of Jack Daniels on her tray — the real stuff, not the cheap one that was sold to those who didn't know any better — as Zeke filled a pitcher of Coors.

Sure enough, a moment later, Dax Castor, the human version of a junkyard dog, with a long snarly face, stringy salt and pepper hair in a pony tail, and his usual ensemble of ratty t-shirt, dirty jeans and biker boots, stormed in, yanking off gloves and a leather jacket. His every vibe screamed, *Do not fuck with me.*

"Zeke," he snarled, "one of these days I'm gonna shoot that fuckin' mutt of yours."

Zeke and Rhonda exchanged a quick glance; boss-man was not happy.

"C'mon, I keep him chained when I'm working," Zeke shot back, forcing a chuckle.

"Fuckin' shit. Rhonda! Usual."

"Comin' right up," she said, giving Zeke a roll of her eyes. He grinned back.

Right behind Dax was JJ Howith, sturdy, fair, burn scars to his neck, in a nicer version of the typical t-shirt and jeans, but atop Dingo boots. He walked with a slight limp because his leg had been burned and repaired. He and Dax went everywhere together, to the extent some people referred to him as Dax's shadow...or version of Loki.

Never to either man's face, of course.

They were headed to their usual booth next to the pool tables when Dax stopped and spun around to Zeke. "You seen Grady, yet?"

The pitcher of beer was almost done.

"Not since last night," Zeke said. "He doesn't usually show till about nine."

Dax huffed and joined JJ in the booth. They whipped out their cell phones and made call after call, most going like...

"It's Dax. Grady been 'round? ... Today, yesterday? ... You sure? ... Shit."

"Hey, Priss, it's JJ. Have you seen Grady, recently? ... When was that? ... Thank you."

"It's Dax. You seen Grady, today? ... When? ... You sure? ... Yeah, thanks. Fuck."

"Hey, Bobby, it's JJ. Has Grady been around? ... Last day or two. ... Thanks. Bye."

What none of them knew was...

A couple hundred feet down The 14, snuck behind an area of scrub and cactus, sat an old Dodge Ramcharger 4x4. It was painted matte black, including over the chrome, so was all but invisible in the darkness, and on its dashboard was a black China urn, the only part of it that was shiny. Seated cross-legged in its back, the tail down, was Carli, dressed nice and casual, a laptop open before her. That radio receiver was next to her, plugged into the truck's AC outlet, and she was wearing earbuds so she could listen to the conversations inside the Cantina.

Seems the night before she had surreptitiously taped a tiny radio mike under the pool table when she crouched down to eye a lineup of balls. Now that mike was so close to the booth, Dax's and JJ's voices were coming through, loud and clear, as were Zeke and Rhonda.

Dax was saying, "Izzy says he picked up, yesterday."

And JJ replied, "He hasn't been to Priss's in two weeks, and Bobby said he's a no-show, this morning."

Carli frowned. Apparently, word was taking its time getting to them. Then she heard Zeke call over, "Say, Dax, want nachos?"

Inside, Dax had slumped back on the bench by the booth's table, but he perked up and cast Zeke a look. "Fresh supply?"

"Got everything in, yesterday."

JJ finished a gulp of beer and chimed in with, "Extra jalapeños?"

"Hotter'n shit," Zeke said.

"An' can you add...?"

Dax cut him off with, "No! No! No! No beans." Then he said to Zeke, "Makes this asshole fart too goddamn much."

In the Ramcharger, Carli smirked. *Pun intended?*

The video of Lara's rape was playing on her phone, showing JJ enjoying himself. She froze it and opened a folder on her laptop labeled *Motherfuckers*. It held a list of other folders; the two labeled Stasi and Grady were highlighted in red. Below them were folders labeled Zeke, Spit, Dax, Nat and JJ, all highlighted green.

A window in the upper left corner of the screen showed a program transcribing a readout of the voices. She ticked into the folder to pull up JJ's mug shot and...

Another chopper roared up The 14, from town.

Carli hunkered down to peek between the seats and watch a young man hop off the bike and remove his helmet.

"Nat Edmonds," she murmured.

He was black, younger than everyone, trimmer, wearing a shirt with a collar and slacks over his untied Doc Martens, no jacket. He also sported an eyepatch and scars on his face.

Carli shifted to a section of the video that showed him as he raped Lara, his trousers unbuckled and loose around his hips, no shirt but a gold cuff, the look of purest bliss on his face.

Carli watched him march inside with that stick-up-your-ass gait so prevalent in ex-Marines, and she all but purred, "And that's the last fucker accounted for."

As Nat entered the Cantina, Zeke slid an open jar of cheese into a microwave. They gave each other a wave then Nat crossed straight to Dax.

Zeke seemed focused on setting up the chips, salsa and jalapeños for the nachos, but he was listening to every word, worried. It wasn't like Grady to be unreliable.

Nat spoke with an educated lilt to his voice. "It appears the last time our charming compatriot, Grady, was observed by anyone is yesterday evening, when he departed this establishment in the companionship of that Elvira-style female."

Dax glared at him and snarled, "Shit, talk English."

JJ was confused. "He didn't hit Bellamere's for dinner? He loves meatloaf Thursdays. Swears the sweet corn alone is worth it."

Nat shrugged to him and said, "There is no doubt he did not enjoy their...um...*questionable* repast, today. I am acquainted with a lovely young waitress in their employ. Eyes of amber, and with the idea my eloquent usage of the English language is quite glorious." He aimed that last bit at Dax. "By her recounting, he has avoided their less-than-fine-dining establishment since — well, since his awkward proposal to her for a night together was rejected."

Rhonda brought over another glass, for Nat.

"Right," she said, fighting a laugh. "What he said was, *Let's you and me get drunk and fuck, some night.* Real class."

JJ shook his head and called to Zeke, "You think of anything else he might've said to that bitch, Zeke? Like where they were going?"

Zeke glanced at them and said, "Just what I told you." But he was not liking the direction this was headed.

Dax huffed. "Shit, some girl picked *Grady* up?"

JJ had to agree. "That'd be a first."

"Oh, Dax," Rhonda said, leaning against the end of the booth table, "she wasn't no girl, no more."

In the Ramcharger, Carli almost laughed. "You bitch."

Inside, Nat slid in next to Dax. "My supposition?" he said. "She descended deep into inebriation, and now regrets her indiscretion, so does all she can to keep it surreptitious until she has departed our fair locale."

Dax snorted. "Fuckin' shit, Nat, you gotta sound like a fuckin' dictionary all the time?"

Nat smirked and pulled an old paperback thesaurus from his back pocket, saying, "This is a more appropriate reference."

Dax glared at him. He hated being shown up, but the kid was so happy doing it, getting pissy would have been like kicking a puppy, and the only dog Dax hated was Loki.

JJ took Rhonda's hand, gentle and easy. "You agree with what Zeke says? That she was pretty? He can be way too nice about people."

Zeke shot a glare at him as the microwave dinged.

Rhonda slipped her hand away from JJ. She liked him, but not enough to let him think he had a chance with her.

"No," she said, "she had tits to here. Ass to there. Her waist tied in so tight it's amazing she was able to move. And so much makeup on, it would've cracked if she'd smiled. Black wig probably means gray hair. My bet is she was wearing a girdle three sizes too small, maybe a bustier tied up, and she all but screwed him on the table, she was so hot for his ass."

Zeke finished making the nachos, saying, "C'mon, Rho, it wasn't that bad. Grady's not exactly bulldog ugly."

She and JJ shared a *See what I mean?* look, then she went to pick up the nachos.

Dax snarled. "If that fuck's dissed us for a fuck, he better have some fuckin' selfies."

"As good as Laila's, I hope," JJ said.

"That's if he *can* get to his phone," Rhonda smirked over her shoulder.

"What's that supposed to mean?" Dax asked.

"Oh, I believe I captured your intent quite well, Rhonda," said Nat, chuckling. "And I would not be the least bit taken aback."

Rhonda giggled as she brought the Nachos back to the booth.

JJ glanced between them. "You think she pulled this shit to rip him off? Get him hot and horny then tie his ass up and make off with the cash he had?"

Rhonda rolled her eyes as she set the nachos on the table. "C'mon, JJ, how's she gonna know he's got a dime on him, the way he dresses and skulks around?"

Zeke huffed to himself. One reason he did not let Rhonda get too close to him was how she loved to talk behind your back.

"Then I don't get it," JJ said. "What's she after?"

Rhonda set down her tray, took hold of his hands and crossed his arms at the wrist, then lightly wrapped her cloth around them and batted her eyes. "Y'know, some girls just wanna have fun," she said as she pulled the cloth away.

He looked at her with complete confusion as she walked away.

Nat did laugh. "JJ, do you continue to retain a lovely memory of Mademoiselle Madeline at *Les Trois Coquettes* in New Orleans? Her little peccadillo?"

Now JJ got it. It took him a moment to get past the ideas flooding his mind, and he still had to force himself to accept reality. "With *Grady*?"

Nat merely shrugged.

That's when Dax's cell phone rang. He checked the number then growled, "Chase, why the fuck you callin' me on — ?" His voice cut off. "What you mean? ... I don't know why he wasn't there. He's never not been, before. ... Yeah, no, no, I got plenty. Usual place, tomorrow. ... You know JJ, right? ... Okay, okay, he'll be there, with me. Nine a.m. ... I don't give a fuck about your test. You want the shit or not? ... Okay, fuck! Four-thirty! Fuckin' right. Shit."

He ended the call and noticed both JJ and Nat were watching him. "Fuckin' Grady missed a meet-up with fuckin' Chase."

In the truck, Carli frowned and flipped through her notes as she listened to JJ say, "Didn't know he had one." She found no mention of a Chase. That was an interesting revelation. She added it to her list.

"He called Grady yesterday," Dax was saying as she used her laptop to open the college student roster and do a search for CHASE. "He's almost out of supply. College brats're freaked over mid-terms. Usin' anything they can to keep calm or stay awake. They were supposed to connect at six, today."

Ten male names with *Chase* in them showed up as being students, with another as a faculty member. It would take too long to figure out which one belonged to the gang, and the only video she had was of the four men raping Lara. TF's research had not dug into other members of Dax's gang. Now she wished they had.

Inside, JJ asked Nat, "What about the other kids Grady works?

You find them?"

Nat slapped a wad of bills on the table. "Tribute to his majesty from our loyal Westside minions. They still awaited our man's arrival when I appeared, and they cursed his name in language I am loathe to repeat, seeing as how there is a lady present."

Rhonda giggled.

"However," Nat continued, "I am, unfortunately, unable to locate the lads known as Luna and Madrigo."

In the truck, that caught Carli's attention. More names she didn't have. Okay, maybe it was a mistake not to expand on their info.

She thought for a moment then dug into a backpack and pulled out another radio mike. She looked up and down the road, saw no more headlights approaching so removed the earbuds, slipped out of the Dodge and carefully snuck up the road to the Cantina's parking area. Under the starlight, Dax and JJ's choppers, two gleaming beasts of chrome with phenomenal paint jobs on their bodies, all but glowed. Nat's bike was a bit more commonplace but somehow seemed better cared-for.

She caressed the chopper with *Dax's Beast* incorporated into the paint, then she stuck the mike under its second seat, after which she scurried back to the Dodge.

Inside, since there was no one else in the Cantina, JJ started counting bills as Dax lit a joint. He was not happy with what he was thinking. After Grady's wreck and burns, Dax had maintained contact. Once he was done with rehab, he'd brought him into the gang. And never once had he reason to complain. Grady did what he was told when he was told. As for Zeke, he was happy running the Cantina and handling the bank. The only person Dax trusted more than them was JJ, and that was because they had both been clipped by the same suicide bomber, near Mosul. Somehow, JJ had managed to keep Dax from bleeding to death, even as his own leg was messed up.

But then, all of Dax's guys were messed up in one way or another, thanks to those two fucked-up wars. Spit had been a contract driver in a convoy that had been attacked, in Iraq, and got his back torn up, while Nat lost his eye in the run-up to the evacuation of Kabul. His father had been Dax's DI, and he had quietly acknowledged that sometimes making a living means a guy's gotta do what a guy's gotta do, since no one was willing to hire any of them for a *legal* job.

That's why he took care of them, because he knew they would do the same for him. Loyalty counted more than ability, and *back me up* had been his only request, which they had done. So Grady vanishing was not something to let pass.

He had to agree with JJ about that bitch. Yes, Grady wasn't exactly hound dog ugly, but he was barely house-trained. And now that he knew the guy might have pulled some supply from their stash for Chase? The whole situation reeked like old fish.

Now, Chase, there was one little sneak Dax didn't trust as far as he could throw him. One of those shitty college brats who had to be reminded, every now and then, just exactly who it was owned him. Could he be part of this? Could that phone call be him just covering his ass?

No. No, he wouldn't dare to pull anything. Not after that shit with Stasi.

Besides, Chase had warned him about another gang that had tried to make inroads with the college crowd. They had offered party drugs at a discount to woo clients away, and somehow, Chase had got some product from them. He'd brought it to Dax and they had found it was diluted by near half. Then Chase had suggested a new strategy.

"I can tell my clients they're buying quality, with us. Saves them money in the long run," he had said. "If we cost fifty percent more than them but you have to drop twice as much of their shit to get going? Well..."

Fortunately, JJ had been with them when Chase made the suggestion, and let Dax know the math didn't work out like that. But it was good in theory, so they'd agreed to charge a third more and emphasize to the clients that since they knew where it was coming from, they could tell it was good stuff.

It was a clever idea from the little shit. What was he into? Advertising? No, something else. But that had worked, and the new guys had been relegated to the poor sections of town.

So, what if *they* were trying a new tactic? Steal Dax's supply and push it off as their own? With that bitch as their decoy? But Dax didn't keep his backup goods in town and the only way they could have known Grady had some on him was if...

Was if Chase had told them.

Was he playing both sides?

Shit, Dax sincerely hoped he was not that fucking stupid.

His train of thought was broken when JJ called, "Hey, Zeke."

Zeke was setting out clean glasses, and did not even look over as he said, "Yeah?"

"'Nother pitcher. An' double up those nachos. Gonna be here reeeaaal late. An' goddammit, I want beans..."

Dax glared at him. "JJ, you start fartin' while we're sittin' here, I'm gonna light a fuckin' match t' you."

The microwave dinged.

"Already got another bowl started," Zeke said. "Beans on the next one, okay?"

He poured the melted cheese over the plate of chips and plopped a scoop of jalapeños on top.

JJ cast him a sorrowful look. "Ain't you got no *Frito Bean Dip*, there? Ain't gotta be warmed up."

Zeke sighed. "Lemme check the cooler." Then he set the plate on Rhonda's tray and added, "Dax, you want *me* to make some calls?"

"Who the fuck you know that I don't?" Dax shot back.

"Bartender at Selena's."

JJ smirked a chuckle. "Shit, Zeke, you trollin' dyke bars?"

"You want bean dip, JJ? Drop that crap! I know her from the 'Stan. She knows Grady, too."

Dax nodded. "Couldn't hurt. Hey, Rhonda, where's the fuckin' J-D?"

"Empty," she shot back. "Want another?"

"I gotta fuckin' beg in my own fuckin' bar? Shit!"

She and Zeke share an amused grimace, then he put a bottle next to the plate of nachos.

"Comin' right up, your highness," she said.

Zeke grabbed his cell phone and said, "I'll give Selena's a call."

In the Ramcharger, Carli muted the receiver, for a moment, and settled back, murmuring, "So, Zeke, you do seem like a nice guy. Are you, really?"

She had kept her interaction with him minimal, the night before. Same for Rhonda. The less attention paid the better for her. Of course, she hadn't been prepared for Rhonda's sharp observations regarding her disguise, but it was dumb not to expect it; women are like bloodhounds when it comes to picking out the problems in anyone they considered competition. Still, it shouldn't matter in the long run because...

An approaching car caught her focus. A Sheriff's SUV. She slid down to watch, from between the seats, as it pulled into the parking area and sat there for a moment.

Then Eldora got out.

This late? Still in uniform? Finally notifying the family?

Inside the Cantina, Zeke looked in the fridge and called, "Got you covered, JJ." Then he pulled out a can of *Frito Bean Dip* and set it to warming in the microwave.

Stacks of bills were on the table in Dax's booth. JJ was counting the last pile as Nat made notes in a ledger. Dax slammed his cell phone down, growling, "Now his voice mail's too full to take a fuckin' message."

That is when the door opened and Eldora strolled in, her eyes locked on Zeke. "What's a girl gotta do to get a drink around here?" she purred.

"Heard you drive up," he chuckled and poured her a bourbon.

Rhonda stayed at the other end of the bar, wary.

Eldora took the drink. Downed it in one swallow. Set the glass on the bar, obviously troubled. Without the slightest hesitation, Zeke poured another, ignoring how her eyes ran him up one side and down the other, like he was a prize stallion she was thinking of buying. It didn't bother him, but Eldora's interest did get under Rhonda's skin. Why, she didn't understand, because everybody knew the Sheriff liked girls, not boys. But she sure liked Zeke. Dammit.

Dax called to the sheriff, "You ain't seen Grady, have ya? Got him locked up some place, you psycho bitch?"

"Perhaps a later rendezvous in a prison environment?" Nat purred, a massive grin on his face. "You in your uniform? Him in a torn jumpsuit?"

Normally, she would have chuckled or flipped him off; this time, she just sighed and took her drink to Dax's booth, saying, "You get the strangest notions." She pulled up a chair to sit down. "So what's this I hear Grady picked up a good-looker?"

"How the fuck'd you know that?" Dax asked.

"Bellamere's. They're trying to figure out if it's true."

JJ chuckled. "Oh, Nat, you little gossip."

Nat shrugged. "They were already aware. I merely added she was a delicious female of the black-haired persuasion, by all accounts. Albeit not of the natural variety, according to our resident stylist."

"If you don't start talkin' normal," Dax snapped, "I'm gonna burn that fuckin' book."

Eldora picked up a stack of the bills and put them in her pocket. The other stacks were wrapped in rubber bands and slipped into a baggie.

"So nobody's seen Grady since last night?" she asked.

Dax took a shot of whiskey then a swallow of beer before saying, "He missed two meet-ups, didn't do all his collections, and we can't find a couple of his boys."

"That," Eldora said with a deep, troubled breath, "is not good."

"Don't gotta tell me."

"Maybe a set-up. Anybody know who his *female companion* is?"

"If I did, I'd of already asked what she did with him."

"And if she's got pictures," JJ said as he took the baggie to Zeke.

Eldora turned to watch him. "JJ, you share digs with Grady, right?"

JJ shrugged. "He drops at a bunch of places."

Dax muttered, "Paranoid freak."

Zeke took the baggie. "C'mon, Dax, you know what that means."

"And it is not a consistent issue, with him," Nat added. "There are full weeks where he's in complete control."

In the Ramcharger, Carli frowned at that. She checked her notes on Grady.

Nothing in his background about PTSD.

She heard Dax snap, "Yeah, yeah. Right. Right. I know. I just — I wanna know where the fuck he is!"

Inside the Cantina, JJ told Zeke, "That's all. Ready for the bank." And he farted.

Zeke jolted back, snarling, "Jesus, JJ — no beans for you, ever again!"

"I haven't had any, yet!"

"Exactly!"

Zeke hurried over to the cooler, a hand over his nose. Inside, shelves of wine and stacked kegs of beer lined two of the walls. Crates of bottle beer were along another wall. A single light, overhead, illuminated the unit.

Zeke pulled a duffel bag from behind some crates of beer and set the baggie into it, next to a dozen similar baggies.

He could just hear Eldora saying, "You hear 'bout the body we found?"

Nat responded with, "The truck stop was abuzz with little else. Their consensus? Some hopeful dreamer died in the crossing."

Eldora huffed. "Their consensus is for crap."

Zeke had to smile as he heard Dax say, "You understood what he said?"

Eldora chuckled. "I still got some English left from school."

JJ piped in with, "Eldora, why're you here, askin'? You...you don't think that body's...it's not..."

Eldora rose from the table. "I need some DNA. Could Grady have brushed his teeth, once or twice, in that rat-trap of yours, JJ?"

Zeke poked his head out the cooler's door, to listen closer.

"Why? What's going on?" JJ asked.

Eldora's sigh could have been heard clear to Phoenix. "You remember Anastasia Deveaux?"

Now every hair on Zeke's body tingled and his leg, which could be problematic but had been fine the last few days, suddenly sent a twinge up his spine.

Stasi? Why was she being mentioned?

He watched Dax pour the last of the second pitcher of beer, saying, "Fuck, wish I could forget the cunt."

"Don't we all?" Said Eldora.

"What's she got to do with anything? She killed herself."

"Did she?"

Dax looked at her and leaned back, in shock. "Shit, you think that body's Grady's."

Eldora just nodded.

"But what do you need DNA for?" JJ asked. "What happened to him? You sayin' that bitch did something to Grady that — that makes him unrecognizable?"

"Goddammit, JJ," Eldora snapped, "you've been here long enough to know how fast buzzards and coyotes and ants can work."

That sent a shudder through everyone.

Zeke staggered back and dropped onto one of the kegs, shaking his head in disbelief. He felt hollowed out as he heard JJ say, "The woman that picked up Grady, it couldn't have been Stasi. We know her. Shit, Zeke knows her, for sure."

"Right, it couldn't have been," Eldora said. "Because she's dead. Remember? I just think it's pretty damn weird her car..."

"Her car?" That was Dax asking.

Eldora nodded. "Deveaux's car wound up next to a body that was about Grady's size, and was tied up like a pot roast."

JJ sat on a stool by the bar, shaken. "But what makes you think it's...?"

"Red eyebrows."

Zeke felt like he had been punched in the gut. Oh, Jesus Christ, no, Grady couldn't be dead.

In the booth, Nat went online with his phone.

JJ could barely whisper, "That's what Comanches did to prisoners."

Eldora shook her head. "Uh, no, JJ, they staked them out. Besides, this is Apache territory. Rhonda, you notice what kind of car that woman drove?"

She was now at the other end of the bar, paler than usual, looking at nothing. "Mercedes convertible. Silver. New."

"Model?"

"Um...C Class. High end."

"You happen to notice the license plate on this one?"

"Um, no. Dealer plate? Maybe?"

"Hmph, that explains somethin'," Eldora said.

"What?" Dax growled.

"Piece of cardboard caught in one of the back license plate's screws." Then she started for the door, saying, "Well, I'm only ninety-nine percent sure it's Grady's body. There's always that one percent. Where's Zeke?"

He jolted and said, "Right there." Then he headed out of the cooler.

Eldora asked, "You hear?"

He nodded.

"I'm sorry. I know you and Grady were close. You get a driver's license off her?"

Zeke headed back to the bar, nodding. "I'll send it over."

"Thanks. JJ?"

JJ rose. "Yeah. Yeah. I'm done here. Follow me."

He grabbed his things, the bowl of chips and can of bean dip, and they headed outside.

Nat nudged Dax to show him his phone, saying, "Observe."

On it was a news story headlined, *LA WOMAN BATTERS MARRIED LOVER; JUMPS TO DEATH.*

Dax snarled, "I heard that. She really *was* crazy."

Nat softly said, "Dax, this happened in the early hours of Sunday. If her car was here, next to Grady's body...I believe the sheriff means us to understand this was not actually a suicide; that she also was murdered."

Dax glared at him. That put a whole new spin on things, to say the least. He was about to light another joint when he heard a car pull into the parking lot, rap blasting on its speakers.

"What the fuck? On a school night?" He grimaced, rose and pulled his things together, saying, "You handle Chase, tomorrow. He knows you, and Spit knows the location."

"But it's my understanding his back — "

"He's got a brace. An' all he's gotta do is get you there. He can take Katty's Malibu. I'll call him. And Chase won't give you no shit. I'll have JJ do Grady's collections, over by the college, around town. I'm gonna find out what I can. Zeke."

Zeke nodded, still shaken, as happy college-boy voices were heard, outside.

Dax rolled his eyes. "You wanna shut the bar?"

"No. No, better if I'm here. Something to do is better. Can I bring in Loki?"

"I ain't comin' back. You know Madrigo and Luna, right?"

"Yeah."

"Sorry, but I'm gonna need your help in the mornin'. Gotta talk to those two."

Zeke nodded his OK. "I'm not sleepin' tonight."

"Yeah. See you 'bout seven. Fifth and Colorado."

Zeke nodded.

Dax headed for the door.

Nat followed him, asking, "What meaning does this have?"

Dax sighed. "Dunno yet, but I'm sure as fuck gonna find out."

Then he and Nat exited.

Rhonda went to Zeke, hesitant. "You wanna talk?"

He shook his head. The boy's voices were heard approaching.

She continued with, "I'm...I'm gonna sit in the ladies', for a minute. Not think. Let it sink in."

He nodded.

"You gonna bring Loki in?"

He hesitated, then shook his head. He found himself unable to think. That woman picking Grady up and then him being dead? How could that be? He'd left so happy and excited, and now?

Now.

Three other men had been in that Hummer when he was hit, and two of them had died. Gone. Bam. Like that. But he had been comatose for so long, learning about it, once he woke up — it hadn't seemed real. He hadn't even begun to think of it as connected to him in any way. But Grady's death? It was like ice water in the face.

Right now, he did not want to even think about doing anything more than let it settle into him, like Rhonda was going to do. Being in the bar felt like that would keep him preoccupied long enough to let this happen.

Then he called, "Rho."

Turned out, she was still standing across the bar from him. "Yeah?"

"Have a Dos Equis?"

She smiled and nodded. She wasn't fond of beer, but this was a special moment.

Zeke pulled out a couple of long-necks and popped their caps. Then he and Rhonda tapped them to each other and took a drink and...

Five Rock-Jocks burst in, laughing and shoving each other, cloned in plaid shirts, cargo pants and Rocklands. Two of them were singing, "We're done, we're done, we're done; we're off to see the sun!"

And another car was heard approaching!

Rhonda rolled her eyes.

Zeke smiled. Maybe tonight wouldn't be so quiet, after all.

Incomplete Pass, Second Down

Carli sat in the driver's seat of the Ramcharger, watching bouncy college geology nerds come and go. Male and female. Thin and thick. All races. Packs of thin, squealing girls...raising the question as to why they were at Nathan Cruz, unless it was to get away from mom and dad and not have to do much to get a degree. But that thought got tossed aside, because her older brothers had bitched non-stop about how hard San Diego State was, and Nathan Cruz was, at the least, on the same level. Of course, TF hadn't once mentioned the level of difficulty at MIT, so maybe it was just a matter of perception.

After a while, she turned down the receiver. The program still recording their conversations as best it could, but she just could not handle how insanely insipid the kids were. *Those tests* this and *this teacher* that and boys who were cute and girls who were hot and whose dad was the greatest and whose mom was driving them crazy and how great it was to be done with mid-terms and how they had three to do, tomorrow.

Which begged a question, *Why're they out, tonight? Not looking good, there, kiddles.*

In the middle of it all, one set of girls, who sounded like they had wound up at Dax's booth, were all but salivating over *Prince Hot Tatts* and Jesus God, the nattering about his cute ass and sweet eyes and fine hands, and questions about how much of him might be tattooed, followed by more than a little egging each other on to see if they could get him to talk to one of them about his leg...it was hypnotic in its murmuring mundanity.

Carli knew they had to be at least twenty-one in order to be enjoying their Daiquiris, but she was shocked at how juvenile they sounded. Had she been such an idiot, at that age? She doubted it. By then, she had been through Basic and stationed at Fort Benning for three years. But even before joining the Army, she couldn't recall such childishness in her actions or attitudes about boys. They were only something fun to play with. She had learned early on that no man should ever be taken seriously.

That attitude was backed up by how obnoxious and idiotic her jock-ass brothers had been during their teen years. Well, the older ones. Matteo, Marco, Luca, and Gianni. As if using the Italian spellings hid how they were named after the Gospels. Buff, beefy, good-looking brats, sports stars, every one, they had given Carli an umbrella of protection while in school. Nobody fucked with the Vincenzo boys or their little sister.

Of course, it didn't hurt that Carli had been her own no-holds-barred-in-your-face type who took shit off nobody. Male or female. She was proud of the fact she'd been suspended at least twice a year for beating the crap out of some boy who thought she could be bullied. And what made it better? Since she was always blamed for these things happening, she got to play the victim with daddy and the bros.

Just not with momma.

"You should behave more like a lady," her mother had once snapped at her. "Then you wouldn't have these issues."

Carli had laughed then said, "Momma, you don't know jack about shit in junior high."

"Filthy mouth! You never learned that sort of language from your father or me."

"Nope," she'd said back. "Just the real world."

Which got her slapped.

That had been the only time her mother physically punished her. When was it? Was she pregnant with TF? No, soon after he was born; that would be about the right time.

Tomaso Federico Vincenzo. Who went by Tommy-Freddy, until he was twelve; then he declared he was TF and would answer to nothing else. And didn't. Like a switch had been flipped and he had no earthly idea who this *Tommy-Freddy* was.

Carli was stationed in Germany, at the time, enjoying the shit out of the beer if not the boys. Well, until she met Val, a lovely Persian Jew whose eyes, alone, put every elegant *kitteh* alive to shame. He got a card for Hanukkah and fond remembrances in Carli's memory bank.

TF had sent her a text with the announcement of his new moniker. Carli had replied, *OK*, and that *was* it. The rest of the family had problems catching up, but soon learned if they did not address him properly, they got ignored. Even momma had to go along, though Carli doubted the name change was really any big deal with her; not after having to deal with TF declaring at the ripe old age of ten that he was gay. Papa hadn't cared, mainly because he already had four carbon copies of himself, but momma had been anything but nice about it. Even threatened him with conversion therapy.

For the one and only time Carli knew of, her father had put his foot down and said, "No fucking way that's happening to one of my kids."

Literally.

Then he, Carli and the big bros had given TF enough support and care to make it to the age of sixteen without being crushed by momma's world of religious intolerance or the brutal, casual homophobia of his classmates. By that point, he was done with high school and such a netizen, he had half a dozen universities vying for him to attend. He once told Carli the main reason he'd chosen MIT was because it was the opposite end of the country from momma, and Manhattan had a nice big gay community.

"Um, MIT's in Boston, TF," she had said.

"Y'know, they have these things called trains," he'd shot back. "Straight shot into Penn Station."

"All right, all right, all right. Should've known you'd figure everything out."

"Never underestimate the planning power of a graphics fanatic."

Now he was twenty-two and already worth five times more than the rest of the family, combined, thanks to two apps and three programs he'd developed.

He was also Carli's backup. In two weeks, he had pulled together info that would have taken her two years to procure. Aimed her at the transcription program to use and what spy equipment would serve best. How to work around the easier passcodes while he handled the serious ones. Not once did she ask if his searches had been strictly proper, nor did he question her need for this equipment. All that mattered? While the whole family was angry and hurt over what had happened to Lara, he was the only other one who came even close to feeling the same cold rage as Carli. And who was willing to go as far as it took to find justice for her.

He was the one who dragged together how Lara had reported the rape, but both Sheriff Parridge and the DA's office had blown it off as a girl who'd agreed to have sex in exchange for drugs, not realized what it meant, and now had regrets. He also located video of Winston Deveaux actually deriding Lara on the state Capitol floor as emblematic of trouble caused by drugs, libtards, illegal immigrants, and everything else under the sun, thus increasing Carli's fury to a white hot level.

Didn't help that the state media also took pleasure in disparaging the victim with headlines like *College Girl Claims of Gang Rape Not Verified* and the like. So much so, even momma had initially been unwilling to believe the full story.

Which Carli had found inexcusable.

She was at Fort Wainwright, by Fairbanks, when it happened. The moment she heard, she had put in for leave. Which had been granted by everyone in the chain of command but the weather. A massive bomb cyclone had locked the area in with wind, ice and snow, so she had to wait till it was done.

Then just as it was letting up, she got a text from TF.

Lara killed herself.

Shaken, Carli had immediately called home, hoping it was a mistake or a typo or some cruel joke. From the very beginning, the conversation was not pleasant.

"Took pills," momma said. "Then sat in a tub of water. She was cold when they found her. TF called her phone while the police were going through her things. That's how we found out."

"Aw, Jesus, momma..."

"Don't blaspheme."

Carli held in her retort and just asked, "How's *he* doing? He won't respond to my texts or answer my calls."

"I have no idea. He won't talk to anyone. Matteo's going to fly up. Seattle wasn't hit as hard by the storm and...and he'll find him and talk to him."

"That should tell you how he feels."

"Should it?"

"Fine. I'll try him, again."

There was a long moment of silence, then momma's voice had taken on a cry of pain as she murmured, "I should have known she was too easy to control. Seen she had that same sneaking streak of stubbornness that reminds me so much of you."

Carli's voice had instantly gone sharp. "That the boys had, too."

"Not to mention maybe some of the same wanton genes, all courtesy of your father."

"I was never trapped in a gangbang, momma."

"You were never one to follow the rules, either. It amazes me you've lasted this long, in the Army."

"When a rule is just, I don't have a problem with it."

Which wasn't exactly true, but the claim fit the moment.

Only her mother's retort had been too on-target. "That's not the way the world works."

"Yeah, and you're proof positive."

She had ended the call.

They hadn't spoken, again, till after the funeral. Just emails and texts noting the burial plans. Most of which got sent through TF, once Matteo got him willing to interact, again.

The full story was slow in coming out. About the video being uploaded to *YouTube*. How a link to it had been posted on the college message boards. How Lara had been harassed by several boys on campus, wanting her to put out for them, too. Not to mention how many girls shunned her. It took less than seventy-two hours to convince her stealing a bottle of prescription tranquilizers from another room and downing them all was the answer.

The funeral's aftermath had collapsed into a vicious affair, especially when Carli raised the possibility of getting an attorney to help them navigate the legal proceedings of the case. Momma wanted to leave it behind and tend to her grief, fearing this would only prolong things.

"But look at what they're doing, down there," Carli had said. "They're making this all Lara's fault."

"Why do you care about her, now?" her mother had finally snapped. "It's not like you wanted her! I'm the one who raised her, who cared for her, who guided her while you were off around the world, enjoying your wanton ways. I was her true mother; you just dropped her into the world and let others handle your responsibilities for you, so now all of a sudden you want to act like she was yours, all along?"

Carli had nearly hit the woman, but three of her brothers had pulled her back. It was TF who'd actually calmed her, his hands on her arm, his voice shaking, "Please, Carli, please, not now, not today, please."

Carli had yanked herself away from them all and glared at her father, who was sitting in his easy-chair in their tidy home, looking at nothing, lost in his own sense of grief. Then she had returned to the burial site to sit on the grass and look around at the beauty of the cemetery. Its ponds and streams and weeping willows and gentle greenery, and cold, hideous peace. Not one tear had drifted from her eyes. Not one word was spoken. She just sat there till dusk approached, then took some of the dirt that covered the grave and put it in her pocket and walked away.

Vowing justice would be served.

That dirt was now in that black China urn affixed to the Dodge's dashboard. And she had not spoken with either her mother or her father, since. She had a feeling she should be sorry for that, but considering her father's constant weakness in the face of her mother's fanaticism, she just could not convince herself the last year of silence had been a mistake.

After all, phones worked both ways, and they had not tried once to call her, either.

Two months later, Carli was out of the Army and ready to push hard at the criminal justice system. She did not yet trust herself to be around those who had dismissed Lara's rape, so TF acted as her surrogate. He met with the county's DA. With the State's Attorney General. Judges. Lawyers. Victims' advocates. The university's lawyers. The full turntable.

When Carli asked him how he was able to face them without

launching into fury, he calmly told her, "I let our lawyer do the talking, because he sees them as people; I don't. They aren't human. None of them. They're blank slates programmed to think a certain way, the epitome of garbage in-garbage out. I'm studying them to see how best to process their limitations."

"And what did you find?" Carli'd asked, more than a little impressed.

"The only fix is to wipe clean and reinstall, and for some stupid reason you can't do that with this brand of idiot."

"So...we shift focus. Right?" And the smile on her face told him she had already worked up a plan.

He'd nodded and shrugged. "I figured you'd already programmed yourself for something. I'll see to it all the glitches're smoothed over."

"It could get nasty. Dangerous for you."

He had rolled his eyes and said, "Carls, I can handle it. Those motherfuckers fuck with me, I'll wipe the fuckin' floor with 'em."

She looked at him. He wasn't built like the Four Gospel Bros, but wasn't scrawny or undeveloped. Just tight and taut, and more than willing to use his hacking abilities to shred his enemies instead of the fist-to-face thing.

In the end, as expected, no one was held accountable. The college hid behind their legal department to avoid blame. The bastards who'd raped her swore it was a consensual encounter and *they really were just as angry about the video*. As everyone reported. So the DA refused to charge them. How anyone could accept that a crime had not been committed after watching the damned thing made absolutely no sense.

Stasi was allowed to leave with a diploma, thanks to daddy, and Carli's lawsuit against Nathan Cruz University, a *much discussed last resort to find justice*, had just been settled. Papers signed, last Friday. Waiting for the money to be transferred, which should be cleared, tomorrow.

In short, it looked like Carli's vow had not been kept.

What too many people failed to understand was, there are many other ways to get justice, if you're willing to take matters into your own hands. And if that was the best option left? Well...

A Thunder Hog roared to life outside the Cantina, its thrump-thrumping startling Carli from her reverie. She realized she was now lying across the back seat, her laptop asleep, her phone showing it was down to seven percent battery.

Had she dozed off?

That made no sense. When she was in the field, she'd learned a dozen tricks to stay alert. Granted, that was a few years ago, but still, hadn't she been paying enough attention to use them?

Not good.

She rose in time to see a couple of bikes race down the road towards town. Then three young men, only one of whom was worth even a glance, stumbled out of the Cantina with a pink-haired biker chick and poured themselves into a Porsche SUV. The woman got behind the wheel. If she was drunk, she didn't show it, while they most definitely were. They zipped away, next.

Then the Cantina's lights went off, and minutes later, Rhonda came out, slipping on a jacket. She hopped onto a Suzuki motorbike, pulled a helmet on her head and started it up. Then she rolled around and...

Headed straight for the Dodge!

Carli ducked down to let her pass, then used the rearview mirror to watch her ride on. She seemed not to have noticed the truck in the shrubs.

So the only person left in the Cantina was Zeke.

Who was on her list.

Carli smiled and caressed the top of her belt, where a sheath had been built inside the waistband of her pants, to anchor that knife.

She smiled and began putting herself back in order.

*****

Inside the Cantina, Zeke tied up his second bag of trash. Now the place was clean and ready for business, tomorrow. It helped that the crowd had thinned out to just a couple bikers and those Rock-Jocks with Laila.

Oh, Laila.

He shook his head. Eventually her actions were going to come back to haunt the joint, but he had learned long ago not to come between boys who thought they were about to be taken good care of and the nice, randy, ready biker babe who was going to do the caring. At least she was smart enough not to take things too far. Just a *big-eyed plea to help her make this month's rent.* Repairs on her non-existent Lincoln, *that she really-really needed to get to work. Hospital bills for her sick grandmother,* who lived in Cleveland and ran five miles a day. Simple things to make simple boys think they were simply doing good. So, let them have their fun.

He turned off the last of the interior lights, except for one over the rear exit. Without the colorful twinklers and tubes of neon bubble and fat round bulbs glowing, the Cantina seemed just plain bleak. He grabbed a pair of icy Dos Equis and the trash bag, and headed outside.

The moment Loki saw him, he barked for joy.

"Hey, Loki-puppy. Almost done," he called.

He dumped the trash in a bin, locked the door, and limped up the incline to the mobile home. Loki gave him more happy woofs as he unchained him, provided some good rubbing pets then let him run around to snap at a few bugs and roll in the dirt.

Zeke smiled. "Y'know, if you get too dirty, you're sleepin' on the floor."

He hated chaining the mutt up, like this, but not two weeks after Lara's rape, Dax had roared up to the trailer, JJ with him, and pounded on the front door, screaming, "Goddammit, you motherfucker, why the fuck'd you tell the cops about that fuckin' video?"

It was about nine and Zeke had only just fallen asleep, so he was groggy and using a crutch when he'd opened the door, saying, "Dax, what the fuck?"

The second Dax had seen him, he'd yanked Zeke outside and punched him. Knocked him down. Was about to kick him when Loki had latched onto his boot and hauled him back. Only JJ catching him kept Dax from falling off the porch, where Loki would happily have shifted his teeth into his throat.

Zeke had scrambled to separate them as Dax bolted up and pulled his gun from a rear holster. Loki had howled and snapped at the man as Zeke had hovered over him, all but screaming, "Get away, Dax! He's just protectin' me! He's just protectin' me."

JJ had shoved Dax away, saying, "Back off. Back off! Zeke wouldn't do that to us. Stop and think."

"He was the only one there pissed off about it," Dax had snarled, waving the gun around.

"Chase was there."

Dax's glare had shifted to one side. "That little fuck wouldn't dare fuck with me. Tell the cops about that fuckin' video? Go against me?!"

By this point, Zeke had pulled himself up to lean against the door, one hand still gripping Loki's collar, ignoring the blood trailing from his mouth.

"Dax, what?" he'd said. "What video?"

Dax had glared at him, Loki still expressing exactly how much he would dearly love to dig into the man's belly.

"That little cunt, Stasi," he'd yelled. "Shot video of the guys havin' fun with that girl. Uploaded it to YouTube an' put the link on the college's message boards."

Zeke had gone weak and whispered, "Oh, Jesus Christ. Oh, no."

Then Dax had eyed him, uncertain. "Somebody told the cops an' Eldora's pissed as hell about it. It's all over the news."

"I never pay attention to that shit."

"You...you really didn't know?" Dax had finally stepped back, shaking his head. "Chase? Fuckin' Chase..." He had put his gun away. "Shit, Zeke, I'm sorry. You're the only one I thought would have the balls to do it."

Zeke had looked at him, confused. Cut to the core. "You think I — you think I'm a narc?"

Dax bristled. "No! No. I — that's what got me so fuckin' pissed off. I trust you an' I...I was sure nobody else would've done it an'...an' I just went nuts. I'm sorry."

Loki had cut down to merely growling, with an occasional bark thrown in for good measure. Dax had glared at him.

"That mutt's gonna go at me, again. I've seen dogs like that. He wants a piece."

Zeke had made himself say, "Don't worry. Don't worry. It'll be okay."

He had promised from then on he would keep Loki on a chain, when Dax might come around, and knew that was the only thing that had kept his pup, alive.

Well, that and the fact that Dax had actually seemed to feel bad about tearing into him. Especially once he'd verified it was the college who had reported the video to Eldora.

Zeke hopped up the steps to his porch, dropped on a padded folding chair right by the door, and pulled off his shoes. Next, he pulled his shorts off then unset his bionic leg. He leaned it next to the chair and sighed, long and easy. He finished his beer while massaging his thigh.

All he had left was from just above where his knee used to be. The scarring on it was mostly hidden by a swirling Viking design that would put *Game of Thrones* to shame. He had two other fake legs, of various designs, and it seemed alternating them helped keep from rubbing him too raw. Right now, while his stub was throbbing, it was not unlivable. Massaging it helped.

But sure as hell ain't goin' two-steppin', tonight, he told himself.

"Whoop, whoop, *Cotton-eyed Joe,*" he actually said, making Loki look at him as if he were nuts. "Wish I *was* crazy," he added.

Instead of feeling trapped.

That idea had been growing stronger and stronger in his head since the rape and suicide, a sense of guilt accompanying it. And the simple inability to decide what to do next.

He did not want to stay here. He had his benefits and money from his tips put aside, but where else would he find a place that was as quiet and easy as here? And after all that Dax had done for him? How could he dump on the guy? Sure, he was an asshole, sometimes, and the only thing standing between them and a raid by the Feds was Eldora, but he was usually okay. And hell, when he wasn't...well, even Grady'd had his moments of freak out, too.

Like this one Tuesday night he had burst in on Zeke. Not six months ago, in full paranoid mode, sure someone was messing with him. Certain it was the Feds looking to drive him nuts.

"I'm gettin' all kinds of shit calls on my phone," he'd muttered. "Calls from all over the States and they don't answer or when I try to call 'em back, it's a banned number."

"Just robo-calls, Grady," Zeke had said in his calmest voice. He'd guided the guy onto the couch and Loki had jumped up to beside him and just lain there, watching them both.

"But the phone numbers are shit," Grady had snapped. "It's the DEA! I know it. I'm gonna go to jail. I never been! Shit, the Army was bad enough."

It had taken Zeke an hour to calm him down enough to where he could watch an old episode of *Lassie* on Zeke's laptop, feeding himself and Loki strips of beef jerky as both locked in on that damn collie rushing back to the farm to bark that Timmy was in trouble.

When Grady had said, "Stupid fuckin' kid, always gettin' himself into shit," he'd known everything was cool, again.

Now Grady was dead.

Dead.

Shit.

And Zeke had to make it through the night. Alone.

Dusk to dawn had never been easy for him, even before he almost died. His mind just would not shut down. Far too often, the thoughts hitting him were vicious, cold and out of nowhere. Like remembering the second the blast happened. Or the pain of physical therapy. Or when he'd had both legs and would go climbing in the hills or swimming in the lakes of Minnesota. Now mixed in were imaginary visions of being jumped by a wild beast intent on tearing him to shreds, visions that sometimes were so real it was hard to convince himself they weren't. That was why one of the greatest blessings he knew was drifting into slumber, because he never remembered his dreams.

Well...that was not going to happen, tonight.

Not with Grady dying.

It had been a two-way street, with Grady. Sometimes in the first few years, he'd just shown up to sit with Zeke, on the edge of the porch, saying nothing as he sipped his beer. Knowing. Just knowing when he was needed. Not a word spoken. Let Zeke run the moments of silence as long as he wanted. As long it took to regain his center.

He'd shown up that day, after Dax's attack, and silently tended his cuts and quietly sneered, "Gonna have another scar, bitch. As if you ain't got enough."

Zeke had smiled and shrugged and said, "Road trip to Juarez, eh?"

Not anymore.

His brain kept drifting back to the horror of Grady's death. Left outside, bound, to be feasted on by the creatures of the desert. It was beyond comprehension that anyone could do that to anybody, no matter how much they hated them. And if he was alive at the time? The pain. The suffering. He could see it. Almost feel it. Made his skin cringe in sympathy.

And now the only person he'd ever thought of as family was gone.

He needed something to shift away from the horrific images that began to pound into him, so opened the screen door and pulled out an acoustic guitar. Still sitting on the chair, he fiddled with the strings, then played a gentle version of *Romance de Amor*.

The melody had been playing in the bar, in Juarez, the night Zeke got the first part of his thigh inked. Grady had pushed him across the bridge in his wheelchair and complained the whole way.

"It's been a rough week. I ain't up for it. My feet hurt. Should've grabbed an Uber. My arms are achin'. Ain't doin' this, again." On and on.

But after the tattoo shop had come beer and burritos, on Zeke, so he hadn't said a word while pushing him back. Probably helped they were both seriously on the drunk side. And that Grady had tried to work his charms on the immigration clerk. Which had nearly got them busted for harassment. It was only Zeke laughing out of control that had saved them.

That and Stumpy being very visible.

The next time they'd gone, Zeke had made himself walk on his new bionic leg. It had hurt like shit, but Grady had been solicitous the whole way. And the steady nudging of the needle had handled a lot of the soreness. That was when Zeke had finally begun to accept he could make it back to life. So he'd bought this plain guitar in a shop near the bridge. For a hundred pesos.

Self-taught, he wasn't as smooth as he would have liked. It took him more focus than most people, he was sure, but that's why he liked playing it. The melodies seemed to come out like they were his, and they did a lot to lift his mood. He'd never make *America's Got Talent*, but he wasn't interested in that crap, anyway, and...

Loki skidded to a halt.

Zeke stopped playing.

The dog turned.

And sniffed.

And listened.

Then growled towards the Cantina and carefully positioned himself beside Zeke, in a warning stance and attitude.

Okay, this was serious. It wasn't Dax returning, because Loki would be barking and tearing off after him. Still...

He carefully set the guitar by his chair and reached back around into the trailer, his eyes scanning the area. He had an old M-16 that was in top condition propped just inside the door. He brought it out and held it, ready to fire.

Into darkness.

Into silence.

Into nothing?

"Careful," he finally said. "Loki don't like surprises."

After a moment, a woman appeared from a shadow.

Zeke tensed. Kept his finger on the trigger. Was it the same woman? The form didn't look right. The hair was shorter. But Rho had mentioned she'd been in disguise. Best play it safe.

"You can stay there," he said, his voice carrying the hint of a quiver.

"Sorry," she said. "Just listening to the music. It's pretty."

"Bar's closed."

"I know, I just..."

"So what you doing here?"

"I dunno. I was bored. Thought maybe I'd find some fun, but I arrived late."

"From where?"

It took her a moment to say, "The college."

"That's twenty miles off," he said.

She shrugged. Moved a bit closer. Ran a finger over her belt.

Loki's growl went low and dangerous.

"You really need to stay over there," Zeke said.

She stopped. Said, "Nice dog. Protective. What's his name?" Then she held up a hand, realizing. "No, wait, you said — he's Loki. Right? The trickster."

Zeke just nodded.

She crouched. Offered to let Loki sniff her hand.

He did not even think about approaching her. Just kept glaring at her. Softly rumbling.

She finally rose.

"You're doing good," said Zeke. "If he thought you were a real threat, he'd have bit you, by now."

"Is that why he was chained?"

"How'd you know about that?"

She hesitated then motioned to the chain lying in the dirt. "I don't think it's there for you."

Zeke leaned back, still wary. "Okay."

"Oh, you...um, you work here?"

He gave her another shrug. Still frowning. Rifle still in hand.

She continued with, "What time do you open?"

"Six."

"A.M.?"

He snorted in response.

She sighed. "Yeah. Right. Makes for a nice, short commute."

"Works okay."

"Your...your leg. Iraq or Afghanistan?"

"It matter?"

"No. It's just I..."

He caught on to her hesitation. Her confusion. His voice became more gentle. "You do a tour?"

She hesitated then said, "Yeah. Logistics. Bagram. Few years ago. I was AMS. Saw guys messed up like that, so many times."

Zeke relaxed a little more. "Marines. Three-three."

"Helmand? Wow."

"How long you been out?"

"Oh, just over ten months. You?"

"Eight years. Y'know, bar closed near an hour ago."

"Did it?"

"Don't you know what time it is?"

"Oh, I...no, I — truth is, I was sitting in my car. For hours. Um, trying to talk myself into going inside. Just for a beer. Then I couldn't even get myself to go home."

He quietly propped the M-16 between his legs.

"Still want one? Shot?" he asked, his voice gentle.

She looked at him. Everything about her said she was deeply confused. She ran a finger over her belt, again.

"No," she finally said. "I, uh, I...I just heard the music and it was nice so I came over. But that was a mistake."

"Yeah. I know. Even one-on-one can be hard, sometimes. How you handle classes?"

It took her a moment to understand the question. Finally, she said, "Not well. Remote. Mostly."

Zeke nodded. "You did more than logistics."

All she did was shrug.

"It'll get easier," he said. "There's a good VA hospital not too far from here. They've worked out ways to get around cuts in funding. I'm Zeke."

"Carli." Then she seemed upset that she had told him.

"Mid-terms're on through tomorrow, but you know that. Good thing is, Saturday night'll be slow, if you wanna try again. Kids're off on Spring Break. Bikers are gone. I tend the bar. I'll comp you one."

"You don't have to do that. But thanks. Maybe I'll take you up on it. Sometime."

"Your choice."

"Okay. Thanks."

She hesitated then backed into the shadows.

Loki did not move.

A few moments later, Zeke heard a truck start up. Saw its headlights flare on just up the road and pull away. He gave Loki a pat and scratch behind the ears, saying, "Thanks, boy."

Woof.

"So you think she's lyin'?"

Woof.

"Yeah, me too. Can't lie to a dog."

Woof-woof.

"We'll deal with her next time she comes. C'mon, buddy, it's chilly out. Let's go in. See if we can find some *Rin-Tin-Tin* on YouTube."

He set the safety on the rifle, used it to steady himself as he rose, then grabbed the guitar and entered the trailer, Loki on his tail.

*****

In the Dodge, Carli drove down The 14. To her surprise, she was shaken. Something about seeing Zeke without his leg, in his undies and shirt. Sock on his right foot. Caught in shadows and the cold night breeze. Vulnerable as he played that lovely melody. It sliced into her. The gentleness in him. The calmness. The quiet. And the casual acceptance of her lies. There was nothing about him that struck her as him being the kind of guy who would even tolerate a rape, let alone commit it.

Plus, there was also one other very important fact.

"He wasn't on the video," she told herself. "Maybe he wasn't even there. Maybe."

On top of this, there was something else that troubled her.

For the first time in her life, she'd felt protective towards a man she didn't know. Hadn't even really met. And that was weird. Yes, she was like that about TF, but he was her baby brother. And okay, she'd been like that about the men in her unit, in the 'Stan, but that was different. That was in a conflict and they were on the same side and knew each other.

But there it was. Deep inside, she did not want anything to happen to Zeke.

Which made absolutely no sense, whatsoever.

Because she had heard him join with the gang in mourning that vile piece of shit, Grady. Like he was a nice guy. Someone decent. Who'd been a good friend. As loyal and trustworthy as that damn mutt. Loki. Right. Which didn't even begin to meld with the image of him grunting and giggling on top of Lara.

Grady, a good buddy?

That also made no sense.

Except, let's be honest here, Carli, it almost sort-of kind-of does.

They kept saying he wasn't the kind to usually get access to someone of the female persuasion. He had even admitted he usually had to pay for his sexual encounters. And on top of it, he was damaged. It wasn't inconceivable that someone like him would get all giggly and awkward in a situation like that, like a randy puppy that's too excited to control itself and pees on a rug.

Like he had started to with her, the night before.

Damaged.

That word stuck in her head.

Zeke was damaged.

Nat and JJ were damaged.

Was Spit? Was Dax? There was nothing about it in TF's info.

Was there something she was missing, here? Some detail she'd passed over in her drive to plot a course of revenge? TF had brought her only the minimum background needed on all of them, all of it criminal, but something else in all of it was how not once had there been previous accusations of rape. Nothing since, either.

No, no, hold on, Carli. Don't go getting all sentimental just because they were soldiers who got hurt serving the military-industrial complex. Millions of others did, too, and they didn't hold down and rape young women.

It's just, there was something else in play, and she needed to dig deeper before she let herself get all weepy and bleeding-heart over them.

Or not.

Because the fact of the matter was, that video was damning.

Was absolute.

And even though Zeke wasn't seen on it...well, that didn't really mean anything. It had cut off, suddenly, and there was the whispering of another voice in the background. A voice she couldn't make out. Plus, Dax had only watched the rapes, from what she could tell. Almost like he was cheerleading. That alone was reason enough to punish him. And if Zeke had done nothing to stop it? If he had been there but had only watched, as well?

Then maybe he should the last to die.

She laughed. That made her sound like the *Wicked Witch of the West*.

"The last to go will see the first three go before him!" she cackled. "And his mangy little dog too."

She drove on, still laughing. Her plan was back on track. A vow would still be kept.

And tomorrow promised to be a most glorious day.

Double Your Pleasure

Zeke met Dax at 7am, not having slept a wink. He'd chowed on grilled cheese sandwiches, for both him and Loki, and sweet pickles just for him, more beer just for him, which always seemed to irritate Loki, and nonstop videos of Rin-Tin-Tin's TV show, from the 50s, which made up to Loki for the lack of beer. At least he was now in jeans topped by a leather jacket and Ninja helmet, and looked scruffily cool.

Dax, however, was fresh and clean, for once, and seated on his Hog at the dead-end of a street that vanished against some railroad tracks. One of many in a run-down neighborhood of old, nearly dilapidated frame houses on the town's south side. A few adobe structures painted in pinks and tans were mingled in. Lots of dirt and sand. Scrub and cactus everywhere. Cyclone fences cluttered with the remains of tumbleweeds that achieved nothing except to make the area look more forlorn. Not a single mesquite tree to offer even a hint of shade; no sidewalks, either.

"You look like shit," Dax snarled the second he saw Zeke. "Didn't you even take a fuckin' shower? They relax you, good."

"Thanks. This is early for you, ain't it?"

Dax shrugged. "Been here since six, but got some cool info from some early birds headin' for work. You know the university bought all these houses?"

"Here? Why?"

"Dunno. But they're all rented, and they're jacking rents up. Drivin' people out."

"University's miles away."

"Railroad tracks. Somethin' about minerals an' assholes from Phoenix sneakin' 'round. Might ask Chase if he knows about it."

Zeke shrugged. He didn't trust Chase, but Dax seemed to be okay with him and there was no need to start issues this early in the morning. "So Luna and Madrigo live here?"

"One of the houses on this street. Grady mentioned it. But you know what they look like, right?"

Zeke took in a deep breath. "Do we know what happened?"

Dax shook his head. "Nope. Body's been transferred to Tucson, an' Eldora's still bein' cagey with the details, but I know a guy at the hospital's morgue. He said...he said..." What he'd been told about the condition of the body played over in his mind. "Shit. Somebody really fuckin' hated Grady."

Ice whispered into Zeke's veins as he murmured, "That bad?"

Dax nodded. "How was last night?"

Zeke took in a long, deep breath. "Busy. Then watched dog shows. Loki enjoyed himself."

"You spoil that fuckin' mutt."

Zeke shrugged, unable to think of anything to say.

"We're gonna find out who did this, Zeke. Then I will personally tear 'em ten new assholes an' piss in every fuckin' one of 'em."

Zeke nodded, then noticed a couple of Latino boys exiting one of the adobe structures. Both in their teens, slim and cocky, black hair and jeans, light jackets and shades against the morning sun. Backpacks over a shoulder.

"Here we go," Zeke said.

Dax saw them, fired up his bike and zipped down the road. Zeke followed.

The boys spun around at hearing them approach, and froze.

"Luna, Madrigo, remember me?" Dax snarled as he pulled to a stop in front of them. "Where you been keepin' yourselves?"

"What you mean?" Madrigo said. He looked about a year older than Luna. "You...you know where we are."

"I ain't so sure I know jack shit about either one of you."

Zeke slipped off his bike then approached the boys, saying, "When was the last time you saw Grady?"

"Night 'fore last," said Luna. His voice had a soft squeak to it.

"Then he left," Madrigo added. "What's he sayin'?"

"Every dollar was there! Swear!"

"When?" Dax snarled. "When'd he pick up?"

"Told you, Wednesday. Like always."

"He took all of it," Luna said. "Even the crap we had left over."

That made Dax stop short. "Grady took leftovers off you? You didn't sell out?"

"No, it's been slow."

"Spring Break's comin' up an' shit, y'know," said Luna.

"But that's always been our busiest time," Dax growled.

Zeke slipped between him the boys. "What time did he show up? Grady?"

Luna shifted so he was better hidden behind Zeke. "'Bout six-thirty, seven. When he always does."

"He waits till after dinner," Madrigo added. "Real considerate."

Zeke turned to Dax. "He got to the bar just before nine."

Dax huffed. "It ain't half an hour's drive, from here."

"Oh, he brought us more stuff, later," Luna said.

Dax was confused. "After he took everything you had?"

"Yeah," Madrigo said. "That shipment was crap, Dax. We got complaints, an' word's gettin' around."

Luna added, "So he was gonna palm it off on some college asshole. Had a meet-up all set. Said those fucks don't know shit about good pot or Ex, like they don't know shit about good beer. Somethin' like that."

"He brought us some of the really good stuff, straight back. Wanted to see if that'll sell."

"But it's only half what we need for the weekend."

Dax glared at them. "Did this Wednesday night?"

"Yeah."

"What time'd he get back?"

"'Bout eight-thirty," Luna said.

"Said he'd get us more, last night, after the meet-up. Had to talk to you."

"We waited till eleven."

Dax exploded. "On a school night!?"

Zeke had to hold him back, again, sighing, "C'mon..."

"We needed more, Dax!" said Madrigo.

"Good stuff," said Luna, "'cause somebody's hornin' in."

"An' they're cheaper an' — "

Dax scowled at them. "Says who?"

"Guy who bought some pot," said Madrigo. "He said the buzz he got from their shit was shit. He's who told us word's gettin' around that ours wasn't all that hot, either. Thinkin' of findin' a new source."

"That's why Grady was gonna get us more of the really good stuff. How'd he put it, 'Rigo?"

"Rebuild our brand."

Dax eyed them, wary. "You sure you ain't just slackin' off?"

"No, Dax, ask the guys on the north side. Shit, at the college."

Dax chased both boys down the street, snarling, "I got a better idea. You two get to school and I get you the best I got, tonight. Then you sell every bit of it by Monday or I ship your butts to a whorehouse in Mexico."

The boys vanished around a corner.

Dax strode back to Zeke, growling like a pissed-off junkyard dog. "Fuckin' cunts. Shit. Think they can pull that shit with me?"

"But it makes sense," Zeke said.

"My product's crap?"

"If somebody's cutting it."

Dax stopped. "Why the fuck would somebody cut pot?"

"Buddy of mine used to do that in the 'Stan. Mix in some parsley, to sell off, make his stash last longer."

Unknown to them, the Dodge was parked near the high school, a few blocks down. Carli slunk, inside, earbuds in. Her receiver picked up their voices, perfectly, as her laptop transcribed their conversation.

She heard Dax snarl, "But how do you cut Ex? Those're pills."

Zeke said, "Crush 'em up. Sell 'em to snort, like Molly mixed with Tylenol."

"You think Grady was doin' that?"

"No, he wouldn't."

"Neither would JJ or Nat."

"Yeah, and Spit? Well...I say it's your supplier."

"Fuck, I gotta test my own product 'fore I hand it out?"

"Might be the only way to know. And if it's good when you pick it up..."

Dax growled. "Whoever's doin' this must think I'm stupid."

Carli smiled to herself and said, "They'd be right."

"Maybe somebody *is* working your supplier," she heard Zeke say. "To move in on you. Maybe one of the guys is helping them."

"Like Luna and Madrigo?"

"I hate to think it. Then there's the idea of a set-up. With Grady. It just sounds...I dunno...too right. He always kept to a schedule. Wouldn't take much to figure out when he's got cash on him. I warned him about being so loose with it, but he was just so sure no one would...no one would bother him..."

His voice trailed off.

Carli was cut by the pain in it, and angered. Still grieving over that bastard? She knew men could be ridiculous bro's with each other, but this?

She heard footsteps, as if Dax was pacing as he said, "You're right. An' with that chick pickin' him up? It screams he was marked. Fuckin' idiot. Thought he was gonna get some tail and wound up killed, instead. Shit."

"God, it's so sudden and hateful. Vicious."

Dax stopped pacing and sat against his Hog, scowling. "Y'know, I had some trouble, back 'fore you came. Couple guys in the Apache community. We made a deal; they keep to their space, I keep to mine."

"That's eight years ago."

"Shit, that long? Really?"

"Yeah. So why wait till now to fuck around with you?"

"Right. And if the day's receipts weren't all that hot, and he had some of the crap stuff on him, if they'd marked him they'd probably know that. 'Course, that's if those two little shits are to be believed and — and shit! That's why he shouldn't have pulled that shit! Goin' off with that bitch."

"Find out anything more about her?"

"No. It's like she don't exist."

Zeke leaned against his own bike, almost lost, then fought a yawn.

Dax noticed. "You finally ready to catch some Z's?"

"Yeah, I guess. It's just, right now it's just hard to think about sleeping."

"My C-O was a night owl. Kept me up, a few times, talkin'. Till he ate a bullet in Anbar."

"That ain't me, Dax."

"Good. Go on home. Get some sleep. See you, tonight."

*****

Carli heard their bikes rumble to life. A moment later, in her rearview mirror, she caught them in the near distance, bursting onto the main road then splitting. Dax aimed for town as Zeke roared off in in the direction of the Cantina.

A slight shift in the mirror showed Madrigo and Luna storming up the street, closing in on the Dodge. The school was a block ahead of her, a blank building in the middle of a dirt lot with a stone wall encompassing it. Kids were exiting cars and entering through the main door as others walked up. All so typical.

She got out of the Dodge and walked around to the back, watching the boys storm along like a couple of scowling puppies, and could just hear Luna saying, "We gotta get out of here. Dax is gonna figure out we're cuttin' his shit."

Madrigo was a lot cooler. "We don't do it that much."

"I told you, sixty-forty makes pot all but worthless."

"We still got a buzz off it."

"Barely. We'll be lucky if all he does is kick us down to Mexico."

"We were born here. He can't deport us."

"Wanna bet? He was gonna do that to one of those college jotos who owed him a bunch of coin."

That made Carli stand up straight. New info.

"That was a bitch," Madrigo half-laughed.

"So?" Luna squeaked.

"So she paid him off, first."

"But if Grady took off with the cash, he'll hold us for it an' — "

"Naw, he's too fuckin' stupid to figure out what's goin' down."

"Shit, I want out of this town. Now."

"We don't have enough cash set up, yet."

They were just even with the Dodge when Carli said, quick and loud, "Want some help building it up?"

They jolted around to look at her. Eyed her, wary.

"In exchange for directions," she continued. "And information."

"Who the fuck're you?" Madrigo snapped.

"An angel with a way out of your troubles," she said. Then she fired up a joint and offered it to them.

The boys looked her over then exchanged glances. Madrigo finally accepted it and asked, "Where you need to go, lady?" Then he took a long drag.

Smoke drifted from Carli as she looked at him and said, "Is there a particular place Grady liked to meet to transfer drugs to Chase?"

"Why the fuck you, askin' us 'bout Grady?" Luna spat. Then he took a snarling drag off the joint, and finally cast Madrigo a quick glance that said, *Holy shit, this ain't bad.*

She reached over to stroke Luna's chin with her thumb, saying, "You should act like a man instead of a mouse."

He jolted and coughed out the smoke, startled.

"What's the cost?" Madrigo asked, smoke drifting from him.

She drew a finger over Luna's lips, saying, "Maybe *I'll* pay *you.*"

Of course, now the boy was too-totally shocked.

Carli smiled. While they were cute kids, neither of them was old enough to be interesting. But that didn't mean they couldn't be toyed with, so she just continued, "You said you wanted to get out of here."

"Yeah," Luna said, "but how?"

"Trust."

"¿Verdad?" Madrigo asked.

She winked at him.

Luna pulled Madrigo aside, saying, "Hold it up, vato, we don't know her. She might be a cop or something."

"Do cops do this?" he grinned, then he blew smoke in Luna's face. "C'mon, vato, don't be a pendejo."

Luna glared at him. "But it...it don't feel right."

"Neither does going to school, right now," Carli said, returning to the driver's door. "Join me? Be my own little GPS?"

With a laugh, Madrigo yanked his backpack off, opened the passenger door, and shoved Luna into the back. He dumped his backpack on him then hopped into the front...and off they drove.

*****

There was a short valley between two outcroppings of rocks just down from the foothills. Another arroyo twisted along one side of it, dry as a bone, a dirt trail running next to it. Carli's Dodge slowly maneuvered along the trail until Madrigo burst from inside, while it was still moving. Carli hit the brakes as he looked around. Luna followed him out.

"This is the place," Madrigo said.

Luna looked around, frowning, then brightened. "Yeah! That rock! Looks like Geronimo."

Madrigo followed his gaze then grinned. "Got it!"

Carli slipped from behind the wheel and looked around.

"You sure about this?" she asked. The area did not look smart. Too many spots for a good vantage point; too easy to set up an ambush.

"Dirt trail curls around to behind the rocks and goes straight into sand," Luna said. "The arroyo's usually dry, but it gets rain lots more than most of the others, so people stay away. An' the wind can get hard, comin' through the rocks."

"My dad brought me here," Madrigo said. "First time he met with some college guy. Grady was with us."

"Then his dad split an' Grady took over."

"Didn't have no car so we worked the school."

She eyed the boys, wary, wondering if they were handing her a line of shit in order to set her up, but then she noticed a set of tire tracks, coming from the other end of the valley. She walked over to look closer. Single set; not fresh, thanks to the breezes and critters crossing, but definitely from a motorcycle.

"This way leads to sand?" she asked, motioning in the direction the tire tracks came from.

"Pretty much," said Madrigo, coming over to her. "There's a foot trail, kinda."

"Yeah, then a dirt road leads to The 14."

She climbed up on a rock but could not see beyond the boulders.

"What'd this college guy look like?" she asked.

Luna shrugged. "Like all white guys. Mr. Ivory Snow."

She snarled, "That tells me nothing."

"Well, he's got a blue Chevy SUV."

Madrigo hurried up, "She wants to know what *he* looks like, vato." He turned to Carli. "You know that guy...he's in the *Marvel Universe*? Cap's buddy?"

"You're full o' shit! He's all blond and Aryan, not like Cap."

"I ain't talkin' 'bout Cap! His buddy in *Avengers, Civil War*. No, wait, wait, um, *Winter Soldier*!"

"Oh, shit, yeah, I get it. I see it. Just blond."

"Bucky! That's it! But just a college guy."

Carli jumped down and returned to the Dodge. "Are you done?"

"Uh, yeah," said Madrigo, following her.

"Okay, I'll drop you home. Do you have someplace you can go, away from here? Like far away?"

"How?" Luna squeaked. "We got no car."

"My dad sold it before he split," Madrigo added.

"Isn't there a bus?" Carli asked.

"Yeah, for Tucson."

"You can catch another out of state."

"What the fuck're you sayin'? Where we gonna go?"

"You got that aunt in Vegas," said Madrigo.

"An' leave my mom? She's been good to you, 'Rigo!"

Madrigo cast Carli a look, saying, "Yeah, and we ain't got that much money."

They were close to the Dodge so Carli went around back, pulled a tool bin close to her, opened it and pulled out a pile of twenties. Then she slapped them into Madrigo's hand, saying, "This help?"

His expression was now both nervous and excited. "This is the bundle we gave Grady."

Luna's eyes went big as he squeaked, "Fuck, right, that twenty with the stamp on it! You're settin' us up, lady!"

Carli's glare shut him up. "You want the money or not?"

Luna started to say more, but Madrigo slapped a hand over his mouth. "Right, lady. Thanks. Bus ride, it is."

Luna pulled his hand down and asked, "Goin' where?"

"Don't tell me," Carli said. "Just be away from here by four o'clock."

"But my mom!"

Madrigo smacked his hand back up over Luna's mouth, saying, "We'll take care of her! Now we gotta pack."

*****

Eldora quietly wandered into a cold, gleaming, room that stank of antiseptic, flowers and death. The coroner's workroom. With her was a tiny man in a brutally white smock, who seemed ready to crack a wicked joke, if he'd had a sense of humor. Which Eldora wasn't sure he didn't have.

"He was strung up like a pot roast," the coroner said, his tone too damned matter-of-fact for her to mention she'd thought the same thing. "Missing a couple fingers, once had a penis, but not anymore. And his prairie oysters..."

That made Eldora have to fight back a laugh, because she wasn't sure he'd appreciate it, and she had learned long ago never to diss a coroner, not if you wanted your results in a timely fashion.

"Nose is half gone, too," he continued, then he stopped at a table covered with trays holding a number of items, one of which was the vibrator that had once been inside of Grady. "I doubt this was very enjoyable to him, considering the tearing in his rectum. But I may be wrong, considering where it was positioned. As for this," he held up the gag showing the part that was in Grady's mouth was dildo-like. "It's what helped cause him to die by asphyxiation. Choked on his own vomit."

"Before the ants got to him?" Eldora asked.

"Maybe. Honey drizzled on him. Most of his epidermis gone. A few muscles bitten off. Probably taken after death."

Eldora shook her head. "Time of death?"

"Midnight to three-am. Toxicology showed Rohypnol. Alcohol and the remains of something I think may have been a meal from Bellamere's. It was about that poisonous."

"What about the car?"

"Like off a showroom, it's so clean. Nothing human in it."

"Cleaned with?"

"Palmolive dishwashing liquid and wiped down with vinegar."

"Not bleach?"

"No. Same for the boards used to get up on the plateau. Tire tracks still visible, but nothing more. People buy those things at Home Depot."

"My guys did a search around the perimeter. Not even tire tracks for the Mercedes."

"It is the desert. With the winds and such."

"But it's been quiet lately."

"I think this counts as non-quiet."

She looked at him, managed to keep from smiling, and said, "Okay, now I gotta call LAPD and fill 'em in."

"California cops. I envy thee not."

"Dealt with any?"

"No, but I know a coroner who has."

"Can you ask him about the Deveaux suicide? See if anything looks wonky, to him?"

"I will ask *her*." And his eyes had glittered with mischief.

"You're gonna out me as a misogynistic pig, ain't you?"

"With glee." At which he smiled. And it came close to scaring Eldora with its wickedness.

This was why she preferred to do everything with him online.

Two For One Ain't Fun

After she dropped them off, Carli drove back to the valley, parked the Dodge well out of sight and did a recon around the area. After brushing away all traces of footprints and tire tracks, using a branch from a mesquite tree, she surreptitiously positioned a couple of mikes in strategic spots then climbed up into the rocks to find the best vantage point. She settled on one nestled between two massive boulders, figured the sun would be to her rear by four-thirty then hauled her materiel up from the Dodge — the receiver, a battery, a backpack full of some *toys*, and the NEMO. Then she went back down to move the Dodge to a hiding place under a mesquite tree, cut off a fresh branch of the tree to swipe away the truck's trail and her own, and slipped back up to the vantage point.

She had a few hours before the meet-up, still, and used that to Zen.

All of this felt comfortable to her, mainly because she'd done so much of it when she was in Afghanistan. Rarely with this much precision, but hiding up in the rocks to keep watch as her guys would carefully approach a village. Mornings, enter from the east; evenings, from the west; Carli in the hills scanning the area for trouble. Which she caught, now and again. She'd only actually killed fifteen in her eight months with the Rangers, but word had spread about the woman sniper in her pack, which meant little trouble. In fact, they had lost only two men; wounded, not dead. Carli was proud of knowing she was part of the reason. To a Muslim fanatic, being killed by a woman meant no virgins in the afterlife, no family to greet them, only shame.

God, men were so delicate; couldn't handle a woman, even in death.

But then her tour ended and it was back to logistics, and it had been hard adjusting. Having always been at the edge of existence. Knowing the men around you would cover your back as tightly as you would cover theirs. A sense of belonging, something she'd never really had. The sharing between equals. Cigarettes. Pot. Pills. Whatever. It was rather hard to find that pack mentality, stateside.

Then Lara'd happened and her focus had shifted to...

A car approached down the valley's trail. An old bronze Malibu in desperate need of a wash and complete makeover. Binoculars aimed at the filthy windshield showed her Spit was driving, Nat in the passenger seat.

And then she jolted.

Because the epitome of a white, blond privileged college lad in two-hundred dollar jeans, four-hundred dollar jacket, and too-trendy, too-overpriced sneakers was sitting on one of the rocks, watching them. And she got the sense he'd been there for some time.

Carli checked the time. 4:38pm? Already? Jesus, she'd lost track of time, again?

This is not handling things, Carli!

She powered up the receiver and propped the NEMO so she could watch them through its scope, then heard...

"About damned time!" burst from college lad.

"Chase, please accept our apologies," Nat said as he got out of the Malibu. "Mechanical issues delayed us."

Spit carefully exited the car, favoring his back, as Nat handed Chase a brown bag with handles.

"I believe you should have something for us, as well?" he continued.

Chase nodded and gave him an envelope, saying, "That's from yesterday, too." Then he looked inside the brown bag and scowled. "C'mon, guys, get real; this won't get me through the night, let alone tomorrow."

"But Spring Break," Nat said.

"Lots are leaving Sunday. Half a dozen parties, tomorrow, and I'm invited to every one of 'em."

"We may be able to double it, in the morning," Nat said.

"That's no good. I gotta have it available, now, or they'll hit these other guys."

Leaning against the Malibu, Spit snarled, "What other guys?"

Chase jolted. "Somebody on campus. Sellin' crap stuff, cheap."

Nat waved Spit off, saying, "Understandable. I will discuss this with Dax, but I can assure you the earliest we can obtain additional supply is in the morning."

"But I go running, first thing, then some guys're taking me to lunch for my birthday. It'll have to be after ten but before eleven."

Nat almost seemed irritated as he said, "Your schedule is quite intense."

"No shit."

"Alter it."

Chase hesitated, then shrugged. "I could put my buddies off to noon. Make it back for the last parties, get some sales in."

"Duly noted. Fortunate for you, *my* diary is open. And happy birthday."

Chase smiled his thanks and started down the trail.

Carli quickly slipped to the other side of some rocks to look back to the road and saw a deep blue Chevy SUV parked at the end of the trail. Through the scope, she could just make out the license plate, so quickly wrote it down.

Then she heard Nat say, "Dax, I fear I may know who targeted Grady."

She spun back to her hiding spot and saw Nat had moved closer to Spit, and was talking on his cell phone. A quick glance at her phone showed *no service*.

"What the fuck..." whispered from her. Did he have a satellite link?

Nat continued with, "Chase claims new dealers are moving in on us. ... He failed to mention who. ... Hold on." He put the phone on speaker and held it so Spit could also hear. "Ready, Dax."

Dax's voice was heard saying, "Just between us, I'm hearin' the same shit from Luna an' Madrigo, but I wanna know for sure if that college shit's tellin' the truth or he thinks he's being clever and rippin' us off. Spit, who's that guy you know in maintenance?"

Spit frowned then said, "At the school? Larry."

"He's been good for info in the past. See what he says about these other guys."

Nat frowned. "Wasn't he once accused of providing the Lady Jane to some students?"

"Yeah," Dax said. "Barely got out of it. But see what you think, Spit."

"Sure thing."

"Nat, see if you can find out some more from that waitress you know at Bellamere's."

Nat nodded and said, "Very well. Oh, Dax, Chase requires more product, so I informed him we'd provide additional supply, early on the morrow."

"What the fuck'd you tell him that for?"

"He was distressed over the minimum we had to give."

"It wasn't a full supply?"

"No. Were I to make a supposition, it would appear Grady raided our local unit to be in readiness for Chase."

"Spit?"

"That's all there was, Dax."

"What the fuck? Okay, Nat, I'll pull more supply down, an' I'm gonna talk to fuckin' Chase, myself."

"He wishes the meeting to occur between ten and noon."

"What the fuck?"

"That is his *only time available.*"

"He'll meet me when I fuckin' tell him to meet me. And the next time he tells you somethin' like this, get names. Shit. You're smart; why've I gotta think of everything?"

He ended the call.

"Now you done it," Spit said.

"Well," Nat purred, "in the words of the great Khalil Gibran, fuck him and the horse he rode in — "

BAM!

The cell phone was shot out of his hand.

"What the?"

Spit jolted and reached for a pistol in the back pocket of his jeans, but...

BAM! A bullet slammed into his back. He screamed. Fell face down.

Nat pulled his own pistol and aimed in the direction the last shot had come from and...

BAM! The pistol was shot from his hand.

He scrambled for cover and...

BAM! He was clipped in the side. He crashed to the dirt as another shot cut him in the neck. He rolled over then forced himself to crawl behind the Malibu to hide, panicked and in pain. He tried to stop the bleeding from his side but blood flowed over his fingers. It also trailed from his neck.

He slowly, painfully removed his shirt. An entry wound was flowing red; no exit wound.

Shit.

He held his shirt against it, as best he could then called, "Spit. Spit, I need emergency care. Fast. Spit?"

Not even a grunt in response. That is when he noticed...

The silence.

No birds crying.

No creatures calling.

Nothing.

Just the barest whisper of a breeze.

He painfully forced himself to look under the car and saw Spit was lying face down, gripping the earth.

"Spit?"

He was answered with a soft grunt.

Then more silence.

Until a buzzard called.

He looked up to see they had begun to circle above him. He almost whimpered from the understanding of what that meant.

Then he heard vague footsteps approaching. Soft, at first then closer and closer. Steady and sure. Seeming to aim straight for him.

He tried to grab a rock but could barely hold onto it, he was shaking and in such pain. The bleeding wasn't stopping. Finally, he looked around to see...

Carli approaching, the NEMO slung over one shoulder, her backpack over the other. Clouds of dust whispered around her like steam rising from a swamp.

She sauntered up to the Malibu, smiling.

"Hello, Spit," she purred as she looked down at him. "Remember me? *Sweet Cheeks*?" Then she looked over the Malibu's trunk at Nat. "Sorry to make such a dramatic entrance, but seeing as how there's two of you and only one of me, I wanted to even the odds."

She squatted and took the pistol from Spit's jeans. Looked at it, with disdain. "Jesus, when was the last time you cleaned this thing?"

Then she rose and dropped the gun into her backpack before continuing, "You're probably wondering what this is all about."

She strolled around to Nat and pulled out her phone. Started the video. It showed him raping Lara as Grady and Spit held her down. JJ was watching, laughing.

"Guess who," Carli snarled. "Spit was just before you. Fucking a girl who'd been drugged and laid out for your fun. And don't tell me you didn't know what was going on. It's obvious. So goddammed obvious, it's sickening."

"No," said Nat. "Don't understand. She was...was..."

The glare in Carli's eyes silenced him.

At this point, her back was to Spit so she did not see he had stopped gripping the earth...

"I don't understand how any man could do that to a girl," she said.

...and was slowly looking up, at her...

"It's like he's proving himself unable to deal with a woman as an equal bed partner."

Glaring at her...

"But instead has to behave like a rutting dog."

Quietly rising to a crouch...

"Big brave boys," Carli continued. "You know, that's rape. And rape is a crime. And where there's a crime..."

Spit grabbed the NEMO and slung Carli around. Yanked it off her and tossed her aside. She tumbled to the dirt then rolled to her feet and pulled the knife from its sheath to sling it at him before he could aim, all in one quick move.

He barely managed to deflect the knife with the rifle's clip, but that gave her enough time enough to bolt up and plow into him. They crashed to the ground and the NEMO flew off into the dirt.

She punched Spit's back, but only hurt her hand.

He grabbed her by her shirt and rolled to get on top of her but she scrambled out from under him then rolled away, looking for the knife.

Nat watched them then painfully glanced around for his own gun. It was not to be seen.

Spit roared and scrambled to his feet. His shirt shifted up to reveal a massive metallic back brace, Velcro holding it in place. It was dented and cut where the bullet hit.

He snarled, "Really helped my back, bitch. Thanks."

He yanked the brace off then snapped it at her. Whap! Caught her in the chin, cutting it open. Whap! Over and over. Forcing her back. Smacking it against her.

She swung a kick at him but he grabbed her ankle and yanked her close and they fought, both of them down and dirty. Crashed to the dirt. Rolled like brawling alley cats. Gouging. Clawing. Howling in anger and pain. Spitting. Snapping. Slamming against the rocks.

Spit laughed the whole time. Even though he weighed twice as much as her, she was twisting and scratching and kicking and howling like an insane alley cat, so he was unable to gain control.

Nat saw the Nemo so, despite his pain, began to drag himself to it. Forced himself to draw closer and closer to it.

Carli noticed, almost managed to break away from Spit and reach it, herself, but he yanked her back and twisted behind her to choke her. She dug her nails into his arms then clawed up to his face and into his cheeks. He howled and she broke free, spun and high-kicked him, again. Pounded him. Hard.

He took the kicks, yanked her to him, again, wrapped an arm around her neck and began to squeeze.

She fought and kicked and scratched and jolted before finally managing to grab his ears and twist and shove back against him, making him lose his balance. They fell and rolled across the ground. She finally spun around to face him...

And punched him in the side of his throat.

He gasped. Choked.

She hit him, again. Straight on his windpipe. Twice. The knuckle of her middle finger slamming deep into it.

He let go and rolled away, gasping, fighting to breathe.

She rose, dust swirling around her like a demon's mist. Watched him stagger back to his feet.

Then crash against the rocks.

Then fall to his knees.

Choking.

Gasping.
Clawing at his throat.
Blood trailed from her cuts. Her face was lost in a expression that could be evil or sexual. She looked around to find...
Nat almost had the NEMO.
She stumbled over to grab it, first. Then she looked back at Spit.
He was still choking.
His face and lips growing blue.
Until he fell face forward.
And bounced.
And died.
Nat watched, horrified. Shaking in fear.
Next, Carli straightened to her full height. The evening sun was dipping down to the top of the foothills. Dark shadows were beginning to stretch across the arroyo. At any other time, it would have seemed restful. A time of peace.
Instead, she found her knife, the cool light glinting off it, and slowly strode back to Nat. The wind swirled dust around her. She had all the appearance of a demon approaching her newest sacrifice.
"He was lucky," she growled in a voice that seemed inhuman. "You? Not so much."
He tried to back away, but the loss of blood had made him weak. All he could say was, "This. Wrong. Please. This is evil."
Carli's smile grew horrifyingly sweet as she murmured, "This is justice."
And she drew closer to him.
And closer.
And buzzards calmly circled, overhead.

Sete de Sangue...or Something

Another clear, still and chilly night in the desert. As it always had been and probably always would be, even with climate change. Carli was hidden between brown-black rock formations that were a hundred feet tall, tens of millions of years of years in age and showed every indication of continuing their jaunt through time, despite their base having been scarred by the modern hieroglyphics of some drug-addled twerp who thought spraying bright neon colors on them was just too cool.

At least those would be gone before the next decade was out.

Here the Dodge sat, a mile from the plateau, its nose pointing into the rocks, engine humming, headlights cutting into the darkness. A hundred feet away, a dirt trail ran parallel to yet another dry arroyo. Atop the Dodge, a portable satellite dish pointed straight at the sky, and almost directly above, up a semi-trail, was the spot where Carli had watched Eldora and her crew deal with Grady and the Mercedes on that low plateau. That tarp was still stretched between the rocks.

She stood before the Dodge, naked, washing blood off her body. She had a five-gallon tub of water hanging between a rock and an A-Frame ladder, above her, and she was rubbing herself down with a blood-soaked rag. She worked slowly. Cuts and bruises on her body. Hands shaking. Mind deliberately blank. A second tub was over a fire next to the rock, heating. She would need it.

With lots of soap to wash away the smell of death.

Then a nice scented lotion, for good measure.

Killing these two, Nat and Spit, they bothered her. Especially Nat. It wasn't that he had bled to death before she could take complete control of him, denying her even the chance of making him experience what Grady had. It was how...well, seeing him drift into death, she had actually experienced an orgasm.

Which, for some odd reason, just did not seem normal.

Because it forced her to admit she had actually felt a bit of a thrill when Stasi had vanished over the balcony railing. And the thought of sending Mikey after her had brought a tingle to more than just her heart. Then there was a nearly guttural release at Grady choking and finally giving up the ghost. Spit had been a fight for survival so had taken too hard a toll to be enjoyed. But now?

Now it almost struck her as foreplay.

Almost.

After all, he really was a disgusting creep.

But Nat?

Poor little Nat.

What had happened could not be ignored or brushed aside. His death had brought a sense of power and pleasure to her that she had never felt before. Exploding from behind her heart in a near animalistic howl. Reminding her of the overwhelming beauty she had felt the first time she killed a man. In Afghanistan. From a thousand yards away. A lovely face with sad, frightened eyes, about to fire an RPG. Whose head had jerked and blood exploded from the back as he ceased to be human. The orgasm had nearly blinded her with its grace and perfection. Carried her for days. Weeks. Months, and she had been unable to achieve that same exquisite torture, again.

Until now.

Grady had been too slovenly to touch her sense of need. But Nat? Bound and bleeding as she tore his clothes open, she had seen he was Grady's exact opposite. Trim. Tight. Not much hair and that was tightly curled in ways she found odd and playful. And his penis? Of a decent length...and circumcised. She had inserted the vibrator then undressed and lain next to him as he drifted into shock.

And stopped breathing.

It hadn't mattered that she couldn't do the same dance as she had Grady. She wasn't even sorry that he would not feel the bites and stings she'd watched overtake his predecessor, just before he died. She just really did hate to hurt pretty things.

Oh, there was no question in her mind that each of these bastards deserved to die for what they had done to Lara. Callous beasts taking joy in the destruction of another human being should be destroyed in just as callous and cruel a manner. Like rabid dogs. They were a danger to others, and she had ended that danger.

I am justice, incarnate, in all her cruelty. And vengeance.

The thought actually jolted her.

Does that make me Samael?

The fallen angel of death.

She had wondered this a couple of times near the end of her tour. Her skill on a target range, in the 'Stan had brought her to the attention of a Field Captain, who had learned how the Taliban and ISIS felt about being killed by a woman. He had talked with her, checked her out, joined her in her bed at her instigation, since he had a Tyrone Power sort of beauty, to him. He had seen she had not only the eye but also the concentration, and had arranged for her transfer to his unit.

All on the down-low, of course. At this time, the Army wasn't ready for a female sniper and besides, things were starting to gear down, over there. But a few words with another captain got it fixed by just using just her initials and her *officially* being assigned to logistics.

No need for any colonel or general to know what they don't need to know.

And she. Truly. Had. Loved. Every. Minute. Of it.

The marches, where she proved she could carry as much weight as the boys. The target practices, where she outshone even the best of them. The few gun battles that screamed for erotic release, once done. The camaraderie, where her being just as forward about sex and fun as the guys made her more like a buddy than just an object of prurient need.

Of course, the Captain hadn't expected her to happily lead more than one of his men into understanding that sex was sex, whether with a man or a woman, or both at the same time. But her kill ratio was too great to let some antiquated sense of morality fuck things up. And he had to admit, his men were a lot closer and morale much better since she had joined.

So if it ain't broke and all that...

But then she had to leave it all behind. Make it something to just dream about. Until Lara had been raped. And died. And Carli's entire persona had shifted. At first, she kept off to herself, brooding and easily triggered into a rage. She would not let a man touch her. And what was worse? At least, to her conscious mind?

She had wanted to go back and kill more of the enemy.

Had needed to.

Had used her time in target practice to pretend it was some man she was blowing away. Had grown to where she exalted in it. Felt a thrill deep in her soul when the bullet hit home. Even if it was just a face on a target a hundred yards away.

Despite her rejection of her mother's religious nonsense, she knew, deep down, this was wrong. Sociologically. Humanly. Morally, even.

But there it was...and she could not get a handle on it.

Then she stupidly got wasted, one night, while at Wainwright, and let a dumber-than-dirt Second Lieutenant, who looked like Glenn Ford, in *Gilda*, join with her. He had wound up being a humpity-humpy type, like Mikey, so she had blown him off. Until a month later, when he got drunk and grabbed her breasts from behind and told her she was servicing him, and she'd broken his nose without a thought.

Didn't look so much like Glenn Ford, after that.

Being a man, he got pissy about it, which meant she was bound for Courts Martial. No matter how much of an ass a Second Louie was, he was still a superior officer.

His attack on her was ignored, of course, but for once the Army, in its wisdom, let Carli take an honorable discharge. That was the only way she would help them avoid getting another black eye over yet another sexual assault allegation being ignored.

Besides, by that point Carli had begun to formulate a need for justice to be served on Lara's rapists. Not being beholden to anyone was perfection, to her.

And here she was, keeping her vow.

She pulled a cord and hot water poured over her. The last of the blood washed away. Vanished into the sand and dirt. Like that of so many men, women and children in the 'Stan. Like some of the men she had known. And now we were out of there, and nothing had been accomplished.

And suddenly she was exhausted.

She halfway realized she'd been so caught up in her thoughts, she had refilled the bucket with hot water and put the pail aside. Talk about zoning. She sat against the Ramcharger's bumper. Let the cold air dry her off. Her clothes were in the fire. Ruined, thanks to the fight and the blood. Dammit, she had really like that shirt.

Shouldn't have worn it, idiot.

But who'd have thought there'd be so much blood, with Nat? More than with Grady? Or that he would bleed to death so fast?

Her phone was on the truck's hood. She took it and unlocked it. Pulled up arrest photos of Spit and Nat, and deleted both. Next were shots of Dax and JJ, all but sneering at the camera. Drug charges, of course. She sneered back.

Then she shifted to one of Zeke. Barely eighteen. No ink. Trying so hard not to look scared. *Possession with intent to distribute* charges. Such a sweet looking boy. Not innocent. His eyes were too aware, for that. Just...well, when TF had first sent it to her, she'd thought he was more *accepting*. Like he figured *This is how it's going to be so fine.*

She almost smiled. She'd like to see how his eyes struck her, now. She hadn't been able to get close enough to look into them, last night, and she'd deliberately kept from glancing at him in the Cantina, even when he carded her.

TF had worked up a damn good ID for that. First fake she'd had since high school.

God, the things she had done, back then. The bars she'd brazened her way into with fake IDs. The boys she'd misused. And, she might add, happily so.

On both sides.

She would have had a lot of fun with a lad like Zeke, at this age.

She was back to feeling ambivalent about his part in Lara's rape. Obviously, he knew about Dax's drug networking here, but there were indications he was wasn't too deeply involved in it. Carli got the impression it was not because what Dax was doing was illegal; it was almost like he just didn't want to make a moral judgement.

Which was an odd thing to think, but there it was.

She needed more info about him, so she made a call.

TF picked up. "Hi, sis."

"Bro' baby," she replied.

He hated when she called him that, but this time it didn't faze him. "Who'd you get?"

She drew in a deep breath before saying, "Nat. Spit."

She could see him doing his jerky little nod of agreement as he said, "Two at once! Wow. Two left."

"Or three. Maybe four."

"What d'you mean?"

"What more did you find out about Zeke Lindstrom?"

"Oh, shit," sighed out of him. "So he *was* in on it?"

"I don't know. Not yet. Could go either way."

"Wow. Okay. Uh, I got more to share. I'll post it on my site."

"Encrypted?" she asked, being snarky instead of really asking.

"Gimme a break. You still got my passcode?"

"Yeah. Thanks."

"You said four."

"A guy named Chase?"

"*Chase*? Really?"

"Yes."

"First or last?"

"Don't know. But he's as white bread as his name, so probably first."

"Just did a search in my stuff. No one came up."

"I've got a license plate."

"Post it on my site. I'll text you when I've got the info."

"Thanks," she sighed.

"Okay, what's wrong, Carls?"

"I'm fine."

"Nope. No. No way. What's wrong?"

She let a long sigh whisper from her then murmured, "I really enjoyed this one. I actually — well, you know how excited one can get and..." Her voice trailed off.

There was silence, for a moment, then he said, "Sete de sangue." Soft and easy.

"C'mon, TF, I don't speak Italian."

"Drop the shit, Carls. You know what it means. Blood lust.

You've had it, before."

"In a different country."

"Your point being?"

"You make it sound like I'm fucking Dracula."

"Well, not sure about the fucking part, but..."

"Shut up!" But he had taken the edge off her mood.

There was a pause before he said, "Honest question. You want to stop?"

She had no answer.

He finally continued with, "I wouldn't blame you. We can take 'em all down without another drop of blood."

She still had no answer.

He noticed. "Y'know, what I learned about Zeke — *Ezekiel*, no less — I really do hope he's *not* one of them."

"Oh, cut the crap; you just think he's cute."

"He *is*."

"Shit, are you really that shallow?"

"Of course I am. But I also think you'll see what I mean when you go over what I got."

"Probably will."

"So?"

Carli rose and looked around at the China urn. "I'm not done yet. That fucking sheriff is in the middle of it."

"We already knew that."

"I've got the proof, now."

"Okay, Carli," and him using her regular nickname always caught her attention. "Be careful, here. We've already figured out how to handle her."

"I know, and I will be."

"No. No. You'll be all clever and crap, but you also don't give a shit, and those bastards in that state, they'll give you the needle over this, no matter what your justification. 'Cause they don't give a shit, either. My suggestion? Add what you got on that sheriff to the file we got. Pop it off to the state's attorney general and get the fuck outta Dodge."

She chuckled. "In my Dodge?"

"No joke!"

"I was just sitting on its bumper. Naked."

"Christ, too much info!"

"No. I've got two left, at least, but I want to talk to this Chase creep, first. If only to make sure that's all."

He took in a long breath, obviously displeased, then said, "Fine. You know the code to send if you get busted."

"And you'll shut 'em down."

"I'll shut down the whole fuckin' state, if I have to. And you know where you can cross into Mexico."

"Thanks, TF."

"No, actually thank you for being a crazy-assed take-no-shit sister. Mom's pissed that so much of you rubbed off on me. I wonder what she'd think about this?"

"I can just imagine. Matt-boy 7:1-6."

"Or Matteo 25:31-45?"

"Probably in tandem. You got any idea how she and papa are doing?"

He took a moment to answer. "I flew down. Sunday. Came back Tuesday."

"That bad?"

"Marco's worried. Thinks dad's gonna need an intervention. Luca and Matt are pretty much in agreement; Gianni, not so much. If you can avoid getting reamed by all the shit you're pulling, we'd like to have a family gathering. Luca says Reno, Tuesday, Wednesday, next week. Nice and low-key. As for mom? Well, there's only one thing she believes in. Even more, now. Seems to help her."

Carli nodded. "Got it. Reno's a good idea. Talk later."

She ended the call.

Then she pulled up a mug shot of Lara. The girl looked young. Scared. Defiant. She had been arrested with a friend who was caught with some Ecstasy on her. After an overnight stay in jail, and a confession from the other girl that Lara hadn't known about the pills, charges had been dropped. But she still had an arrest record, and momma had been angry about it for weeks. No ranting and raving; just her usual vicious little comments about *choices of friends*. But it had pretty much blown over by the Christmas before her death.

She shifted to a video, on the phone — Lara before a Christmas tree, looking sweet and innocent and happy as she said, "Hi, mom. Happy New Year. Sorry you couldn't stay longer. Must be a pain to fly thousands of miles just to be home for a couple days. Especially this time of year. The Army sucks. Miss you. See you at graduation. You are gonna make it, right? Got five months to get ready, then it's off to college. You ready for that? Bye. Love you."

The video ended.

She hadn't made the graduation, thanks to Russia pulling more of her shit, so she'd ordered a gift and card, and...

And six months later, Lara was dead.

And Carli felt raw and evil for not seeing her, again.

She rose and turned to look out over the empty, never-ending desert. This was wrong. Standing there. Naked. In the shadows, like a scared coyote. She rounded the Dodge. The ground was hard and pebbles and bits of tumbleweed dug into the soles of her feet. The breeze was chilly. The silence expansive in the darkness. All perfect for the moment. She began to feel alive.

And even more wrong.

She had just slaughtered another man. One she was almost sorry to do because he was rather pretty, with the dark tattoos against his creamy brown skin. And the deep red blood from the bullet to his side and cut in his neck. And his one eye wide with fear and pain.

He knew what was coming. And he'd tried to fight it, but was too badly wounded to do much more than struggle and use every word in his vocabulary to plead for his life, his voice growing softer and softer.

And now the ants were feasting. And the coyotes. And soon the buzzards. And God only knew what else, out here.

And she was not sorry. She was jubilant.

But for the first time, she was also just a teensy bit afraid of herself.

No Picnic in a Park

Another day done at the Cantina. Now everything was in order and it was quiet, except for Rhonda's perky boots tippy-tapping over the boards. She was slipping on her jacket, helmet on the bar, when Zeke carried a case of assorted beer from the cooler.

"Y'know, I would've done that for you," she said.

"Thanks, Rho, I got it."

She huffed. "My gramma called people like you independent to a fault."

He shrugged. "Keeps me in shape."

She shook her head, slung her purse over a shoulder and grabbed the helmet, saying, "Won't take help from nobody. I'll let myself out."

"Thanks, Rho. See you, tomorrow."

She exited and nearly slammed the door behind her.

Zeke set the case down and rubbed his leg. It was sore so he was limping a bit more than usual as he headed around to the door...

And it opened.

He stopped and backed behind the bar to grab a pistol he kept under the cash register as he said, "We're closed."

Carli entered, clean and sleek and looking lovely.

"Zeke?" she asked.

He hesitated. Kept the pistol hidden, still wary. "Hi. Uh, Carli, right?"

She smiled and nodded. "You remembered."

"Would you lock the door behind you? Just turn that knob in the deadbolt."

She did then turned back to him. Keeping the pistol hidden, he shifted to the back door to make sure it was locked, then returned to the bar, saying, "What's up?"

"I, uh, it, uh, the place is nice and quiet, now, and I was — I was hoping it's not too late for that beer. With a shot?"

He eyed her, for a moment. She was raw and unfocused. Skittish, even. He put the pistol away and asked, "Got a particular label?"

"Nah. Whatever whiskey."

He drew a Coors for her then poured two shots. "Can't sleep?"

"Too keyed up. You know how it goes."

He smiled and picked up one of the shots, indicating she should do the same, then said, "Here's to politics and religion, and the hell they bring us all."

"No shit," she chuckled.

They downed the shots, then Carli sipped her beer as he refilled the beer cabinet.

"How many tours did you do?" she asked.

"This happened three months in, my second."

"Messed up your career, didn't it?"

"I only enlisted to get out of jail. You?"

"Oh, had nothing else to do."

"How long were you in?"

"Fourteen years. Almost fifteen."

"That's a lot of *nothing else*. What brought you down here?"

"Here?"

"To this school? The Cantina? None of it's convenient."

"It was recommended. Archeology. Digging up the past. And here? It's a place to go. Where nobody knows your name."

"Mm. But you keep showing up after closing."

"I know. But that way I don't have to deal with people. They get so stupid when they're drinking."

"I'll give you that."

"But you're right. I should go."

He hesitated. Saw the confusion in her expression. He really wanted to be alone, right then, but how can you abandon a fellow vet? So he simply said, "No. No, you know what? I got a better idea. You, uh, you like picnics?"

"Here?" Carli asked.

"No, I'm done. Got a helmet." He pulled a rather battered ninja-style with a cracked visor from behind the bar. "Guy named Frank left it. Rode off, never saw him again. That was four years ago. I hang onto it in case he ever comes back."

"That happen a lot?"

"You'd be surprised. C'mon. We'll take my Harley. Loki. It's not all that far."

He led her to the back door, helmet in hand. She noticed his limp was more pronounced, almost weary, and to her surprise she began to hurt for him.

A quick mental kick warned her, *Don't grow weak. Not now.*

He ushered her out then turned off the lights, and exited.

Loki saw Carli and grew very still, then he saw Zeke and gave a *woof.*

"It's okay, Loki-puppy," Zeke said. Then he undid the chain and patted a doggie seat on the back of his Harley. "It's Friday night."

Loki hesitated, still eyeing Carli but not growling.

"I dunno, Zeke," Carli said, watching the dog.

"He'll be okay. Just don't try to cut my throat. He wouldn't like it, and I wouldn't either. Out in sec."

He slipped into the trailer.

Carli stayed focused on Loki, frowning. "You really love him, don't you?"

The dog just kept eyeing her.

"My mother hated dogs," she continued. "Preferred cats. They're just as judgmental as her. Sitting on their perch and disapproving for hours. Do you like cats?"

Not even a flick of his ears.

"Battin' a thousand, ain't I?"

Zeke came out with a bag, now wearing a pair of jeans and his jacket. He put the bag in the doggie seat, then he scooped Loki up and set him beside it. The dog huffed.

Zeke huffed back. "If you're gonna act like a puppy, you'll get treated like one." Then he swung his good leg over the bike and pulled his own Ninja helmet on. He turned to Carli. "You up for it?"

The Harley thrummed to life, its deep growling engine ready to go, now, now, now.

He looked at Carli, waiting. Half hoping she's say no.

Loki looked at her, wary, also waiting. Half hoping he'd get to rip her throat open, if she tried anything.

She slipped the helmet on and slung a leg over to sit behind Zeke then held onto the side handles. Her knees touched his hips and thighs, sending a cascade of elegant shivers rambled through her in ways that made her catch her breath.

"You never rode a bike, before?" he asked.

"Ten-speed."

"Yeah, this is a little different," he chuckled. "You can hold my waist, if you want. I promise not to take advantage, if you won't."

She made herself laugh. "Didn't want to seem too forward."

She slipped her arms around him then he set the bike in motion. Smooth and easy. Nothing crass like the Hogs, the night before. Just another light thrum, and in moments they were whispering past the Cantina and onto the road.

Carli almost gasped at the rhythmic heartbeat of the Harley's engine. The exquisite gentleness of the ride as they sliced through the crisp cold breeze. The tenderness of it. The sensuous caress. The very essence of life diving into her like a world of beauty and peace.

She looked left to watch dark scrub and even darker mountains in the distance almost appear to be pacing her in ways that seemed too real to be right. To her other side, the space was more open. The dark cacti and bushes extended all the way to the end of the world so they could meet the sky. Looking up revealed the deepest, blackest velvet gleaming with stars enough to put the overwhelming lights of the LA basin to shame. The moon had yet to rise to give them competition, and she was in no rush to see it. She loved the sense of midnight all around her as they sped along under a blanket of all-enveloping peace.

Without thinking, she lay her chin against Zeke's left shoulder. Strong and so welcoming. The leather of his jacket seemed to rejoice in her presence, and the smell of him...the casual humanness of him...she felt close to drunk from just breathing him in. But what was even better? Even nicer. Not a cringe or shiver at her touch, like so many men had when she took charge. No discomfort. No wariness. Just him as anchor to keep her on the bike. One human supporting another.

The emotions running through her were intensifying. Almost terrifying in how overwhelming they threatened to become. This moment — this pinpoint of time — she felt as if she were caught in poetry. The world as it should be. A connection between two people, surrounded by nothing but the deepest empathy. Purity caressing them both. Her drawing on his warmth in a way that grew more and more wonderful as the ride continued. It made her almost delirious with happiness.

How long had it been since she was with a man? And not one used merely to scratch an itch, but one she felt was worth being with? Liam? Her laughing Aussi, who'd been named after that Irish actor and had a lot of his look and attitude, but with dancing eyes and a perpetual grin instead of that sad sack aura. Probably came from being raised in Brisbane instead of Dublin.

She had joined his Aikido classes in LA, and watching him demonstrate his moves was like watching art come to life. He was ten years her junior and seeking a career in Hollywood but was finding that since Covid all doors were closed to newcomers unless they came with more than just a nice face. And while Liam's was very, very, very nice, that and his body were the only things he had to offer the business, at the moment.

Oh, but what a body. Trim and easy. A stride like a tiger instead of a lumbering ox. She'd had fun with a few too many of the latter, who were lovely to look at but not delightful to know.

Liam, however, was just a happy tomcat that loved to curl itself around your neck and shoulders, and sit there. Purring. Especially after sex and just before sleep. Too damn few men really understood how post-coital cuddles were just as wonderful, just as important as the old *in and out*. The holding, melding together, making you seem as one, if only for a few moments. A man who wasn't interested in that got ghosted pretty damn quick.

Initially, she had thought Liam would just be fun for a night, so had put out the hints of interest. Not the silly girl kind where you giggle and act coy and cute as you twirl your hair in your pinkie. No, just straight looks. Direct. He had picked up on them and asked her to stay after class, one day. Three months later she had still been enjoying his cuddles.

But then he'd landed a part in one of the superhero films shooting in Australia. Apparently, him being from there and looking like he could stand up to his fellow Aussie, that Thor guy, would help the production with its tax breaks, so he had packed up and moved home.

In the space of a week.

With no chance for one last cuddle. Dammit.

Sure, there had been a couple of bed partners since then, but she missed Liam. His hands had known where to go to drive her wild. His lips had always done the exact right thing. His body next to hers had felt real and alive instead of perfunctory. And drawing her fingers along his lightly tattooed back and skin made soft and smooth by liberal use of tanning lotion. It was almost heaven. No one had pleased her nearly as much, since. Since five, six months ago?

Jesus, had it been that long?

Shit, could that explain her sudden love of slaughtering men? Not that these three hadn't deserved it, because they most surely had, but the thrill she'd gotten, was it just from being in total control of a man? Or did she just miss cuddling?

Cuddling with a man I'm killing? One might call that psychotic.

Of course, then Samael popped back up. An angel deciding life and death.

That could make for a God complex. Or devil. Whichever. Yep, definitely psycho-killer, qu'est-ce que ç'est.

But now she was wondering if she could do that to Zeke, if he did turn out to be one of them. As a sniper, not once had she hesitated. No matter how young or pretty her target. But here? Now? Holding him? She felt something shifting. Felt her heart quiver. Noticed an odd hollowness had developed in it that was now being filled, at the same time, with whispers of new possibilities.

And she did not want to even think about that.

She looked at the back of his neck. Well, what she could see between the helmet and jacket collar. Tattooed on one side, not the other, sure. But this close. His skin so clean and smooth. His hair cropped tight so you could even see the point where his skull flowed into his neck.

And where his spine began.

To her surprise, she wanted to kiss it, and would have if the helmets weren't preventing it. Liam's hair had always been too long, and brushing it up or to the side only made that area seem ill-kempt. Not very sensual. The one thing she hadn't liked about him.

But Zeke...

Dear God, she wanted to touch his neck, just to verify what she was seeing was real. But something told her this would not be viewed in a positive light, by him. Or Loki. True, he had invited her to hold him close, but he had also set up other boundaries, and for now it was best to respect them.

For now.

Yes, because right here, at this singular moment, she had this amazingly gentle ride to brush every question away, like they were vile, unimportant, childish notions.

How could being on this bike be so lovely and beautiful and elegant? How was it possible for her to feel so free and alive, without a care in the world? With no past to hold her? After all she had done? Anger gone to nothingness. Pain barely a memory. Nothing but a future of promise and grace.

Which was ridiculous. Seriously, what was so different about her, at this moment?

Granted, she knew more about Zeke's past, now, thanks to her brother's research. His father a Lutheran Minister, unforgiving in his demands to conformity. Her own mother was the Catholic version, so they shared that. The IED, she knew about. The years of physical therapy to get back to normal? She didn't need to be told about that. How long he'd been at the Cantina, she knew about. So it wasn't the research she had on him.

It was his ease with her. His calmness and center. His willingness to accept her at face value. Trusting, but not completely. Not looking at her like someone he wanted to fuck. It disarmed her. Made her step back and question herself. And she both loved to do it and hated it.

She looked back over her shoulder at Loki to find he was watching her, still wary, his eyes all but screaming, *You try one fuckin' thing wrong with my boss, bitch, and I'll rip your fuckin' throat open.*

She chuckled.

Don't worry, puppy. Sete de sangue was satisfied, today. And I trust your boss enough to wait and see and...

Holy shit, that was it. Deep down, she trusted Zeke. Which made no sense. She had barely spoken to him, so had no reason for it; she just...she just did. Because he let her feel he cared. And he trusted her enough to take her on a quiet ride into the middle of nowhere in a soft attempt to restore her soul.

Which seemed to be working.

Oh, dear God, if only it could be so.

*****

Much too soon, Zeke slowed the Harley and turned to pass through a dilapidated gate onto a dirt road. Under the gleaming starlight, Carli could just make out they were approaching yet another of those ubiquitous outcroppings of rocks. They were heading north, over the uneven trail. At a slower speed, yes, but still rumbling along as if on a magic carpet.

"Carli," broke through the quiet. It took her a moment to realize it was Zeke talking.

"Yeah?"

"Hold on."

She pulled herself tighter to him as he aimed his bike up a vague trail along the side of the rocks. Up they rode as it curled around to end near the top. There, he stopped, and the sudden silence was unnerving.

He propped the Harley up and unmounted as Loki jumped out of his doggie chair, shook himself, then stayed by Zeke's side, still casting wary glances at Carli. She took off her helmet at the same time as him, and in the midnight glow Carli almost gasped at the picture he made. Even in profile, she could see he was relaxed and his face was open. She followed his gaze to witness...

Desert stretching to forever, before her. Breathtaking. Empty. Cold. Dangerous. Beyond it, the edge of oblivion.

"This is my place," he whispered in near reverence.

"Your sacréd land?" Carli asked, not really joking.

He looked at her, smiling. "Dunno. I just like it here because it helps clear my head. And I need it, tonight."

"Oh?"

He hesitated then said in a soft voice, "Some bad news."

"I'm sorry," whispered from her before she could work up the where-with-all to realize he was referring to Grady.

"Sometimes I even sleep out here," he continued.

She had to turn away from him to be able to find her voice. "Well, there's lots of rocks for pillows."

"Naw, I got Loki for that. *Woof.*"

Loki woofed, back, then looked out the vast desert like a king surveying his domain.

She looked at Zeke then nodded. "You have trouble sleeping?"

He shrugged a *yes.*

"Cluttered up with the past?" she continued.

"With everything. You know how that works."

She turned back the desert, trying to ignore a strange feeling building in her. It was neither sexual nor erotic, just a deep longing to share. To explain. To let him know she understood. And have herself understood.

Not good, right now, Carli. Careful.

She covered it by asking, "How long've you been coming here?"

"Saw these rocks when I was ridin' in. Look. See? Those headlights?"

Carli noticed the merest hint of beams zipping in a straight line probably a mile away, to her right.

"That's The 14," he continued. "You can barely see these from there, but for some reason the sun was hittin' 'em just right and I...I dunno...it sounds crazy...but it's like they called to me. So I pulled off and came over. Now I come back every Friday night, to keep myself steady."

"I'm glad you brought me."

"It was that or kick you out of the Cantina, and that wouldn't have been right."

"How *did* you wind up at that bar?"

He shrugged. "Gotta be someplace.

"Not home?"

He hesitated. "Gotta be welcome."

"But you're such an even guy. What could've happened to make your folks not want you around?"

It took him a moment to answer. "They weren't my folks. They just raised me."

He turned to the Harley and pulled the bag out along with a blanket that was folded in the base of the doggie seat. He set the bag down and unfurled the blanket then stopped, short.

"Whoa, whoa, see that? Rim of light? The moon's startin' to show...and she's full, tonight. Completely full."

Carli could just see the tip of the moon's crown appearing in the distance, giving the edge of the world a stark clarity. She froze to the spot to watch it rise and fill the landscape, growing larger and grander and almost alive in its pale golden beauty. Never in the history of the world had there been a moon so elegant or heartbreaking. She knew this to the very depths of her soul and wanted nothing more than to just stand there and watch it rise and rise and rise and...

"Here," jolted her.

Zeke nudged her arm and handed her a paper cup with some wine. He raised his own, softly saying, "To whatever passes for the eternal."

"To forever," whispered from Carli without even thinking it.

By this point, the moon had separated from the land to be surrounded by nothing but black velvet. Gleaming and bright, casting the stars into momentary shadow. Carli knew as she drifted higher and higher into the sky, she would shrink in importance, then drift back to the world and grow, but for some reason she never seemed to be as large as when she first formed.

And it was a travesty.

"It's so beautiful, here," Carli said. "The Afghan desert was ugly and brown, and drank so much blood."

"Same as it ever was," Zeke said.

"You know what's crazy? How much I miss it. The guys in my unit."

"C'mon, dinner is served, and Loki will not touch his kibble until we begin."

She turned to see the blanket held paper plates of cheese, crackers, bread and apples. A bottle of wine anchored paper napkins in place against the breeze. He'd been busy while she'd been zoning.

"I should've brought a heavier coat," she said as she sat on one edge of the blanket, cross-legged. "I forgot how the desert can get, at night."

Zeke pulled off his jacket and dropped it over her shoulders.

"No, Zeke."

"Last name's Lindstrom. I can handle the cold." He went into a ludicrous sing-song as he added, "Raised in Minnesota."

She almost laughed. "You a Vikings fan?"

"Total. All that Viking blood in me."

"But they're ocean oriented, and you're in the desert."

"I know." He lay on his back to look at the stars, nibbling on a slice of apple. Loki huffed then dug into his own plate, still careful to watch Carli.

"Do you miss Minnesota?" she asked.

"Sometimes."

Carli slipped a bite of cheese into her mouth, fighting herself, but she had to ask, "Why *not* go back?"

"Don't want to."

"Was what happened to you so horrible?"

He looked at her. "Does it have to be?"

"No," she said. "So how're you doing? Now?"

"Making it. You will, too, y'know."

"You think so?"

He looked back up at the stars, sighing. "You're stronger'n you let on."

"That...that's good to know." She wrapped his jacket tighter around her. Looked back up at the moon, now so much smaller but seeming even brighter than before. And the stars were pushing their way back into prominence.

And the breeze was softer.

And a couple of coyotes were yipping at each other in ways that added to the sense of tranquility.

And Carli felt close to tears.

"So beautiful here."

"Welcome to it, anytime," Zeke murmured. Then he took in a deep breath. "But maybe we better head back. I'm feeling ready for a pillow. Ahead of schedule."

She removed his jacket, rolled it up and set it under his head, saying, "Go ahead."

"Gonna get colder."

"I'll be fine."

"Fair warning. When I sleep, I sleep."

She gazed upon him, that feeling of protectiveness enveloping her heart, mingled with a sort of tenderness she hadn't felt in years.

"Not like this is a first date," whispered from her.

He gave a soft, mumbling chuckle. "Some first date. Drag you out to a cold rock. Watch the moon come up. Then I crash on you."

"I have no place else to be."

"Does anybody?" And he drifted to sleep.

She watched him.

As Loki watched her.

She whispered to him, "They say a dog knows if you're decent and can be trusted. Is that what you're saying to me? Him, you trust and love? Me, you don't?"

He just watched her, remaining wary.

She looked back out over the desert. Heard more coyotes. Owls whispering past. Even bats squeaking. All in harmony. A balance she no longer felt within.

She had read what her brother posted on his site. Apparently the Reverend Lindstrom published his sermons in a weekly paper, in their town, and they were archived online. And TF had found the ones that dealt with Zeke. How he had been a perfect boy until the devil took possession of him and turned him against his guardians.

Not his parents; his *guardians*.

Earlier sermons were more like self-praise for how the man and his barren wife had taken in an unwanted child to raise in the ways of God and the Spirit and on and on. She recognized every reference he made to the bible. And not in one of them was there even so much as a hint of love. What kind of a life had that been, for him?

To have no parents. No family. Just prison guards.

No matter how much Carli disavowed the beliefs and attitudes of her mother, or wondered at the acquiescence of her father, never for one moment had she thought they tried to guide her through anything but love. They'd disagreed with her actions, but they had also supported her in ways that she now felt the need to acknowledge.

Carli was fourteen when she had Lara, and it was beyond her ability to accept. So she had been an unholy terror throughout the pregnancy. Fighting over the best foods to eat and against the no drinking, smoking or running around rules. Rest. Frequent trips to the gynecologist and pediatrician. Lamaze classes to get ready for the birth. She had hated every minute of it. But thanks to this, the delivery had been quick and easy. A couple weeks late, true, but over and done with in less than an hour.

It wasn't until she spoke with other women, in the Army, who had children at such a young age that she understood how lucky she had been. Some of them had truly difficult births due to a lack of all these things, or their child was born with problems or the delivery was horrendous or even the baby was born dead.

As one of them told her, "Well, since your momma didn't let you get rid of it, at least she made sure it come out okay. Not like these assholes who say *fuck you for gettin' fucked.*"

What was better? Momma had taken over rearing Lara. "Just till you're done with school." Which Carli had been happy to let her do. Even pumped her milk so it could be fed to the baby.

Which was a weirdly sensuous experience.

When Carli had told her she wanted to join the Army, *to get money for college and benefits for Lara*, it had been, *Just till you're done with that.* Only they both knew, by that point it was more of a permanent situation.

That hadn't been fair, dropping everything on her mother. She was going through menopause, at the time. And if it hit Carli as hard as it hit her, she figured it might be best to be living on the North Pole so as not to commit mass slaughter.

Like she was doing, now.

No, this is serial murder, Carli, in the name of justice, which you can't put on anything but your own hate and anger. No one to blame but yourself.

"No one," she whispered.

The first hint of sun appeared in the distance, startling her. She looked at her phone. It showed 6:34am.

What the hell? We've been out here nearly four hours?

She looked at Zeke. He was deep into slumber, which brought a smile to her face. He was so innocent, there. So peaceful, she hurt for him.

She looked away. Reached for the helmet she'd worn. Slipped it on then lay back and turned onto her side to look at him. And saw Loki was still half-awake and half-watching her, his head on Zeke's belly. Waiting for her to prove she couldn't be trusted.

She felt so ashamed, all of a sudden. So sorry for everything.

"I couldn't hurt him," she murmured to the dog, without a thought. "I never will, no matter what. I promise you."

He didn't seem to believe her.

Tears trailed from her eyes as she continued, "It's over. It's over. It's over."

That is when the dog gave a soft huff and closed his eyes.

Carli wrapped her arms tighter around herself, stunned at what she had just promised. And truly amazed at how much she meant it. Because it was more honest than anything she had ever said or felt or believed, before.

She would rather die than let Zeke be hurt, ever again.

The sun had just risen and Dax was dog-tired when he rolled up the long ragged driveway to a rambling duplex on the northern outskirts of town. It was surrounded by four acres of desert scrub, where cacti and rocks rubbed against succulents, and mesquite trees provided a modicum of shade.

He owned the place, living in one side and using the other for his office. On occasion, he would let couriers stay there, if they arrived late, so the bedroom and bathroom were blocked off for sleeping; the rest of the unit was a massive desk, three CPUs and monitors, and state of the art tracking system, which no one had access to but him. Like any good businessman, Dax always wanted to know exactly where his guys and his product were. And like a good paranoid freak, make sure no one else did.

That was why he'd been so worried about Grady. Nothing had shown up on the system after he left the Cantina. At the least, his cell phone should have given them a trail, but it had gone dead, on The 14. Dax had spent Thursday afternoon searching the area of the last known signal and finally found the remains of one that could have been Grady's. Totally wrecked, in an area of nothing but open country and a few abandoned homes. It wasn't adding up.

Then Eldora had filled him in. And everything else was scrambled up, too.

Shit.

So Dax had hopped up to his storage unit in Tucson to get more supply for Chase. He spent the night because he hated getting up before the crack of dawn to do anything. He also wanted to connect with his source for a new line of supply, but learned they had been raided just hours before.

"Can't find out who narc'd on us," said the guy, "but we're workin' on it."

"How bad?" Dax had asked.

"Two mules from Nogales and four dealers. Don't call me, again. I'll call you. If you don't hear from me, I'm no longer here."

"Got it. Good luck."

So Dax spent the night in a cheap motel, testing the product. All good quality. Then he sent Nat a text, telling him he'd handle Chase's meetup, but got no response.

At first, Dax didn't worry. Nat has prone to turning off his phone, when he didn't want to be disturbed, then forgetting to turn it back on. And Spit only had his on him half the time, the fuck; something was definitely missing in that piggy little brain of his.

Still Dax should have received a text or call or something, from Nat, this morning. He was always good about touching base, once he woke up. So Dax had gone straight to Katty's, but neither guy was there, nor was the Malibu, though Nat's Hog still was. So he'd headed out to the meeting point.

To find stains in the dirt that could be blood. And tire tracks from what was probably the Malibu. And another shattered cell phone.

That brought on a call to Eldora, an hour of the two of them scavenging the area to find something that would explain away Dax's worries, and getting nowhere.

"I sent JJ up to Loretta's to see if they went up there," Dax told her.

"That place still in business?" she had asked, wary.

"Doin' better'n ever, thanks to the fuckin' Republicans. They love to fuck around in ways nobody knows about."

"All politicians, Dax."

"No shit."

"Okay, I'm gonna put out a *locate only* report. See if we can find them that way. But..."

"No, I'm not goin' for that, yet," he'd snapped. "There's a dozen other places they could be and I'm goin' to every fuckin' one of 'em."

"Waste of time," Eldora had sighed.

"Yeah, well, it's my fuckin' time, ain't it?"

Then he had left her to the place. But he could no longer ignore the very, very bad feeling he had about this.

A feeling that increased when he saw a FedEx tag on his door.

A tag that should *not* be there. His official mailing address was a drop box on the west end of town. He rode straight up to the door to hop off the Hog and grab the tag, not at all happy.

No information on it, of course. Just *Available after 9am*. It was almost eight-thirty. Shit. Barely time for a breakfast of Adderall.

He checked his phone, again. No messages or emails that mattered. That got him to wondering, again. This was the second time Chase had been connected to Dax's guys going missing. Couldn't be coincidence; Dax didn't believe in that shit. Once he had picked up this delivery, he was going to pay a little visit to young master Chase and find out if he was double-dealing him, again.

Chase had made that mistake, once, and it had cost him an ear.

Dax had thought the little prick had learned his lesson, but it seemed privileged white brats didn't really think the rules applied to them.

Like that little cunt, Stasi.

She'd thought she was so fucking cute. Chase had been dumb shit...or horn-dog enough...to let her run a tab for coke before he'd cut her off. She'd come weeping to Dax, thinking she could use the same shit attitude to shrug off making payment.

"I just don't have it, right now," she'd said in her dismissive way. "Daddy says I'm spending too much so he's cut my allowance. But I've been such a good customer you'd think — "

Dax had grabbed her by the throat and slammed her against the wall and calmly said, "You got till Monday to get me the cash, or every one of my guys is gonna fuck you. And if you think you can run from me? Watch how fast you get your ass busted for possession and daddy finds out he's got a cokehead cunt for a daughter."

"He won't believe you!" she'd choked, surprisingly angry. "We've got lawyers who'll fuck you up so bad..."

"Maybe. An' maybe I got video of you. Make daddy think twice about fuckin' with me."

That cut into her attitude. "What video?"

"Oh...you snortin' a line. An' maybe, if I go down, I take you along as one of my pushers, and you get sent to Joliad. I hear the women in there absolutely hate little cunts like you. Be fun to see how long you lasted."

"You wouldn't fucking dare! My father knows guys who'd — "

"Yeah, yeah, yeah, they'll fuck me over. Like I don't know people who know people, for myself. Right."

Then he'd squeezed her left breast, making her howl with fury as he'd sneered. "Shit, these ain't even real. Maybe I should let Spit pop 'em like balloons. All he'd have to do is put his belly on 'em as he's pumpin' inside you. Just be sure you're on the pill; he don't like condoms."

That was getting through to her. "No, no, you can't do that."

"An' Grady? He's had an eye on you for a while. Even Nat thinks you'd be a fun time. An' I hear he's got a big one. I'll have him go last. Tell us all how it feels to fuck a girl who's nothin' but silicon and bullshit."

"But I really don't have the money!"

"Hock something, or your Monday night's booked."

"No, no, what if I — I can get you another girl?"

"Who'd be dumb-shit enough to help save your ass?"

"She wouldn't. She's one of those anti-drug assholes, on campus. Pushing for more security. Tighter watch on who's into what. A holier-than-thou bitch who ruins everybody's fun. She's one of the reasons things are getting slow, for you."

He squeezed tighter on both neck and breast. "Who the fuck told you things were slow?"

"Chase! Chase. When he cut me off. Wouldn't sell any more to me. Told me he couldn't afford any more cuts in profits."

That stupid little fuck. He couldn't keep his fuckin' mouth shut? That had to be remedied.

Stasi had continued with, "What if I...what if I bring her to the Cantina? To show her Prince Hot Tatts? Drop a little something in her drink?"

"He ain't there, Mondays."

"She won't know that. And she's real. All of her. I've seen her at the pool. Couple years younger than me. And I bet she's a virgin, she's such a tight-ass."

Dax had released her. She'd barely kept herself standing, gasping and whimpering.

He'd hated to admit it, but the little bitch had a good idea. That new group on campus *had* been hurting sales, more-so since the beginning of the semester.

"Virgin, huh?" he'd said, deep in thought.

"I...I think so." Stasi had rubbed her neck, her voice full of desperation. "She's first semester."

"What's her name?"

"Lara something. Italian. Vinnenzo? Vienteo?"

"Fuckin' shit, Stasi, ain't she in the school directory?"

Stasi had nodded and opened her phone.

As she searched, Dax had considered her proposition. Stasi was into him for three grand, but the guys needed some fun. If he played this right, he could remove not only a problem that was building for his college clients, but also bring joy to his boys. And if Stasi was dumb-shit enough to think that paid off what she owed? Well, that wasn't his problem. In fact, he might even charge some interest.

So it had been set up for the following Monday. And he'd made sure Chase was there to be part of it. And it had gone like he expected. Making like he's the bartender. Sneaking a roofie on her. The boys doing their thing.

What he hadn't expected was for Zeke to show up and toss a fit. And even worse? For Stasi to record it and put it up on the university message boards, and then dare him to come after her. The double-dealing little bitch. It was only thanks to Eldora he and the boys hadn't wound up in prison.

And also thanks to her he hadn't cut the little cunt's throat.

But now she was dead. And so was Grady, dammit. And he was very worried about Nat and Spit.

What was that old saying he'd heard or read or something, somewhere? *You can be so clever, you wind up in hell.*

He was beginning to wonder if that's what he had done.

*****

Half an hour later, Dax was fed, hyped up on speed, and standing at a FedEx desk with the tag. The clerk was one of those way too nice and helpful morning-person types he so hated, especially evident when he looked at Dax's driver's license and perkily chirped, "Dexter Castor?"

Dax growled and grunted *yes* so he could keep from adding *motherfucker*.

The clerk bounced, said, "Fantastic," and all but skipped back through a pair of double-doors. Two seconds later, he came out with a small rectangular box. "Direct signature required." He pointed to a modem next to the register.

"What the fuck does that mean?" Dax growled.

"Only you can sign for it." Said with the saddest puppy eyes possible.

"Who the fuck's it from?"

The courier pointed to an address on the mailing label...

A. Deveaux, 22 Wilshire Parkway, Los Angeles, CA 90003.

Dax could have made ice just by touching water, he suddenly felt so damned cold.

Oh, mother-fuckin' shit.

It took him a moment, but he signed and accepted the box, then slammed out the door before Little Sir Early Bird could say another word. He hopped on his bike, propped the box on the handlebars, stared at it for a good five minutes, his inner paranoia exploding all through him, then pulled out his phone and called Eldora.

When she answered, her voice crackled in and out, like she was on the moon. "What is it now, Dax?" she asked.

"I just got a delivery from Anastasia Deveaux," he said, his eyes locked on it.

"Don't bullshit me."

"It's on the fuckin' box! Overnight. From LA. So it wasn't sent till after she did that jump. An' I had to sign for it, nobody else!"

"Oh, shit. Don't open it. Bring it to the station. Raymon knows how to check for explosives."

"It's kind of small for a bomb."

"How big does it have to be to kill you?"

"Good point. I'll have it there in ten minutes."

"Make it an hour. I'm still at that meeting place, with the

coroner's men."

"Coroner?!"

"Yep. Found a bullet in the dirt. Some blood on it. And they also have the DNA results."

Dax slumped, shaking his head. "That body. It *is* Grady."

"Yes," she said. "Sorry."

"Fuck, fuck, fuck, fuck, fuck."

"My sentiments, exactly. See you in an hour."

Dax ended the call, slipped the box in his saddle bag, fired up the Hog and headed for The 14, aiming straight for Cantina Madriza.

He needed some JD, right now.

*****

At the other end of The 14, Carli rode with Jake and Loki, heading towards the Cantina. Her head was on his shoulder and Loki was in his seat, still watching her. The morning air was chilly but clean and clear, and neither of them seemed to feel it. The sun was bright and glorious, but the visors on the helmets provided more than enough shade for their eyes.

Never had Carli felt more at peace. She had no explanation for it except she'd slept for an hour next to Zeke. And awakened at the same moment as he. And they had shared a breakfast of stale cheese and bread, and wine. And apples. And never had anything tasted so wonderful to her.

"This *is* a spiritual place, she'd said.

"I like it," was Zeke's only comment, but his gentle smile told her so much more.

To her shock, she knew, deep down, she could actually love him. Whether or not she actually *did*, yet, was another question. But as much fun as she'd had with other men, as much as she'd liked some, Liam included, Zeke was the first man she'd felt more for. And that was without even the suggestion of sex! She had absolutely no idea what to say or do about it. So had stayed quiet.

Zeke had said less. Hadn't even tried to get into her pants, as her bad-boy-brothers loved to put it. Just let her be, like one human with another.

If that's your way of seduction, buddy, you're kicking ass.

So they had mounted the Harley and ridden down the trail with laughs and giggles, and now she felt as if she were going home.

Home.

That had always been an abstract term, to her. Moving every couple of years from one post to another. Even before she joined the army, she hadn't enough of a real kinship to where she was living to refer to it as home. More like a prison or a halfway house. But now? Heading for a ramshackle joint in the middle of nowhere? That was like returning to a place she felt safe and comfortable in? The very idea was ridiculous.

But then she saw the Cantina approaching, and she could see the Dodge in the parking lot, and she felt it was much too soon.

It wasn't the Cantina that was home...

Jesus, Christ, Carli, you know this guy five minutes and suddenly it's Ozzie and Harriet? You gonna start reading romance novels next? With Fabio on the cover? Bare chested, his flowing locks long and blond?

She had to fight to keep from laughing out loud.

"Nice," he said, eyeing it, pulling up next to the Dodge.

Carli jolted, then said, "Thanks. It sucks gas but it works good, out here."

"Do much off-roadin'?"

"Sometimes," she said, getting off the bike.

"I got a feeling it's gonna be busy, tonight. But if you want to drop by..."

"Okay. Thanks. Sleep well."

He nodded to her. "Already did."

He headed to the back. Loki huffed a reluctant sort-of farewell.

Carli watched Zeke go. Watched him get off the Harley. Watched him go inside. His limp actually seemed to add to his beauty...and being away from him, she felt lessened, for some stupid reason. She unlocked the Dodge and got in, angry with herself over all this sudden rush of emotional weakness and...

The distant rumble of a Hog caught her attention.

She saw it coming from town. But why would a biker be heading out this way so early in the morning? Unless.

Oh, shit. Unless it was Dax. She closed the door and dropped to the truck's floor.

Moments later, the bike stopped next to her and she heard Loki howl and bark.

Oh, shit. It *was* Dax.

"Loki!" It was Zeke calling. "Loki! Here! House! Dammit, Loki, house!"

"Goddammit, Zeke, that fuckin' dog!"

"I got him, Dax. Shit, what's going on? You're never here, this early."

"I need a drink."

Between Loki's barking and howling, she caught the jangle of keys as Dax walked to the entrance.

"Somebody forget their car?"

"What? Oh, thought she'd be gone, by now."

"C'mon in. I need to talk to you."

"Okay. Be there in a second. Loki, cut it out!"

She heard the front door open so peeked over the dashboard to see Dax enter. Zeke was back at the trailer, attaching Loki's chain and saying, "It's just for a little while, buddy."

She positioned herself behind the wheel and slammed the key into the ignition, but Zeke saw her before she could make a getaway. He cast her a questioning look as he walked back to the front, so she shrugged and indicated she'd needed to take a pee. That made him even more confused, because he motioned to the trailer as a place to do that but she waved him off and backed away and headed for town. In the rearview mirror, she saw him shake his head then enter the Cantina.

The moment he was inside, she pulled off the road and fired up the receiver and heard...

"Already on the JD?" That was Zeke's voice.

"Zeke, can I trust you?"

"What? You know you can. Why you askin' that? What's up?"

"That box, on the table."

Ooooooooh, look what got delivered.

"FedEx? What's it — ?" She heard him gasp.

"Yeah. But here's the crazy part. It went to my *home* address. Nothin' goes there. Only JJ knows where I live."

Tell that to TF.

"Shit, you're in that part of town?"

"Shut up."

"You gonna open it?"

"Eldora wants me to bring it in. Check for explosives."

"Oh..."

"Don't worry. I know ordinance, an' if FedEx didn't get it to blow the way they handle shit, it's safe."

She heard him pour himself another drink.

"This box." It was Zeke talking. "You think maybe it's her dad fucking with you? Like maybe he blames you for what happened to her?"

"Thought crossed my mind. He's somethin' of a psycho prick, so I wouldn't be surprised. But how'd he know where to send it?"

"State records?"

"He probably would have access. Tell me, you seen Nat or Spit?"

"No. They didn't come in, last night."

"Katty ain't seen 'em, either. JJ's headed back from Loretta's..."

"Since when does he go there on Friday night?"

"I sent him, this mornin'. Lookin' for 'em. They ain't there. I've told him to text me where he is, every fifteen minutes."

"Why're you looking?" His voice was wary.

"Can't find 'em. Oh, an' it's official about Grady."

She heard Zeke drop into a chair. "I know. I know." He sounded like he was close to crying, and it nearly tore her in half.

"Have you thought more 'bout that woman who picked him up?"

It took Zeke a moment to answer. "Yeah. Her license. It was Nevada. And I'm pretty sure her first name was...was Orneta...or maybe her last name. Something like that. All I really look at is the picture and birth date. License number. I sent all that to Eldora."

"Okay. I'm headed to meet her. Get the box looked at. You gonna be okay?"

"Yeah. Yeah. I mean, I knew it, but I kept hoping..."

"We all did."

"Dax. Grady liked the desert. I don't think he'd want a burial. I think...I think he'd like to be cremated and mixed in with it. Can we do that?"

"I'll check. And from the sound of things, cremation might not be a bad idea. I'll talk to you later."

"Yeah. Later."

She heard him walking to the door, so quickly started the Dodge and zipped on down the road.

It sounded like her actions were having the desired effect on Dax. What TF had learned about him all but screamed how easy it would be to torture his piss-ant brain, like this. Paranoid freak. What tempered her pleasure was the pain in Zeke's voice, over Grady.

He *cared* about the fuck. That made her uneasy, again. Unsure about him. How could any man feel loss over scum like that man and not be the same?

Only she got no sense of Zeke being that way. It confused her.

Her older brothers were a pack of randy little shits. She had accidentally overheard them comparing notes on girls they'd had or wanted, and she'd been irritated by their stupid macho crap. But she loved them. Knew she'd protect them as much as they had protected her. So maybe Zeke and Grady and the others saw themselves as a band of brothers kind of thing.

It's just, it tainted Zeke, in her eyes.

Or did it make him even better because he felt so strongly about a sleaze like Grady, despite what he was?

Damn that little shit. He'd brought uncertainty to her plan for justice, and it was messing her up too damn much so...

Her phone buzzed with a text from TF.

Got him.

She smiled, all other concerns flying out the window.

First to her campsite, for fresh clothes and brekkie, bit of preparation. And then? Time to pay Chase a little call.

*****

The Sheriff's office was at the end of a strip center near the five block long downtown. It consisted of a reception area, two offices, a locker room in the back and four cells to house inmates. A back door led to additional parking, for easy loading of felons to be carted off to Tucson. Only the misdemeanors and drunk college brats were kept in-house to await a circuit judge. Everything about it was plain, white, cheap and functional.

Outside by the back door, Reymon leaned over a heavy table shoved against a thick cinder-block wall. He was focused on the box, a pair of padded mitts on his hands as well as a helmet with a face mask and body armor. Next to him was a monitor, into which he had just slipped a swab. Dax and Eldora stood well away from him, watching.

The monitor blinked and Reymon said, "No explosive residue. And I don't see anything that looks like a trigger."

"Can you open it?" Eldora asked.

He shrugged and pulled a utility knife from a drawer.

"Proof is in the cutting," he said as he carefully sliced into a side of the box, away from its strip pull. Slow and easy, feeling his way. Then down at each end to make a flap. Finally, with a deep breath, he pulled the side of the box down and looked inside.

"There's a tube wrapped in paper, in it."

He carefully pulled the tube out. The mitts made it difficult, but he was able to unwrap it...then suddenly dropped it with an, "Oh, shit!"

Eldora and Dax came over and saw what looked like a hot dog, all bloody and shriveled with a lump on one end. But they all knew instantly what it was.

Grady's penis.

Dax spun around, snarling, "Mother-fucking son-of-a-bitch!" He stormed off into the desert behind the office, all but howling in anger.

Eldora watched him go then said, "Reymon, get this up to the coroner, right now. Box checked for everything they can think of. Give 'em your gloves, too. Tell 'em those're the only things have touched it."

He nodded and put the remains back in the FedEx box. "Guess

the coyotes didn't get this part," he said.

"Yes," Eldora said. "Now go."

He took off his gear and headed on.

Eldora followed Dax. Found him sitting on a low dune, joint fired up. His hands shook and he had a thousand yard gaze going. She nodded, took the pot and drew some in as he continued, "I still can't get hold of Nat or Spit."

"That's not good," she said, sighing.

"Understatement of the year." He took the joint, huffed some in then snarled, "What the fuck's goin' on, Eldora? You think maybe it's those assholes, gone off the reservation?"

"Don't be an idiot."

"Then why was Grady done like that?"

"My thoughts? I bet this is about you and your buddies havin' some fun, a year back. Like, did you know that Vincenzo girl's mother was Army?"

"C'mon, why would she wait so long to go after us?"

"No idea. But the girl who set it up and recorded it is dead. Her car's by the body of one of the guys who did some of that rapin' — "

"It wasn't — "

"Cut it out, Dax! I saw the goddamn tape!"

He huffed then snapped, "What about that woman that picked up Grady? Maybe she's helpin' Stasi's old man. Maybe he thinks we killed his little bitch!"

"Maybe. He has got the connections, and Orneta Hughes died in a car wreck three years ago, in Carson City. And was black. Bein' that sloppy about a fake ID suggests it was rushed. Or deliberate."

"Fuck!" He began to pace in a circle, his mind shooting a thousand directions. "Man, if I'd known that bitch was recordin' it..." And the tone of his voice was clear that she'd have died a lot sooner than she did.

Eldora nodded, silently agreeing it would have been better for them all if he had. "My money's still on Vincenzo bein' involved, at least with Deveaux's murder. Maybe that set off the girl's father. A buddy at Fort Bliss is checking her record, see if she has the where-with-all to do any of it. And I got a call into California's DMV. See if she's got a license there. If so, they'll have a picture and Zeke might recognize that. But it bein' the weekend..."

"You think she's comin' after me?"

"Wouldn't be surprised. For all I know, she's pissed at me, too, for not haulin' your asses in. I should've. But you don't kill the golden goose."

She flicked his head.

He huffed, his gaze now locked on the desert.

"She couldn't do all this shit on her own," he said. "The way Grady was found? I bet she recruited those assholes I had trouble with, a few years back."

"Christ, Dax, *that* was eight years! Half of them are dead, already, dammit. Just give me a chance to see what I can dig up, first. Soon as I find out somethin', I'll let you know."

A deputy stuck his head out the back door and called, "Sheriff, we got a call just come in! You need to get there."

"Be right in," she called back, then she yanked Dax after her. "Come on. Standin' out here kickin' dirt won't do a damn thing."

She released him back to the rear door and went inside.

He leaned against the table, pulled his phone and dialed.

"Yeah, Dax?" It was JJ talking.

"Where are you?"

"At Spit's. Katty's finally gettin' worried."

"Fuck. Stay there. I'm gonna go find Chase; I want to ask that little fuck a few things. Come on by my place, about three. We need to figure this out."

Then Eldora appeared at the back door, nearly breathless.

"Dax, I think we found your boys."

He scowled at her, but the look on her face shattered his attitude and made him cold enough to freeze water, again.

*****

Twenty minutes later, Eldora's SUV roared up to the same plateau where Grady's body was found, Dax behind her on his Hog. Atop the plateau was the old Malibu, with two dark mounds next to it. One very large; one trim. Now Dax knew why he hadn't been able to find them, and the fury in him was beyond explosive.

Reymon's SUV was already on-site and he was talking to a pair of young dirt bikers. He saw them approaching and headed to meet them. Eldora said not a word as she burst from the truck, dust still swirling around it. Dax stopped right behind her.

"I got the call on the way to the coroner's," Reymon said, "so swung over."

"What's your thoughts?" Eldora asked.

Reymon looked at Dax, uncomfortable. "All the same as last time. Car's facing east-southeast. Both bodies parallel to it. Got up that same trail, same way. New boards are there."

She nodded. "And the bodies?"

"Not as — not quite as bad off as last time. Both half stripped. One black, one white. Both...both used to be male."

"My guys," Dax growled.

Reymon just nodded.

"There's some significance to this piece of land," Eldora said.

"It's county property," Reymon said.

"No, it's somethin' else." Then she nodded to the dirt bikers. "What's up with those two?"

"Just out bikin', from what I can tell. Saw the car and came closer to look. Found the guys and ran off to catch a signal. Crap cell phone-age. I had to talk 'em into comin' back, but they were up on the plateau so..."

"Tire treads and boots in the middle of it all. Lovely. All right. Give me your notes, then you head on. Coroner's guys're still at the other location; I'll have them come over here."

"Funeral home'll be here in a minute."

"They'll have to wait. I want this place scoured for evidence, first. Should have done that with Grady. I want you to drop off that box, completely separate from this, then find out more about this property."

"I'll need my phone for that."

"What d'you mean?"

"I recorded their statements on it and you wanted — "

"Oh, shit, right. Transcribe everything, soon as you can."

"Already on it."

He headed for his SUV as she looked at Dax.

"Think you're up for makin' an official identification?"

He glared at her. "I was in Iraq."

She shrugged and they strode up to the dirt bikers, one beefy, one ragged, both in need of a bath, then Eldora said to them, "Thanks for stickin' around. Coroner should be here in a few minutes. Once we have impressions of your bikes' tires and boots, you can head on."

The beefy dirt biker nodded his head up the plateau and asked, "This some Indian thing?"

Eldora glared at him and said, "No." Then she led Dax up the side of the hill.

There lay Nat and Spit. Bound. Gagged. Half their clothes torn away. Castrated. Covered in blood. More bits of their bodies gone. Crawling with ants. Two empty honey bears between them.

Eldora held Dax in place then did her little walk around the plateau. When she was near the bodies, she motioned to him.

"Follow my footprints. Careful."

He did, eying the remains of Nat and Spit, cold as ice. In Iraq, he had witnessed far more hideous tableaux. Usually missing limbs. Heads. Bodies torn in half. Not always the enemy. But that was war. This? This was more than just jockeying for drug sales. It was nothing but a sick form of...of what? Vengeance? Over some girl's rape?

The guys hadn't known about the deal he'd set up with Stasi. They'd thought they were getting another stupid twat who was paying off a drug debt the only way she could. That she wept and struggled wasn't unexpected; what mattered was, they *had* enjoyed themselves.

But he had always done that for his guys. Taken care of them in every way he could. Nobody else would bother. Kind of hard to get a decent job when you're damaged like they were. People didn't want to be reminded of the realities of war. That not everyone who was hit by the enemy died. That some came back without an eye or with burns or missing a leg. Some form of damage that was just too damn visible to be comfortable around.

And that was what really mattered, wasn't it? One's own comfort. Still brought a sneer to his lips.

But now three of his men were dead. Butchered because he gave them a good time. That probably meant JJ was marked, too, as was he. They might even think Zeke had been part of it.

No. If Chase was behind any of this, he knew Zeke wasn't around till the very end. Plus, the guy had freaked out over what he saw. Dax was sure he'd shut the guy down, but could he still be helping with this? No. No, Zeke would never hurt Grady. Not like that.

But Chase might. After all, if a little rat squeals on you, once, they'll do it, again.

Still, that was a big maybe. Dax needed to find out more. So when he was done here, the first thing he planned to do was find that little fuck and get him to talk.

Actually, that wouldn't be the hard part; it was getting him to shut up that would be.

Chase'd...Not Chaste.

Next to Nathan Cruz campus was an absolutely adorable area of upscale condos and fine apartments built for the better class students to live in. All fresh, new and well-kept. Walls white and roofs tiled. Streets paved, with curbs and sidewalks. Ash and Oak trees shading yards made of pretty gravel pebbles lined by lovely neat bricks. No car dared park anywhere except a driveway or assigned parking; the ruination of the roads' lovely curves would not be endured.

It was in this area that Chase both lived and went running, three times a week, always in a sleeveless crop-top, cargo shorts, and too-cool high-top sneakers with black socks peeking over them. He never strayed from his very safe course, ever, because security in the area was really tight. He had also worked out that going up and down these particular streets worked out to five miles, if done twice. So with his phone playing his *hip-hop-don't-stop* music mix and the wire to his earbuds slipped up through his shirt, he was happy to keep doing it. Mainly because if he didn't he could easily balloon to over three-hundred pounds instead of maintaining a nice even one-seventy-five.

He also knew some girls in the area liked the way he looked, running by. Good form to his legs. Ass that's neither too big nor too small. Trim tummy. He'd managed to pick up a few of the little chickie-doodles over the last few years. Cute things that lasted till they either went home after term or found something better on Spring Break, or they just grew bored with each other. What was funny was, she was always the one who did the breaking up, never him. He was happy to have her around for bed and showing off and to hit movies or concerts with, but when it came to conversation? Expressions of love? To anything more than the absolute basics? Well...he just wasn't that kind of guy.

A Rock-Jock, he already had a job lined up with an oil company in Tulsa. He figured that after a while he would marry a pretty secretary, have two kids, two cars, an oversize house in the suburbs, six trips a year in the field, a girl on the side, and would finally achieve his middle-class dream, leaving this crap with Dax long behind.

And damn the bastard if he didn't agree.

Didn't hurt that Chase had his escape planned for the night of graduation. Soft, sweet and sudden. Dax wouldn't know he was gone till long after he was gone.

He almost wished he'd never started with the son-of-a-bitch. The previous guy Dax had on campus had been his dorm mate, but he had wound up using too much of the product he needed to sell. One day, he had simply vanished, leaving his things behind. Some said he went into rehab. Some said into prison. Some said, a desert grave. But since no one really knew, the school had bundled up his stuff and Chase had been more than willing to take over. Otherwise, he was looking at a six-figure loan for his degree. Keeping that from happening meant he'd be way ahead. Especially since he considered drugs were for losers with no self-control. Our Chase had no intention of ever having to go back to Lake Havasu and work in his mom's souvenir shop. That would be the worst of dead ends. So drugs were a no-no.

Things had been good for a year, till Stasi started her bullshit. *Just a hit for the party, Chasey-baby, c'mon. I'll pay you back, Tuesday.* Done in a simpering little-girl whine as she trailed her manicured nails down his chest to his belly in a way that always got him worked up.

Problem was, Tuesdays seemed to be her day to vanish, and when he'd see her at other times, she'd say she was out of cash so he'd have to wait till Daddy's next bank deposit was in. Which was always *another day away*. He'd fallen for it six times before he cut her off, cold — which was five times too many.

Once she'd realized she couldn't get around him, again, she'd gone straight to Dax. How she knew Dax was his supplier was one of those mysteries you don't want solved. She had simply managed to be at the Cantina when he was and had done her little schtick, and thought the guy was falling for it. Only it turned out that just was his way of reeling her in. She had come to learn, too late, she was hooked like a barracuda.

An appropriate fish metaphor, there.

That was the year Lara had started school. A nice casual figure in nice casual clothes, nothing high-end. Hair cut short and easy. Little makeup. Fully confident. A way of talking *to* you instead of *through* you or being manipulative. She was in a Geo-physics class with him, and she seemed to have the brain for it. Problem was, he'd caught on pretty quick she also had a serious hate for drugs that he felt was kind of overboard. Until he learned a close friend of hers in high school had OD'd on Fentanyl. Lara felt she should have noticed the signs in time to stop her, so had taken on the crusade and would brook no opposition. She had even joined an anti-drug group that was already on campus, and gotten them to start making real noise.

Fortunately, Chase had always been careful to know who was in that group, because sometimes they would come to him to see if they could buy some pot or speed, just because *somebody told them he was a good source.*

"You believe gossip about me?" he'd snap. "You think I do that shit? You know how much of a slap in the face that is?"

And they had always backed down.

The fact that he had a nice SUV and a nice condo to live in and nice clothes to wear is what drove the gossip, because for some reason that crowd chose not to believe they were thanks to his dad. Granted, he had no relationship with the tight-ass; he disapproved of Chase's choice of career so wouldn't give him a fucking dime, but he was also way up the chain in a bank in Phoenix. Normally, all people needed to find out was that daddy had dough and they'd accept he was just one of the spoiled, entitled few. But the few who actually were of the opinion they were entitled were the ones who were buying stuff off him, and had figured out that was how he was paying his way. That fact kept him separate from them, like he was trash, and was what raised questions about his financial situation.

Little hypocrites.

Still, things had gone fine, until Stasi, the most entitled of them all, appeared. She had left UCLA because it was *full of fakes*, but he knew it was bullshit. He'd met her type in high school — mean girls best dealt with by remaining on their good side, or being usable to them, in some way. Maybe you'd even be all right if the little bitch didn't care about you. But man, if she didn't like you, then you became a mortal enemy.

And Stasi absolutely hated Lara.

Gossip was, the problem stemmed from something to do with one of Stasi's male minions. He'd connected with Lara, and she had actually convinced him to drop the chemicals. So mid-Fall semester, last year, he'd told Chase he was no longer a customer.

"But don't worry," he'd added. "I'm no narc."

"Lara's not dumb," Chase had snarled, fearing his income was about to be slashed to nothing and prison bars were his next abode. "She'll catch on and then it's death for me."

"Chase, she don't know about you. They all think the main source for the party drugs is some guy in maintenance."

Chase knew who he was referring to and thought it was funny. That dude — Larry, was it? — he'd only sold crap pot that was half parsley to some dumb freshmen, and then only because they'd bugged him about it for days. Of course, then they'd complained because the high they got wasn't so great.

Still Chase had played it safe, selling only to people he was absolutely sure about, and the rumors about him stayed just that —

rumors. His interest in Lara had drifted away more out of worry that she might catch on to his line of work than from her not having any interest back.

So when Stasi started snarling about how much she hated her, he had shrugged it off.

But then came that night.

Ten days after he'd ended Stasi's access. Grady had relayed a message that Dax wanted Chase to join him at the Cantina.

"Dunno why," he'd said as he stuffed the mid-week receipts into his backpack.

"But it's closed," Chase had growled.

"Wants us all there. Big surprise."

"Crap, you know how long it'll be? I got a class at nine am."

Grady had shrugged. "Good thing is, you can have some beer. Or wine. Or some of the good JD. *Prince Hot Tatts* won't be 'round to hassle you. He's headed up to Scottsdale."

"I'm gonna beg off. I'll send Dax a text."

"You want him pissed at you? See you 'bout seven. Don't need to dress pretty."

That last said with a wink. Then he'd hopped on his Hog and driven away.

Chase had still debated about going, since it was a half-hour drive, each way, but finally headed out just after eight.

The first thing he'd noticed, when he got there, was Stasi's E class in the lot. That did not bode well, but several Harleys were there, so even though the sign had said *CLOSED*, he'd knocked on the door.

It had been opened by Dax, who'd snarled, "'Bout fuckin' time," as he'd been yanked in.

He'd staggered across the room. Then heard grunting and groaning.

And had looked around to find Lara on the pool table.

Weeping and trying to struggle.

With Spit on top of her.

Grinding into her, fast, as JJ and Nat held her in place. Every part of his body jiggling as he grunted and growled.

And Stasi had been seated at a nearby table. Watching.

Chase had been slammed into a chair next to Stasi, facing what was happening to Lara. He'd shifted his eyes to the floor, but Dax had pulled up a chair, grabbed his chin and forced him to look.

"Just want you to see what happens to people who fuck with me. Even pretty boys."

"I...I...don't understand," Chase had gasped. "I haven't."

"That's good to know." And the coolness in Dax's voice mixing in with Lara's whimpering had torn deep into Chase. "But I'm hearin' you and Stasi got problems."

Chase had cast her a quick glare. She hadn't looked back. Then he'd said, "She's in for a lot of — "

"I know. But she's makin' up for it. She brought my boys a playtoy, and she's still gonna pay off every fuckin' dime."

That had made Stasi jolt and glare at him to snipe, "That's not what we — "

"Shut up," shot out of him, hard, low and cold.

She'd shut.

"So what you're gonna do, Chase, is let Stasi have whatever she wants. Keep a runnin' tab. Let me know every time she comes to you. And she's gonna pay us off every fuckin' Friday, in cash. Plus twenty percent. Or she's gonna wind up on that table. You know what's funny is, I think she'd actually get off on it."

It had looked like Stasi was about to snarl at him, but the glare he shot her would have killed a charging buffalo at a hundred paces.

"Are we understood?" he'd finally asked.

That was when Spit had finished and Nat stepped in to take his turn. His shirt off. His pants around his hips. His dick at full mast. With a wink and a kiss to Stasi, he'd got down to business, chuckling.

"Stasi," Dax had said, far too sweetly. "Are we understood?"

She had looked straight at him and said, "Why wouldn't we be?"

He had eyed her then risen and rounded the table to glare down at her. "That's not an answer," he'd said. "You think I'm some dumb fuck don't know when you're tryin' to fuck with me?"

"No, Dax," she'd said, now nervous. "It's just another way of saying *yes*, that's all."

He had squatted before her, taken her phone from her hands, eyed it, then calmly pressed it against the side of the table. Broken it. Then he'd handed it back to her.

"So long as we're in agreement," he'd whispered as he handed it back to her.

She had nodded.

It wasn't until later that Chase learned she had actually been recording the rape on her cell phone, and had shut it down just as Dax rose and went to her. His suspicions and breaking the phone had achieved nothing. She'd simply pulled it down from the Cloud and uploaded it to YouTube then linked to it on the school's boards. When the dean had asked her about it, she had simply called daddy, told him she was done with school so send some men down to get her things, and left.

For that, Chase was relieved beyond belief. Because once Dax found out about the video, his anger was totally focused on her. Until he learned Dean Trevarian had told Eldora about its existence, and blamed him for that mess. He hadn't set a foot out of line, since.

What had happened with Lara bothered Chase. A lot. But staying on Dax's good side...and staying alive...was way more important. At least until he had his degree. So for the last year, and up through the next few months, it was and would continue to be a careful trade-off. But when you deal with the devil, and all that.

Fortunately, he was no longer worried about meeting up with Nat. Fewer kids were at the parties than he'd expected, so he would be fine, tonight.

He finished his run just after eleven, dripping with sweat despite the chill in the air, and bounded up the stairs to his one bedroom condo on the third floor of one of the older white and tiled structures. A massive Oak partially obscured the view from the balcony, but he loved it because its shade also kept his cooling bills lower. As for his furnishings, they were rented. Easy to dump. Posters were taped to the walls. The kitchen's main utility was the microwave over the stove and the fridge, where he kept a nice stock of beer, for him, and white wine for any girl who deigned join him in a king-size bed that filled the room.

He knew the owner and considered letting the guy blow him a couple times a month was a fair trade-off for having to pay only half the rent. Of course, he told everyone his dad had bought it for him to live in; image to keep up, and all that, even though no one believed him. Seems the old guy had a few other condos set up the same way.

He bounced around the walkway and used a key-fob to unlock his door and enter. He was stripped by the time he hit the bathroom and had the shower running seconds later. He hopped in, loving the first sensation of hot water pounding down on his skin. This had been a good run. Blood flowed through his muscles and into his balls, and he loved the feel of the soapy suds whispering over him. He thought for a moment about jacking off, but he wanted to save it for after lunch. One of his buddies had hinted they'd be going to Tucson, to a Chili's, then possibly up to Loretta's, where maybe they'd pay for him to get taken good care of and...

The curtain ripped aside and he yelped as someone put a knife to his throat and snarled, "Hello, Chase."

He almost slipped, but the point of the blade was cutting into his skin and some deep instinct told him if he did fall, his throat would be sliced open. Didn't want that. He managed to keep on his feet and lock his eyes on...

On hers? It was a woman!?

Who looked scary as shit in a black, full-body onesie and Balaclava on her head. And she didn't care that he was naked and water was getting everywhere, including on her.

"What the fuck?" was all he was able to get out.

"I have some questions for you."

That made him cold to the core, despite the hot water and steam billowing about. "Oh, fuck, fuck, did Dax send you? You gonna kill me?"

"No, no, no. I mean, not if you're a *good* boy."

"Huh?"

"What do you know about what happened with Lara Vincenzo?"

Chase wiped water from his eyes, saying, "I don't understand. That was over a year ago, and Dax already got me for that."

The woman hesitated. "Dax *got* you?"

"Who *are* you?"

She scowled. "What do you mean *Dax got you* for Lara?"

"I don't understand..."

"ANSWER ME!"

He began to shake, from fear. "I — I — I was a dumbshit and told the dean about the video!"

That seemed to surprise her. "*You* informed the university there was a video on their site of Lara being raped?"

"Yeah! All I did was let 'em know about it! Didn't say a fuckin' word about him, nothin' 'bout what I saw, that night, but that bitch sheriff let him know so he cut off my ear."

The woman stepped closer, now wary. "You were there, that night?"

"Oh, shit...shit...what're you gonna do to me?"

"Did you join in?"

"No! Fuck, you think I'm an asshole?"

"Did Zeke?"

"Zeke?"

"The bartender."

Chase was taken aback. "That's his name? Really?"

Her voice held a serious warning as she said, "Chase..."

"Man, we all just called him *Prince Hot Tatts* 'cause he's always actin' like he's above us an' — "

"CHASE!"

"No! No, he wasn't even supposed to be there and he didn't show till it was over, and he freaked when he saw it and — what the fuck is this?!"

She stepped back, knife still ready, and said, "Dry off. Wrap yourself in the towel, nothing more. I want you to tell me everything that happened, that night."

"But Dax..."

"You said he cut off your ear. You still have both."

Chase shook his head, shivering despite the hot water pouring on him. "Look closer. Left one."

"Show me."

He hesitated then turned, slowly, and held the ear flap away from his skull. The scarring was now evident.

He continued with, "Dax threw the real one in a garbage disposal. This doctor in...well...in some whorehouse made a mold of my right one and attached that."

"He did a good job," she said.

"She did. It's pigskin. Like a fuckin' football."

She drew close. Touched it. "I've heard about that." And she seemed truly interested.

"That's why I keep my hair kind of long," he said. "Hides it better."

Her voice was soft as she said, "Seems everyone associated with Dax is scarred, in some way."

"That's his thing," Chase said, nodding. "His way of control. Feelin' like some kind of king or shit."

She nodded and stepped back, then pulled off the Balaclava. "Come on. Shut off the shower. Get dry. Let's talk. I promise, I'm not going to hurt you."

He finally got a good look at her and wiped his face.

"Wait, you...you look familiar..."

The woman smiled. "Come on. Get to it." Then her voice took a gentle purring air. "Before I decide to take advantage."

The sudden shift in tone jolted him and he said, "Huh?"

"You're a pretty boy, Chase, and sometimes pretty boys can be fun. But first, your story."

Now Chase was completely confused. He turned off the shower, worked himself over with his towel and wrapped it around his waist, all as she stood in the doorway, watching, then he let her aim him to his dining table. He sat on one chair and she the other, and he told her everything.

Including how Zeke had come into the Cantina after the guys were done with Lara, and seen she was drugged.

The woman stopped him. "How did you know she's drugged?"

"It was obvious. She had that roofie kind of look about her. Saw that on a girl at a frat party."

"Now, Chase, don't make out like you're a good boy. You've been selling pot and pills on campus."

"Happy drugs, that's all! Stuff to help people get through all the shit they gotta do to make it. This ain't an easy school. Sometimes you need some speed to stay awake and a couple joints to mellow you. And X. A little coke. That's why people keep coming back to me, and I have a very discerning clientele. I'm happy drugs. Party drugs.

Everybody has fun when I'm around. But roofies? Shit, those are for rape. Dax was cool about me not wanting to sell 'em. I think he used Larry, in maintenance, for that crap; I don't know. Didn't want to."

"So you sell pot? That's pretty much legal, isn't it?"

"Not in this state. And New Mexico's hard to deal with and Colorado's too far away. Same for California. It's just easier to come to me, and my prices aren't all that much higher. Factor in gas and time, works out close to even."

She nodded. "Tell me about when Zeke came in."

"I can't get over his name's Zeke. People ask me if I'm named after that stupid bank. But him? A name like that. Shit." He huffed, hurt. "That makes him even cooler, don't it?"

"Chase..." Growled with a warning.

"Right. Right. Well he wasn't supposed to be there, 'cause when he came in, it was at the back door. Dax went straight over to him, and he was pissed."

Actually, Dax was infuriated.

"What the fuck, Zeke, you're supposed to be at Loretta's for a couple days."

"She's got a big party in and I didn't want to stick around and Orin wanted to know if he needed to drop by, tomorrow, and I came in to see what kind of mess you made...and..."

And he saw Chase sitting at a table, looking ill, and next to him was Stasi with her usual cold glare on. Nat was standing by the pool table, buckling his belt around his pants as JJ held his shirt.

Then Zeke saw Lara roll to the side of the pool table, her jeans around one ankle, panties half torn off, mumbling. She half tumbled onto her feet.

And blood ran down her inner thigh.

"Dax, she's hurt," Zeke said.

Dax looked around and snarled to Stasi, "Take her home."

"No, Dax," Zeke said, "she needs a doctor."

"Stasi! Go! You, too, Chase."

Stasi got up and coolly helped Lara pull her jeans back on. Chase just sort of stood there, lost.

That's when Zeke got a good look at Lara and shot quick, angry glances at Nat, JJ, Spit and Grady. All had smiles or smirks on their faces. He pulled in a deep, growling breath and cast a vicious glare at Dax, snarling, "What the fuck's goin' on, Dax? What'd you do?"

"What I said I was gonna do! You knew what was goin' down, tonight. Said you didn't want in on it."

"You said you were getting a working girl..."

"Which is what I fuckin' did. Who the fuck're you to — ?"

Zeke started past Dax, saying, "This one's a freshman, looks like, and she's drugged and she can't even stand and — "

Dax howled, yanked Zeke back and punched him. Knocked him to the floor. Then straddled him to hit him again and again and again, screaming, "Who th' fuck you think you're callin' a liar"! Me? Me? Nobody fuckin' calls me a liar!" Over and over.

Nat and JJ scrambled to pull Dax back. It was a struggle.

Grady knelt by Zeke, who was bleeding from cuts to his face and mouth. "Fuck, Zeke," he said, "what'd you come in for? You shouldn't of come in."

Dax shook Nat and JJ off, snarling at Zeke, "Everything I done for you an' you're gonna tell me how to do my business? How to handle my guys? You don't like it? You can get the fuck out, you little fuck, spitin' on me like this."

Grady helped Zeke to his feet, carefully. "C'mon, buddy, let's go back to the trailer."

"Not so fuckin' fast," Dax growled, then he shoved Grady aside and grabbed Zeke's shirt. Went nose to nose. "So am I a liar? Huh?"

Zeke looked down, saying nothing. Just pulled away from him and stumbled to the bar to put some ice in a rag and hold it to his mouth.

"That's what I thought," Dax said. "Go back to your trailer to clean up. An' let Oren know we'll need him, in the mornin'. I want this table cleaned off."

Grady went to Zeke and guided him out the back door, murmuring, "C'mon, buddy, let's go see Loki."

Then Dax noticed Chase standing by the pool table, watching it all, wide-eyed.

"What the fuck're you still doin' here?"

He scurried out the door.

"Zeke was right," Chase added, leaning his head against a hand propped on the table. "We should've taken Lara to the infirmary. But Stasi had her in her car and told me to fuck off when I tried to tell her. I didn't know what else to do, so I came home. Couldn't sleep. Missed my class. It all spooked me, so much.

"I thought about talking to Lara, that week, but shit came up and I...I just didn't. Didn't know how. Didn't see her around campus. Then Saturday night, I was at a party. Caught Stasi showing that video to everybody. Calling Lara a skank who did it for drugs. That *Little Miss Suburbia* thought she was a bad girl, and that her being all anti-drug was cover for herself. I got sick and left. Let Dean Trevarian know about the video, Monday."

"That's why it was available for so long?" the woman asked.

He nodded and it took him a moment to continue. His voice was softer, shakier when he said, "Dax caught me on my run. Couple days later. I used to go in a different area and...and he drove me up to Scottsdale. Spittin' all kinds of scary shit at me the whole way. Got me in a back room. Cut my ear off. Said if I ever told anything to anyone about him, ever again, my dick'd go, next. The girls just watched. Then cleaned me up. The doc came in, like she was on call. I stayed there till she fixed it. Missed a week of class. Told 'em I had Covid, so I got some remote shit done. From then on, I did as I was told."

She eyed at him, impassive, then asked, "Did Dax enjoy himself with her, too?"

"Lara?" Chase shook his head. "Something about a grenade messing him up. Maybe an IED. I don't know the full story, but he doesn't have anybody that I know of."

"So he just arranged it."

"I don't get it. What's so important about Dax? He's an asshole, but he didn't kill Lara."

"He might as well have." She rubbed her neck, knife still in hand. "Chase, you don't belong in this business."

"Gimme a break. Min-wage don't even cover books and my old man won't give me a dime."

"You won't be able to finish college if you're in jail."

"Aw, shit, are you a cop? I need a lawyer?"

"No. Because you are going to tell everything to the state's attorney general."

"Are you fuckin' crazy? They'll tell the sheriff, and she's the reason I lost my ear and Dax'll — "

"I'll take care of Dax. And Sheriff Parridge."

He looked at her for a long moment, no longer shivering. He almost felt hopeful. "You gonna kill 'em?"

She smiled. "How much money do you have on you, now? Cash."

He hesitated then shrugged. "About seven thousand. But eighty percent is Dax's."

"Take half of that and what drugs you have on hand to Phoenix, to this address." She handed him a slip of paper. "Tell the AG you...oh, you *found out about these things being sold on campus*. That you did what you could *to get information on it all*. Tell the AG everything, in that way. It's best to end all this shit, right now."

"That means I won't finish up. The job I got requires a degree and..."

"I'll talk to Trevarian. Suggest the same deal she gave Deveaux's daughter. I bet you get one."

"You do?"

"I'm dealing with her and the university on some *legal issues.*

They will be only too happy to help me in any way that I deem appropriate."

"Lara!" he yelped. "You look like Lara! That's why you're familiar!"

"Do I?"

"And you'll kill Dax?" He almost looked like a playful puppy as he said it.

Carli smiled. "No telling how things will turn out."

He eyed her, still on the wary side. "I hear Stasi killed herself."

"Did you?"

"And something about a body in the desert."

"I've heard there were three."

"Three?"

Her expression was inscrutable.

Chase almost laughed. "My mom'd freak over me saying this, but good."

She smiled. "Then we're in agreement?"

"I'll call off my buddies; tell 'em I got lucky. I'll head straight out." He rose. So did she. "What? You gonna watch me get dressed?"

Carli all but purred as she said, "I'm keeping an eye on you right up to the point you leave for Phoenix. And believe me, I'll know if you don't go all the way there. And if you don't, I'll see to it you *do* go to jail. Okay?"

The look on her face said he had no choice.

What could he do but grin, in agreement?

Jumping the Gun or Shark

Eldora was driving down The 14, towards town, when Reymon called. "What's the word?" she asked him.

"It *was* Grady's dick in that box," he answered.

She shook her head, not surprised. "Anything else?"

"Spit and Nat's bodies just arrived, but looks the same. Clean cut on the genitals and...vibrators. Coroner says Nat was shot; probably bled to death."

That sent a chill through Eldora. Nat was a cute kid, almost as cute as Reymon. And he was trying to better himself. Like with that stupid thesaurus. Dressing nice. Having good manners, though she was fairly certain those were from his probably-abused mother, if she'd read his father right.

The old man had come down to meet with Dax, son in tow. She'd been asked to be at the Cantina, as a go-between, just in case things got dicey. But it turned out daddy was a pragmatist.

"One eye gone means no more Army career," he'd scowled. "Top that with being black an' just a GED, he can't even get a job at fuckin' McDonald's. I'd kick his ass down to his momma, in Brownsville, but that'll just make her have to support him, while he's in college. If he goes. I don't know what the fuck else to do."

Eldora had watched Nat sit there, blank and quiet, hearing but not listening. Patch over one eye. Couple scars that would never be unnoticeable.

"Ain't he got somethin' comin' from the Army?" Dax had asked, actually confused.

"Not in long enough, and they don't consider his injury debilitating. Motherfuckers. Betcha five bucks the Republican fucks try to fuck even me out of my pension, when I hit thirty years."

Eldora had noticed Nat's jaw clench so stood up and said, "We all need a drink. C'mon, Nat, you can help me."

Then she'd motioned for Dax to keep the discussion soft. He had nodded, with a hint of a smirk. To which she'd responded with a middle finger, and a smile.

She and Nat had gone behind the bar, out of earshot, and she'd grabbed the good JD. "Want one?" she'd asked, setting out four glasses and starting a pitcher of Coors.

Nat had only shrugged, but she picked up on some wariness in his eye. His lovely eye. The one now under that patch had probably been just as lovely.

"How 'bout a Coke, instead?" she'd asked.

Head nod, in response.

"Don't drink much, do you?"

Head shake, in response.

"Does your daddy?"

No response, at all.

She had nodded and, while filling a glass with Coke, said, "Don't go hard on him. Drill sergeants are always in control, even when they aren't supposed to be."

"He don't want me 'round. I'm shameful to him."

"No..."

"Not in country three days and this shit happens."

Without a thought, she had caressed his cheek, just under the patch, and said, "Life sucks."

He had reacted like a kitten to having its ear scratched.

Poor kid, she'd thought.

Dax had taken him on. Set him up with JJ to live, at first. And Eldora had given him the thesaurus. Then taken him to bed. And made sure he felt every bit of being in control, even though he wasn't, really. But once he saw how joyous sex could be, she had watched him blossom into a fine young man...who was part of a minor-league drug gang, granted, but capable of going places and doing things.

Now?

"So he was shot in one place and ferried to another."

"Looks like," Reymond sighed. "Thing is, they haven't found any blood in the Malibu. Got a colleague coming in from Phoenix with some special equipment to check on that."

Eldora sighed and nodded. "Like to know, sooner than later."

"Find anything more at the crime site?"

"Nope. Too goddamned clean. Tony Chavez is standing watch, tonight."

"He likes to camp out."

"He also thinks the desert's full of ghosts."

"It is."

She chuckled at that, then asked, "What'd you find out about that land?"

"Like I said, it's county property," he replied.

"But?"

He nodded. "It used to belong to the university. They transferred it over, last year."

Eldora nodded, remembering, "In exchange for a plot near the Coahila Flats. I heard about that, but didn't know it was that exact location."

"Council kept it low-key, because it's worthless while the Flats might have minerals to mine. And as I understand it, the University is, um, *drilling for water*, out there."

"That could be even more valuable, in this area. You know who facilitated the deal?"

Reymon looked at his notes. "I found the name of a dean? Yeah, here, Trevarian."

"I know her."

"She was workin' with somebody; don't know who. But in the minutes of one of the meetings, she referenced help from Phoenix. Lawyer, maybe?"

Eldora rubbed the back of her neck, in pain. This was turning into a massive fiasco and she would dearly love to just let it drop, but she now had to know, "Can you find out if Winston Deveaux was involved in any way?"

"Um, his name didn't come up, that I could tell. But didn't he make a really nice donation to the school, last year? Maybe around the same time?"

"Yeah. Dig deeper. I want to see if his hands were on this transfer in any way, whether as a legislator or through his real estate office. In fact, focus on that office, since it might not be him actually handling anything."

"Eldora, this was all just a few months after that girl killed herself. Maybe it's connected. Deveaux's daughter was involved in some way, and as I understand it, the guys who were accused — "

Eldora's voice went sharp. "Raymon, I will not speculate on a goddamn thing until I have all the information before me, and I very strongly suggest you do the same."

Then she ended the call.

Damn that boy for being so damn clever. Because there was now no question in her mind it was mingled together, and all she was waiting for was evidentiary confirmation.

She nearing Cabrillo, but reality was, she did not want to return there, just yet. In fact, she wanted to get the hell away from town. This situation was turning into a real nightmare, all off it due to that entitled bitch daughter of Deveaux's.

Stasi had just dumped Lara outside her dorm and driven off. A fellow freshman named Trini was heading inside when she saw Lara standing by the road, not moving. They knew each other, slightly, so she called over, "Hey, Lara, you okay?"

Lara had turned to look at her...then fallen to her knees. Trini had rushed over. Seen the blood in Lara's jeans and called an ambulance. She was in the hospital for two days, one to stabilize her, one to repair her. A rape kit was done and handed over to Sheriff Parridge, who gave it to the coroner, who gave his findings to the DA's office.

During the interview, Lara had been vague and disconnected. Could remember nothing about the rape except some men she didn't know sitting around a booth, looking at her.

"I went to that Cantina," she said. "With Anastasia. She invited me. We haven't been getting along. Thought we could mend some fences."

"They're closed on Mondays," Eldora had said.

"It was open."

"Who tended the bar?

"Um, dunno his name. Old guy. Long hair."

Which had instantly let Eldora know this had been one of Dax's sneaky-assed set-ups. But she kept even and calm as she asked, "How did you get home?"

"Don't remember. All so fuzzy."

"What drugs did you take?"

"I don't do drugs."

"They ran a tox-screen of your blood and some interesting things showed up. Coke. Ecstasy."

"No. No, they're wrong."

"You were busted for possession, once."

"No, I was with someone who had something. I was arrested. They checked. Didn't have any. In my system or on me. Charges were dropped."

"Okay. Could you recognize the men if you saw them, again?"

"Don't know."

"Bartender?"

"Maybe. Blacked out. I don't remember any of it. Not till I was here."

"Well, don't push yourself. Get some rest. Here's my number."

She'd left a card and headed straight to the Cantina. Of course, Dax wouldn't be there; she left a message with Zeke for him to contact her. She also noticed the guy had a cut lip and bruises on his face.

"Were you here, Monday night?" she'd asked.

Without looking at her, he'd said, "I went to Scottsdale, Monday. With Loki."

"What happened to your face?"

"Me being stupid."

And that was all she'd been able to get out of him, but she could add two and two, and the sum of it made her even angrier.

When Dax had finally contacted her, she had let him know if he ever did anything to any girl from that school, ever again, she'd see to it he *vanished into the desert.*

"And don't you think for one second I don't know how to do that," she'd added, with a growl.

He had only shrugged, acting all tough and unintimidated, but she could read in his eyes he knew he'd screwed up. That was all she needed, right then.

Then the county DA had proceeded to do everything he could to kill the investigation. The original rape kit was *misplaced.* Dax's boys had their stories set. And Stasi lawyered up, thanks to the DA's gentle hints. It all would have drifted away if that conniving little bitch hadn't uploaded that video to YouTube and linked it to school's boards.

That made it impossible to control. Then the Vincenzo girl killed herself, sending everyone into crisis mode.

One of the Vincenzo sons, a fine-looking young man named Federico, who was sadly gay, came out to deal with the school's administration, his lawyer with him. They wanted acknowledgement that Stasi should never have been allowed to add outside video to the university's message boards, so were in error.

Dean Trevarian had let Eldora know he was coming, so she was in the next office, watching through a crack in the door in case there was trouble and she needed to barrel in.

There wasn't. That boy had a tight control of himself, despite his obvious anger. He just sat there like a statue. Even when the school's lawyers stupidly blew off his attorney with a lot of legalese that even Eldora had known was bullshit. The idiots weren't paying attention.

He had expected their blank refusal to be held accountable. This meeting was just a formality to show his side had tried to settle everything amicably. So he had gotten up, at the end, and walked out of the room. And his attorney had followed. The lawsuit was filed the next day.

And now, after — what? Over a year of legal wrangling? Word was they'd come to a settlement. She didn't know what the terms were, but it looked like the school's administration had given in, completely.

She had already wondered if that cool, quiet Italian boy might be the one behind the sudden explosion of trouble and death. She knew he lived in Seattle, so had made a preemptive call to a buddy up there. Got a spot check done...and been told that he was in town. Which killed that idea.

Surprisingly enough, it's rather difficult to butcher three men from over fifteen hundred miles away.

Unless the family hired someone. She'd watched *The Sopranos* so knew how Italians could be. *You fuck with me, I fuck you twice over*. Could that woman be their hit man? Murder girl? Or maybe a sister? But Lara had no sister. There was an aunt, but something was off about that whole family dynamic. She hadn't dug into it because she hadn't thought it would matter, at the time. Now she needed to.

Meaning crank up the coffee and make herself read pages and pages of crap. Lovely way to spend a Saturday.

She could see her office, just ahead, when...

A black Dodge Ramcharger passed her.

Going the opposite direction.

With California plates.

Being driven by a woman who reminded her of Lara Vincenzo.

Without a thought, Eldora swung her SUV around, snapped on her lights and raced after the Dodge. She caught it at the edge of town. It pulled over, nice and easy. Eldora took a moment to input the plate number on her car's computer. An instant later, up popped the owner's name.

Holy fucking shit.

Eldora got out of her SUV, the safety strap on her pistol undone, her hand on it. She walked up to the driver's door and said, "License and insurance, please."

Inside the truck, Carli already had them in hand so gave them over. Her eyes locked on Eldora as she said in a voice so innocent, it was almost silly, "What's the problem, officer?"

Eldora caught her tone and snapped, "Driving erratic. Is this your current address?"

"Yes."

"Do you have insurance?"

Carli smiled. "You have it."

Eldora just glared at her then read off the driver's license, "Caralina Angelica Vincenzo. What're you doin' in town?"

"Why're you asking?"

"Answer the question."

"Not until you answer mine."

Eldora stepped back, snarling, "Okay, out of the car. C'mon, Vincenzo."

Carli calmly stepped out of the Dodge, almost smiling. "It's Master-Sergeant Vincenzo, United States Army."

"Wrong. You got discharged last year. For attackin' a superior officer."

That made Carli grin. "Wrong, yourself. I broke his nose because he thought my tits were his personal property. But there was no courts martial; I was honorably discharged. It was his wife who beat the shit out of him, when they sent him home. But I do find it interesting you've been looking into me. Why is that?"

Eldora suddenly realized she'd made a tactical error, so she straightened to her full height, plus three inches thanks to her boots' heels, and snarled, "How 'bout *you* account for your whereabouts over the last week?"

"Why should I?"

"'Cause if you don't, I'll haul you in."

"Do it. My attorney'll rip you to shreds. This is going to her website." She held up her phone. It was recording everything into an app. Actually going to TF's site, but no need to quibble about details.

Eldora blinked. She wasn't used to this sort of pushback. "Turn that off," she snapped in her best controlling voice.

"No," Carli calmly replied. "This is a public street and you are a public servant. I have every right to record you doing your job, in public."

Well, Eldora told herself, *so much for Italians being emotional creatures. Just as cold as her brother.*

Eldora glared at her, have herself a quick little *Fuck it*, then said, "Does your attorney know you're connected to the deaths of three men?"

Carli's innocent expression returned. "I am?"

"And a young woman in Los Angeles."

"Oh. My. Why, I sound positively dangerous. Maybe you *had* better arrest me." Then her voice went low and vicious. "If you have any proof I really *am* linked to those deaths."

"They were connected to a *claim* of rape filed by one Lara Vincenzo."

BOOM!

Right through Carli's defenses, sending her into near battle mode. "*Claim* of rape?"

Now it was Eldora's turn to smile. "I saw the little junkie's arrest record. Her mug shot."

The smile gave Carli the hint that Eldora was deliberately provoking her. She latched onto that thought, even as she gently caressed the knife in her belt, and forced herself to calmly ask, "Are you saying that justifies a young woman being sexually assaulted?"

Snap, right back at you, bitch.

Eldora nodded. *In for a dime, in for a dollar*, and she had no idea where that stupid phrase came from except her asshole father had used it so many times, it was seared into her brain. *So let's jump, Eldora.*

"*Sexually assaulted.* Some stupid little party girl gets herself into a situation she can't handle, and I'm supposed to blame everybody but her?"

Carli's voice was like ice. "Cops, even when you don't have a dick, you are one."

"Careful."

"Every one of you thinks, *Girl gets raped, it's her own damn fault. She gets drugged, held down by four men and it's her own damn fault.*"

"Like mother, like daughter."

"Now *you* be careful."

"Got a nice little trail of your own. Shoplifting. Property damage. Assault."

That shattered Carli's anger, replacing it with wariness. "How did you find those records? They're under the juvenile system, which are supposed to be sealed."

Okay, Eldora, second tactical error...but too late now.

"Yeah," she sneered, "protect the little felons all you can."

"Why were you even looking into me?" Carli snapped. "Are you working with the university to fuck up the settlement?"

"They have attorneys for that."

"Which doesn't mean jack shit. Why were you digging into records you shouldn't even have access to?"

"Simple," Eldora cooed. "The second I heard about Anastasia Deveaux's *suicide*," and she drew that word out, "I started wondering if you were involved. Now I'm pretty damn sure."

Carli was close to losing control, and Eldora knew it. Hoped for it. Waited for it. One punch and this bitch was hers and so was her phone and...

Dax roared up on his Hog, snarling, "Where the fuck you been?"

Both women turned their glares to him. If he had been the least bit capable of awareness, he'd have run for the hills at seeing their expressions. Instead, he hopped off his Hog and stormed up to Eldora.

She all but growled at him, "What you doin' here?"

"I been tryin' to get hold of you, an' you're handin' out fuckin' tickets? At a time like this?! Look!"

He showed her a slip of paper.

It was a FedEx delivery tag.

"Another box," he said, "tried for delivery. Today. Saturday!"

Eldora glared at it, angry, then turned back to Carli. Who was eyeing Dax with cold satisfaction. That simple glare...that expression in her face gave Eldora all the proof she needed that Carli was behind it all, and the goddamn bitch was toying with them. She was not going to put up with it.

"Get it and I'll meet you back at the office," she said to Dax, her voice soft, "then we'll discuss..."

"Fuck that. Get it, yourself!"

"I don't know when it's available."

"Driver's back at the facility, five-thirty."

"But you have to sign for it."

"I ain't touchin' the fuckin' thing."

"Dax!"

He just hopped back on his Hog and rode off.

She turned to find...

Carli watching her, cool, calm and dangerous. Advantage lost.

"Where you stayin'?" Eldora snarled.

"None of your business."

"I can make it my business."

"You can try."

Eldora huffed. What she did not want was having to explain shooting Carli Vincenzo to the county, the state and the media. Not yet. So she started back to her SUV.

Then she heard, "Sheriff, my license and insurance."

Eldora glared at her and tossed them back to her.

Carli caught them with minimal effort, made herself smile, then shoved them in her pocket and got in the Dodge. With all deliberate care, she drove away, headed west.

Eldora input Carli's information onto her phone and texted it Reymon before calling him.

"I want you to check into someone else," she said, the moment he answered. "Just sent it over. Caralina Angelica Vincenzo. She's Lara's mother, and she's in town."

"Oh, shit. But you got a lot on her."

"I want you to go deeper."

She could almost see him nodding before he said, "Thought you might wanna know. The company that handled the deed of transfer on the title?"

"You got that, already?"

"Yeah, on my phone."

Eldora sighed. "Jesus, I gotta catch up to the world."

"It's one of Deveaux's subsidiaries. Way down the food chain, but still connected."

"Figures. I'm headed to the office. I'm goin' back over that Vincenzo girl's complaint. The University's statements. See if I missed something."

"By the way, Luna and Madrigo; they're in Las Vegas."

"You sure about that?"

"Luna's my cousin. I finally got hold of my aunt. They're at her place. Why'd you need to know?"

"Oh, stop it, Reymon. You know as well as me he's a skanky little fuck who worked with Dax. But he does know some of Dax's meeting spots. Can you get him to come back?"

"Why?"

"Because if he did lead that bitch to where Nat and Spit were killed, that's a link between her and their murders. And I would love to wrap her up tight, in them."

She ended the call, got in her cruiser, started it up and did a U-turn to head on to her office.

She finally felt she was running this show instead of it running her.

Fully Zeke'd

Zeke fired the M-16 into a target a hundred yards away, over and over and over. It was propped up against a rocky part of the foothill behind his trailer. The remains of several beer bottles gleamed under an outcropping, next to it, having proven less than satisfactory when being shot.

He hadn't changed clothes, from last night, except to take off his jacket. The air was still chilly, but he didn't seem to notice. Just kept aiming and firing and refilling the clip. Loki watched him, lying atop a stack of wooden pallets by the steps to the trailer's rear door.

This was how Zeke kicked back, sometimes, on the nights he couldn't sleep. Or days he couldn't stop thinking. Something to keep him occupied until the Cantina opened and he could shift his focus to that.

But it wasn't working, this time.

Grady was definitely dead.

He'd tried calling Nat but only got voicemail. Not even JJ was picking up, which was making him nervous. All of a sudden, Zeke felt isolated and alone. He'd grown up with that feeling, way down deep inside, but had lost a lot of it, first thanks to the guys in his unit and then Grady's friendship. Now? It was back to haunt him, and not even playing his guitar had driven it away. Firing the M16 was the only thing he could think to do, otherwise.

Yet it kept coming back to Grady really being gone.

He had been so damned much help, at Beaumont. Caught in despair, still healing in some places, especially after several rounds of surgery, not one fucking word from the Lindstroms, a vicious sense of worthlessness growing in him, darkness surrounding him, Zeke had been feeling more like a wounded animal than a man.

Grady had pulled him out of it. Hell, dragged him out, kicking and screaming. Had to make him go on their first jaunt to Juarez. With Zeke in a wheelchair. Grady'd even let Zeke watch as his ink was added to.

"Hides the scars pretty damn good," Grady had said over those beers, afterwards, and a pile of scary-looking nachos between them that tasted like heaven.

"I looked through the books they got," Zeke had murmured. "Designs. Saw a couple I think are Viking. Norse. Somethin'."

"You like that shit?" he asked as he sat across from Zeke.

"I am that shit."

"You don't look like a fuckin' Viking."

"What do fuckin' Vikings look like?"

"Thor! *Marvel Universe.*"

"Oh fuck that. I had my hair long, like him, once. Never again. Too much trouble."

"You'd be real pretty with long hair."

"What the fuck, bitch. You after suckin' my dick?"

"Fuck, no. But there's this one little nurse, he's givin' you some looks."

Zeke had leaned back in his wheelchair, stretching. "Yeah, that's all I need, now. Change my sexual orientation. That'd really piss the Lindstroms off."

"Cut it out. A mouth's a mouth, when you're in need."

"Done your own research, huh?"

"You could say. Iraq. My unit's corpsman. He took care of us and we took care of him. He's in Malibu, now. Surfin'. No. No, it's, uh, what the fuck? It's Manhattan Beach."

"Wish I'd done some surfin', before this."

"Still can. Get a leg that's waterproof."

"Yeah, right. That'll work."

"You ain't gonna know till you try."

"I'll think about it." They had sat there, for a few moments, then Zeke had added, "I think I would like another tatt. This really cool one had a wolf's head in all kinds of design with a helmet mixed in. Covers half your arm."

"Then you better get to walkin' with a fuckin' leg, 'cause next time we come here, I ain't pushin' that fuckin' wheelchair."

That had given Zeke the impetus to start testing various prosthetics and find there were all sorts that made it easy for him to get around. And the next time Grady went to get a tatt was when Zeke had walked with him. He'd still had to use a cane, and he limped like a drunken sailor, and his leg had wound up sore as shit, but he had walked all the way there and back. With Grady calling him Chester, from some old tv western show and...

And now Grady was gone.

And Zeke felt completely alone.

He hadn't really connected with Dax or JJ. They were a couple of guys he felt it best to keep at arm's length. Nat was cool enough, and had been around a few years, but he was young and very uncomfortable around Loki. Not because the mutt had done anything to him; he just didn't like dogs. Something about a run-in with a K9 cop; he never did get the full story. As for Spit, nobody wanted to deal with him, if they could help it. It was a minor miracle he'd wound up with Katty. So Grady was his best and only real bud.

And now Grady was gone.

He could not get past that thought.

He finally stopped firing and sat on those wooden pallets. Loki just watched him.

Grady was the only other person Loki liked. The only other one he'd go riding with. Or play with. Or just sit next to when he was needed. And now?

Zeke rested his hand on Loki's back, murmuring, "Our buddy's gone, puppy. It's just us, now." And the loneliness was overwhelming.

He got a soft sigh, in response, and a nuzzle from Loki's nose.

Then he heard a car pull into the parking area, and he rolled his eyes. *Just stay back here*, he thought, *and they'll catch on the joint's closed*. But footsteps approached the trailer and Loki rose to his wary stance and...

"Zeke?" It was Carli's voice.

He rubbed his face, rose and went to the corner of the trailer to say, "Back here."

"Hi," she said. She was halfway up the steps to the front porch. "I'd have called, first, but I don't have your number.

He pulled out his phone, saying, "What's yours?"

She held up her phone with the number showing. He input it and sent her a call. Her phone rang, she smiled and answered, "Anyone I know?"

He sort of smiled back. "There you go."

"You all right? You seem kind of down. I thought you were all Zen, this morning."

He shrugged and said, "I'll be okay. I got my dog. Woof."

Loki gave a *woof*, in answer.

"How long've you had him?" Cali asked.

"Eight years, almost nine."

"He sticks by you."

Zeke eyed her. Noticed how her hands didn't stay still. He finally said, "You look like you could use a drink, and I know I could. I got whiskey, wine, water, beer. Dr Pepper."

She looked past him, taking in a deep breath. "Is that a target range?"

"Yeah. A little practice, now and then. You want to fire off a couple?"

Carli looked around at the vast emptiness and smirked. "Won't it bother the neighbors?"

Zeke shrugged and leaned around the side of the trailer to yell, "Hey, Oren!"

Carli saw an old, old man pop his head out the back door of the Cantina. He had a hammer and chisel in hand.

"What?" he snapped.

"Gonna practice some."

"Still?" Then he popped back into the Cantina.

Zeke turned to Carli and said, "He's fixing some shit."

Carli nodded then said, "I think I'd like a whiskey."

Zeke headed for the back door of the trailer. "Sounds good. It's gonna be a long day."

He limped inside.

Carli noticed Loki was looking at her. "What?"

He gave her a *What* look, right back. She hesitated then tried to scratch his ears, but he shifted away to lie down, still watching her.

"Smart puppy," she said. "Don't trust anybody."

A moment later, Zeke came out with two glasses of whiskey. He gave her one and tipped his own to hers.

"To old friends," he said, then downed it.

Carli nodded, said, "Absent friends," and drank her own.

He took his M-16 from beside the pallets and handed it to her, saying, "Used one of these?"

She smiled and nodded, accepting it. Looked it over. Almost caressed it.

"This is your baby," she murmured."

"Think so?" he asked.

"Very well-maintained. Beautiful."

She hefted it to her shoulder. Swung it around.

Loki rose to his feet, casting a wary eye at her.

"You always take care of the things that matter most," Carli continued. "You want them to be protected and stay exactly like they always were. But sometimes...sometimes you lose sight of that and...and..."

She whipped the rifle around and BAM-BAM-BAM. Emptied the magazine. All into the bulls-eye.

Zeke whistled.

Even Loki huffed that he was impressed.

Zeke took a box of bullets off the pallets and offered them to Carli. She refilled the clip so fast, it was like it hadn't been empty, then she fired into the bullseye, again.

That is when she lowered the rifle, saying, "You've got a true site, on this. That's rare."

"Keep on, if you want. I buy my ammo in bulk."

"No," she chuckled. "No. That's all I needed."

She handed the rifle back to him. He kept watching her, wary. Trying to decide if he should reveal what he was thinking.

Finally, he said, "Y'know, there was a guy brought into Beaumont just before I was discharged. He liked to tell stories. One was like how this one Ranger unit had a girl sniper."

"*Girl* sniper?"

He nodded. "Word was, she could hit your spit in the wind, from a thousand yards."

"That's ridiculous."

"That's soldiers. Lots of bullshit. Besides." And he gave her a long, very deliberate look. "Army says they got no female snipers."

Carli did not look at him as she said, "They're right."

He set the rifle back by the pallets, not looking at her.

"I know who you are," he said.

She tensed but said nothing.

"It took me a while, but you look like her," he continued.

She still could not look at him. "You knew Lara."

"Just...just that night."

"That night?"

"Yeah. Yeah. It's scarred into my brain. As much that IED."

She looked at him to ask, "Why?"

He met her gaze and could barely get the words out. "Because I...I didn't do anything."

That confused Carli. "Were you there?"

"Doesn't matter. I knew Dax was getting some fun for the guys, that night. He's done it before. Pick up somebody off the street, in Tucson. Or Nogales. Let 'em act like crazy kids. I mean, he'd pay the girl good and he even offered me a go. But it's not really my thing. That time, though...I dunno, it...it sounded weird, the way he put it."

"How *did* he put it?"

"*This one's gonna be lots of fun. Just you wait, she will be.* So I headed up to Loretta's, but they were busy and I wasn't really up for anything so came back. And saw Stasi's car. And the hogs. And this dumb little SUV. All like the Cantina was open. And it bugged me. I was still going to let it go, but I chained up Loki and made up some stupid shit excuse to go in and...and I saw what they'd done to her..."

His voice trailed off.

Carli's focus on him was harsh, sharp and intent, a finger caressing the knife in her belt.

He finally continued, "I should've gone straight in. I should've taken her to the ER. But I didn't. I had a feeling what'd happened, and I didn't do anything. And I didn't say anything to the cops."

Carli could not take her eyes off Zeke's face. He was still torn up about it. Blamed himself. Even though he'd actually done nothing wrong. Not really. Now she knew, without question, he was innocent. But she couldn't say that to him. She didn't dare. All she could say was, "Not say anything to Sheriff Parridge? Don't blame you."

"Yeah, she...she's not somebody you want to deal with. But I should've. I should've done something. 'Cause when I heard what she did...when I found out..."

"Zeke, it's hard to know what to do sometimes."

"That's just a bullshit excuse. I knew what to do."

"Maybe. But I do not blame you for what happened."

"Then why're you here!? Why now? With everything blowin' up?"

The pain in his voice cut into her. She barely managed to keep herself even as she asked, "What do you mean?"

"Friend of mine. He died. Was killed. He wasn't a perfect guy, but he was always there for me. Probably saved my life. Did you have something to do with it?"

Her heart dropped to her toes. "Me? Why're you asking me?"

"A woman picked him up. Looked a little like you."

"You think I killed him?"

"I don't know!"

He was torn up over Grady's death. Saw that piece of shit as a friend. How was that possible? Here he was, acknowledging how horrible this had been for Lara, so how could he not see that snake deserved to die? Was he that blind to the man's true nature? Just because he'd been supportive and...

And treated Zeke as a friend.

Saved his life...maybe...

For some stupid, truly insane reason, something in her said that this was actually almost admirable of him. That he accepted Grady, faults and all. Appreciated what he'd done for him.

Which certainly put a new spin on everything.

So she found herself asking, "When did this happen?"

"Wednesday night."

She let out a deep breath...and deliberately decided to lie. "I wasn't in town till Thursday. I'm here to finalize a lawsuit."

He blinked. "I...I heard the family was suing the college over what happened."

"They finally agreed...that video, they should have monitored their platform better. Should have handled Lara's trauma better. But it's done, now. It's over. I ended it. It's all done."

"Oh." He dropped onto the pallets, shaken. "I'm sorry, what I said. I'm not thinking straight."

She looked him. Saw the pain in his eyes. The tears. The guilt he'd been carrying, ever since, and she couldn't accept that he was taking the blame for what Dax and his bastards had done because he was the only one who actually was sorry for it all and it wasn't right and she could not keep from crouching before him and reaching over to caress his face, tenderly, tracing her fingers from his eyebrow to the line of his jaw then over his lips and he looked so confused and lost and lovely and...

She could not help but kiss him. Soft. Easy. Lips to lips. The hint of whiskey still on him. The warmth of his breath whispering into her. Giving her strength and humanity and...

He pulled back, startled, saying, "Carli..."

She took hold of his face, with both hands, her eyes burning into his, and she whispered, "You are not to blame for any of this. You are the only one who isn't, and I hate that you think you're guilty in any way."

"But I..."

She put a hand to his lips. Tears streaked from her face. She could not let him do this to himself. Her voice was so soft, as she continued, it was like she was sending him nothing but thoughts as she said, "I *was* a sniper. I can't tell you how many men I've killed, because I was good at it. And I had the excuse that I was protecting my own from them. But the hell of it is, I also grew to love it. Love the power of it. God-like power. *Will I let this one live and that one die?* And when I was assigned back to the states, I found I missed it. Like a junkie misses his fix. I finally left the Army because...well, it scared me. Terrified me. There have been nights where I can't sleep, I miss it so much. Like I went cold turkey off a drug, not realizing what a powerful hold it had on me. I saw others like me. No remorse. Joy in the killing. Love of it. No care for anyone else. Just animals, like I was. I know the signs of evil. I've seen them in too many men. And there is none of that in you."

"But that's not..."

"Zeke, you're decent, inside. You care. You hurt for others. That's what I see in you. I know, without question, if you'd had any real idea of what those bastards were doing to my daughter, you'd have stopped them. You'd have saved her. You cannot blame yourself for any of this. I won't let you."

She went in for another kiss.

This time, he did not pull away. Let her hands hold him in place. Let her mold herself to him. Felt her breath grow sharp and shallow. Felt with her every touch, every caress that she wanted him.

Needed him.

He let his hands slip around her waist. Then up her back. Then pull her close. And hold her tight...tight...tight...

Finally he whispered, "Carli, what I said..."

She put her fingers to his lips and murmured, "Shh."

They kissed, again. Deeper. More wanton. Her jacket sliding off her shoulders. Her breasts crushing against him. She pushed him back. Guided him to lie across the stack of pallets and...

Woof.

Loki bolted up and away from them, with a huff, startling them both.

Zeke laughed as Carli leaned back, and he said, "Y'know, I got a bed."

She pulled him up into another kiss, then whispered, "That sounds perfect."

They rose and entered the trailer as Loki huffed, again, and lay back down on the pallets.

Carli barely glanced at the basic furnishings and casual mess as Zeke whispered, "Wasn't expectin' company."

In answer, she kissed his neck and his lips and his chin and his ears. They wandered down a short hallway past the bathroom into the bedroom. She turned his back to the bed then worked his t-shirt up, revealing smooth skin with just the right amount of hair on it and the completion of the tattoo on his left arm, minimizing the pockmarked scars it covered. The tracheotomy. She caressed them. Felt the unevenness of them, the ridges they bore, as if in awe. Kissed them.

Then pushed him onto the unmade bed.

He laughed, startled. "What the fuck?"

"Stay down," she said, a deep laugh coming from her.

Then she straddled his hips. Pulled at his belt. Unfastened his jeans. Opened his fly.

And stopped, to caress his sides.

He squirmed under her and started to pull his jeans down.

"Lemme take my leg off," he said.

She silenced him by grabbing his wrists and pinning his arms over his head to lean in and kiss him, long and deep and full, her breasts caressing his chest, then whispered, "Don't. This one's for me. Let me run it."

She rubbed her groin against his. Felt him growing, even more.

Breathless, she rose, still whispering, "Keep your hands above you. Keep your hands above you."

He looked at her, confused, but did as she asked.

She trailed her fingers down his arms. Then over his chest, making him chuckle. Then down his sides, again, and back to his fly and slowly, oh so very slowly, lowered the zipper to reveal a pair of simple white Jockeys. She undid her own jeans and lowered them. Shifted her panties to open access to herself. Then pulled the Jockeys down to release him.

He was ready. His dick flopped back as if to say, *Take me, take me.* And it was pretty. Nicely formed and ready to go. She caressed it. Ran fingernails along the length of it and traced the veins and tickled his pubes. Made him squirm from the amazing intensity of it. Then, when he was throbbing, she lay on top of him, her breasts still in her shirt...

And guided him into her.

She held her breath as she felt him fill her, and he all but groaned from the exquisite beauty of her surrounding him.

She sat back, slow and easy, to settle down on him, still straddling him, and finally gasped at how lovely he felt. He wasn't the largest man she'd ever had, but he was the first who had given in completely to letting her lead, from the very first moment. Not even Liam had been willing to allow her this much control.

She began to rock on him, grasping at him as she rose then letting herself just slide back down, repeating, over and over and over, mimicking waves rolling up to a beach. Up and back and up and back.

He tried to caress her body but she grabbed his wrists and returned them to above his head, almost snarling, "There...keep them there..."

He was breathless as he gasped, "Carli...please...wanna hold you. Touch...you. Kiss..." Then he fell into a groan.

She giggled. "Greedy." Then she tightened herself around him.

He jolted and cried, "Oh, shit," and jammed against her.

She froze in place, whispering, "Not so fast. Take some time."

Her voice was soothing and gave him time to hold back. Then she began to rock on him, again.

Oh, dear God, how she loved the look of him under her, and the sensation of him in her. Especially being only partially undressed. His jeans tickling at her pubes. Her jeans caressing her thighs and rear. Her shirt drifting over her skin. Her being able to shift him to where he was rubbing her in just the right spot. The perfect spot. Sending electricity through every fiber of her body. It was more than sensuous or erotic; it was lust, depraved and wanton.

Zeke let her do what she wanted. Liam might have been a prettier man, but he was unable to completely give in to her being on top. Fortunately, the rest of their love-making was so good, it hadn't mattered. But the truth was, she enjoyed being in total control as much as anything else.

And Zeke had given that her.

Almost like a gift.

He did not even try to fight her, now. He gulped in breaths and let ragged gasps escape him. And there were more than a few *Oh, God*'s mingled in, as well. His legs, both the full and the incomplete one, began to dig at the bed to get better leverage to push inside her.

Now she had full ownership and was moving quick and hard. She remembered how fast Mikey had been going with Stasi, that night, and chuckled, deep and sexy. Oh, God, how lovely it was to set her own pace, to the point Zeke's eyes were all but rolling back in his head.

She dug her fingers into his pecs and pulled at his nips and dragged her fingers down his sides to hold his hips and her needs grew more and more demanding.

To go faster.

Faster.

Faster.

She loved it. Loved it. Loved it. He was hers to do with as she wanted. Ride him hard and cruel. Use him like so many had used her. Used all women and...and...and oh-my-god this was so wonderful and she was careening to out of control, and he began bucking into her, hard and sudden, and beyond amazing because she felt every nerve in her being shiver and explode with joy and send screaming lightning throughout her body as waves a hundred feet tall crashed over her and she screamed from the pleasure of it.

Over and over.

And then the waves whispered back into the ocean, and she was gasping for breath.

And he was looking straight at the ceiling, gulping in air.

Both of them drenched with sweat despite how cool it was. Drifting on a calming sea of beauty and emotion. They lay there for what seemed like hours. Minutes.

Until Zeke laughed. Joyous. Almost in disbelief.

"Oh, fuck, Carli. Fuck."

"Are you feeling Zen, again?" she all but chirped.

"Oh, shit...yeah...oh...fuck..."

Her smile was lopsided. "I'd say...that...is what we did."

"No shit." He could not stop laughing. "I'm soaked."

She loved seeing the joy in his face. His heartbreaking smile. How deep his laugh was. She wanted to just sit here, on him, forever, but she did need to know something.

"Do you happen to have a washer and dryer, available? I'm kind of wet, too."

He laughed even harder and rose to embrace her. Bury his head between her breasts. "In the bathroom," he managed to gasp. "So I get to...to watch you walk around...naked?"

He looked up at her, a wicked grin on his face.

She caressed his head and nodded, saying in a sing-song voice, "Only if you do the same."

That ended the laughter but not the joy in his face.

"You sure you wanna?" he asked. "I'm not as pretty as you."

She leaned down to kiss him and murmur, "Thank you for lying."

When she finally pulled back, his eyes were closed. Then he finally said, "Deal."

And for the moment, the loneliness in him had vanished.

And in her, the Angel Samael, was at peace.

One Step Closer to a Mighty Chaos

After he left Eldora, Dax rode straight to Chase's condo, but he didn't answer when the security guard at the gate called him. The guy thought he'd seen Chase's SUV drive away an hour earlier. Dax had to accept that and head back to his place, where he called Chase, but only got voicemail. Finally, he sent a text to call him, ASAP. If he didn't hear from the little fuck by six, he'd track him down.

Finally, he set to work at his computer setup. JJ joined him at three. By that time, Dax had a dozen windows open on his monitors showing everything he could find out about Stasi's father.

"What's up with him?" JJ asked as he entered.

"My bet?" Dax shot back. "This motherfucker thinks I kicked his daughter off her balcony for pullin' her shit with me."

"Dax, c'mon."

"Wait'll you see what I got, 'cause it makes sense, now. It finally makes fuckin' sense."

"But she was killed just a week ago. Funeral's not till tomorrow. That's awful fast work for an old fuck, like him, and that's if he'd take time away from grieving for the little bitch after arranging to get her body back here and all that shit."

"I fuckin' know that! But recognize that name?"

Dax emphasized a window with a mug shot of a broken-faced, ratty-haired, pissed-off beast of a man named Edward Smythe. It took JJ a moment to place him.

"Wait, he's the asshole who tried to muscle in — what, nine, ten years ago?"

"Eight. Got him busted 'bout a month before Zeke got here."

"*You* got him busted?"

Dax let out a long, complicated sigh then sat back and shrugged. "With Eldora's help."

"What? Didn't he offer her enough of a cut?"

"Stupid son-of-a-bitch wouldn't pay a dime, so off he went. But it did make his buddies see the *reality of the situation.* We made peace. She got her cut. An' he got parole, last year."

"...Okay..." But JJ was still wary.

"Guess who he does *security* for." He pulled up another window with *Deveaux Security Systems* as its header and Smythe's much more charming visage down the menu as an employee. Hair cut. Skin nicely tanned. A smile on his face that would still scare small children and chihuahuas. And a suit and tie.

Which made JJ drop into a chair, in shock.

Dax continued with, "He started workin' for Deveaux about six months after that daughter of his split for LA. Day after his release. Seems kinda convenient, don't ya think?"

"The day after? Shit."

"Deveaux might even have had something to do with it goin' through." Dax tapped on the monitor. "This motherfucker hates my guts. Hates all of us. Even hates his own gang for turnin' their backs on him. One of his guys got busted and sent to the same pen. I hear he got punked and passed around for cigarettes."

"Wait, wasn't that...I mean, the only one of that gang I knew got sent up was — was it Milton?"

Dax nodded. "Huerra."

"But he's fat and ugly."

"He was a mouth, till he cut his own throat."

JJ almost laughed. "You so sure he did it to himself?"

"No, but that don't matter. Word down low is, Smythe was the one set him up. An' now I find that bastard's with Deveaux? An' a few days after Stasi does her jump, Grady shows up dead. Tortured. Next day, it's Nat and Spit. Found on that same fuckin' plateau. Same shit. Pointed away from Phoenix and at the Cantina. I worked out the line."

He shifted to another window that showed a map of lower Arizona, a dot in the center of Phoenix, where the capitol was, and a line from it to the plateau's location, and then to the Cantina.

JJ murmured, "Like it's a sign."

"I think Smythe's been plannin' this for a while, to get back at me for kickin' him to the curb. Then he'd take over."

"Deveaux wouldn't go along with that."

"Maybe," Dax snarled. "Or maybe Deveaux wanted to shut me down because Stasi was afraid I'd turn on her, or somethin'. Little cunt never did pay me what she owed. After that Vincenzo girl offed herself, I let the little bitch know I hadn't forgot. That I still wanted it. But then she up an' split."

"You think what happened to her kicked this into gear?"

Dax nodded. "Eldora's all about the Vincenzo girl's mom, but she abandoned her."

He shifted to another window, showing the university's website and an old story about the anti-drug group. It included a reference to Lara being raised by her grandmother.

"Her mom went in the Army. Eldora's lookin' into that part of it, but I really can't see any bitch who dumps her child as the kind who'd come after me. Goin' after Stasi? Maybe. But that condo she had was high-tech and real secure. Can't get in without a lot of backup. So far as I can see, the only reason Eldora thinks that bitch is behind it is because she's here."

JJ looked at him, confused. "Huh?"

"That's why she's so hot for it. Can't see the shit for the shinola. Too busy givin' out speedin' tickets. Shit."

"She's here? That girl's mother's here? Could she be the one picked up Grady?"

"C'mon, JJ, Grady might be desperate, but for some middle-aged bitch old enough to have a daughter in college? No. No, it's this motherfucker, an' he's comin' after us, next. I can feel it."

"Shit, what you wanna do?"

"In war, if you sit around waitin' for your enemy to attack, you lose. We gotta stop this, before it goes farther. " He shut the screens down then put a hand on JJ's shoulder, saying, "Tell me, you still got a buddy in the National Guard?"

JJ nodded.

"It's time we take the fight to them."

JJ almost smiled. "When?"

"When's that funeral, again?"

"Tomorrow."

"Sounds perfect."

"You sure about it being him?"

Dax nodded. "You think some dumb-ass woman could take down three of our guys? Tie 'em up an' torture 'em, all by herself? Naw. And she sure as hell wouldn't be helpin' this bastard get to us, not after what his bitch daughter did. It's gotta be them."

JJ nodded, anger beginning to take over. "I'll give my guy a call. What you want?"

"Couple grenades. That's all. Minimize collateral damage."

JJ let a dangerous smirk come to his face as he said, "That will be so easy."

*****

Carli was seated on Zeke's bed, naked, hair still wet from a shower, playing his guitar...very badly. He was in the bathroom, pulling their clothes from a small front-load washer and put them up into its twin of a dryer, all without his bionic leg, just a crutch.

"How long've you been playing this?" she asked.

"It was part of my therapy," he replied, glancing around the bathroom door. "Focus. Align my mind to dexterity. That kind of shit."

"You got good at it."

"It was the only part of that crap I enjoyed."

She set the guitar aside. "Sounds like a rough time."

He started the dryer going and maneuvered into the bedroom, saying, "That or wind up a shriveled old man in a wheelchair."

She sighed at seeing him. A nice, trim body that was fully human. Strong but not taut. Well-formed. Tattoos that seemed to emphasize his beauty. Smooth, gleaming skin on his right. She started to get up to join him, but he pushed her back and lay on top of her. Kissed her.

"Hungry?" he asked.

She shook her head as she caressed the tattoos on his shoulder. "I had a heavy lunch."

He kissed her, again, then murmured, "Like my ink?"

"Beautiful. Which is funny, because I don't think it really adds anything to a man..."

He chuckled. "Yeah, don't see none on you."

"Almost got a butterfly on my right shoulder. But thinking about it, I didn't want something that dumb on me, forever."

"No scars to cover?"

"Everybody has scars. But yours are visible."

"Not much I can do about that."

He lay on his side and circled her nipples with his fingers, one after the other. Finally, he said, "I've got to open the Cantina soon. How long you gonna be in town?"

"I was going to leave, tomorrow, now the money's been transferred."

"Settlement?"

"Buy off." She was quiet for a long moment, then the words whispered from her. "I tried to get justice the normal way, but finally, I sued. My little brother was the only one willing to back me. He even came down here to confront them. I didn't dare. I'd have wrecked it."

"Nobody else helped you?"

"I've got four older brothers who have their own lives. Families. And my folks, they were too crushed by it. I think they knew the college would fight back, down and dirty. Which they did. But when they saw TF and I wouldn't give in..." She shifted closer to him, nestling like a cat might do. Finally, she continued, "Nothing will bring Lara back, but at least they'll make some changes. Keep it from happening, again."

"You're kind of young to have a daughter in college."

She looked at him. "Oh, you know how to speak to a girl." Then she caressed his face. "I got pregnant very young. Thanks to a cousin who could talk a snake into shedding its skin. He got pats on the back, for being a randy boy; I got refused an abortion. So I forced my mother to raise her."

She took a moment to maintain control. "I'm not proud of that. I was a brat. Angry. Hurt. I joined the Army the day I turned eighteen. I told everybody it was to get Lara benefits. Send money home. But I really did it to get away from my mother. Motherhood. Responsibility. And I stayed away. Got used to staying away. Most of her life. I'd come home every now and then, but..."

The hollowness returned to her heart. The understanding of how completely she had all but divorced herself from her own child. That was cruelty defined, and she halfway wondered if that was why she made such a good sniper. That hardness in her heart. That willingness to kill from a hidden space and take pleasure in it. She wished she could find some way to explain it to Zeke, because then she might be able to explain it to herself.

"My mother is very judgmental," she continued. "I know she loved Lara, but her comments can be *unthinking* and casually hurtful. I think some of the things she said added to Lara's pain. Not meaning to. But sometimes I wonder if that's why Lara took that final step. She couldn't face the possibility she had disappointed my mother. She needed someone to be there for her, but I was thousands of miles away, so couldn't be. And so she died. And the university used that against me. Said I was never really her mother. Now I feel like a monster."

"They had no right to say that."

"Why not? It's true. If I'd just been with her...if I'd been someone she could talk to..."

"She didn't have anyone else she could call? Not even a friend?"

"I don't know. I didn't really know her." The pain in her voice was sharp. "You're right. I should've known...someone...been there..."

He flopped onto his back, sighing. "Shit, Carli, I didn't mean that. I get it. You only need a minute of despair to make the wrong choice; then it's too late to take it back. Almost got to me, too."

She caressed his bionic leg, asking, "This?"

"Naw, that was rough but I never got to the point of wanting to end it. I just...I know what Lara went through." It took him a moment to continue. "I, uh, I was in Appleton, one of those nice private prisons, where you're just a dollar sign to the people who run it. In for drugs. The judge offered me the chance to join the Marines, instead of prison, but I blew him off. I was all *tough and I could handle it.*"

He grew quiet.

He looked at the ceiling, unable to continue. Memories slashed into him. He felt as if he were floating. Was surprised he was letting it out, because no one knew about what happened to him in that place.

No one.

Well, except for the three men who had forced him into that corner. Yanked his pants and boxers down as he'd struggled and yelled and called for help and no one paid any attention.

And then...

Each of them...

One after the other...

Before leaving him crumbled on the floor. Bleeding. Unmoving. No one caring.

It was after the second time they took him that he'd contacted the judge and asked if the marines offer was still valid, and had been told it was. He was out before they could get to him, again.

He honestly felt like he'd been saved. Especially since in basic, him being a felon had bought an extra measure of respect from his fellow Jarheads. And his DI nicknaming him *Ex-Con*? That made it official.

That made him part of their family.

A real family. Not just guardians.

He had liked that.

Carli rose to one arm and put her hand on his heart, soft and easy. He had revealed his own nightmare to her, and trusted her to keep it between them. She dared not say a word for fear this sudden bond might be broken, so just watched the memories play over his face, knowing whatever it was he was thinking, he'd tell her, soon enough. Feeling all he needed at that moment was her just to be there and not say anything.

His voice was soft as he continued. "It haunts you. Digs at you. Shreds you. Makes you wary. But I got lucky with a counsellor at Pendleton. She helped me get past the darkest part of it. And things were good, the two years I was in. I probably would've stayed."

Carli thought of the few Marines she had bothered to pay attention to, during her time in Afghanistan. Taut and built but too damn full of themselves to be fun. Except, they did have a sense of being. Of belonging, that she had found fascinating. Perhaps even admirable. You knew without question they would die for each other, no matter how much of an asshole they were. And that had cut through their bullshit to make them surprisingly sexy.

And here was Zeke, showing he still carried that sense of duty to his buddy. To fucking Grady. And it became so clear, simple and acceptable, she loved that he was this loyal.

Finally, he said, "Maybe Lara didn't have a chance to see what her options were. Maybe if I'd told Dax to fuck off and taken her to a hospital, instead of letting Stasi do it, I could've talked to her. They could've talked to her. Let her know her choices. Told her it'd get easier. Get better."

She lay her head on his heart and whispered, "Zeke, it wasn't the rape that killed her. It was people who saw that video and snickered about it and tortured her with it."

"I still should've done something. But I didn't. I couldn't. Couldn't go up against Dax."

"Jesus, what kind of hold does he have on you?"

It took Zeke a moment to respond. "I...I can't explain it. He's...he's been like a father, to me. Gave me a place to stay when I finished rehab. Welcomed me in."

"You really couldn't go home?"

A crooked smile came to his lips. "I haven't spoken with Mr. Lindstrom in ten years. He doesn't want me until I'm a *good boy with the same value system* as him. Same beliefs. Won't sell drugs, anymore. Church on Sundays. Marry a nice girl and have a job at Lowes. He thought I joined with Satan just to spite him. Same for my ink. So I won't hear shit from him, not till I kiss his ass and have them removed."

"What? Why?"

He grinned as she caressed his inked arm.

"It's prohibited in the bible," he said. "All my Viking crap is."

She grinned. "Must be why I like it so damn much."

"Two little devils joined at the hip, ain't we?"

She giggled. "Joined at more than that."

She rolled on top of him.

He gave her a wary look. "Are you gonna do that to me, again?"

She batter her eyes at him, all innocent. "Do what?"

"Molest me."

"Didn't you enjoy it?"

"Oh, it was fine. First time I was ever the bottom instead of the top." Then a cloud passed over his eyes as he remembered that was not exactly true and he said, "Well...I...I mean..."

She kissed him and rolled him over to be on top of her.

"We can always switch it up," she said.

"So, I wasn't a disappointment to you?"

She let a throaty chuckle whisper from her as she said, "You were exactly what I needed."

"Talk about the right thing to say to a guy, after sex."

He kissed her.

"Jerk," she said.

"Sometimes."

"...Never."

She drew him into another kiss and their hands began exploring, again.

They were still at it when the dryer rang that it was done.

*****

It was almost six when Carli and Zeke exited the trailer, both re-showered and fully dressed. Loki was with them and went to sit by the chain.

"It's too bad you have to do that to him," Carli said.

"He's got food. He's got water. He's got shade. He'll be okay. And it's better than if he takes a bite out of Dax and gets shot." He walked her around to the Dodge. "Gonna drop in?"

"After-hours?"

He batted his eyes.

She swatted his rear. He yelped then drew her into a kiss. When she finally pulled away, she cast him a wink, got in the Dodge and drove away. Then he returned to the back door of the Cantina to let himself inside.

Neither noticed Rhonda approaching on her motorcycle, down The 14. She caught only a glimpse of who was behind the wheel of the truck.

Still, she was not happy.

*****

The FedEx office was set to close at six. Eldora dropped by about five minutes beforehand to collect the box that had been shipped to Dax.

"Kinda smells," the clerk said as he brought the box over. "Like old hamburger."

She caught a hint of it and frowned, recognizing the scent. She also noticed the return address on the box was the same as before. She pulled on latex gloves to handle it, which made the desk clerk snicker.

"What?" the guy asked. "You think it's contagious?"

"Might be," Eldora replied with a vague shrug. "Where'd it actually ship from?"

The clerk stopped snickering. He checked on his computer. "Uh...Phoenix. Yesterday."

She nodded, slipped the box into a heavy-duty padded bag with a zipper, and said, smiling, "If there's anything wrong with it, we'll let you know. Thanks."

Then she walked out, leaving the clerk to huff and worry.

She took the box straight to the office, where Reymon was waiting for her. He caught the scent, as well, but still x-rayed it. There was nothing inside except what looked like more tubes. He opened the box, wary, and withdrew what Eldora instantly recognized as two more male appendages.

"These need to go to the coroner's," she said. "Make sure they match the bodies."

Reymon cringed then said, "Y'know, the tox-screen on Grady showed evidence of pot and low-key stuff. And Benzodiazepine..."

"Roofies, yes. The other two?"

"Nothing."

"Shit. They done with the cars, yet?"

"No prints or DNA. No blood in either one. Did find a strip of plastic in the Malibu's trunk. Could be from a sheet like painters use, but can't say when it was put there."

"But if they were wrapped up in it, that could account for no blood. Means we're lookin' for a couple people. 'Cause Spit's what? Three hundred pounds?"

"Two-eighty-six."

"And to wrap Nat up? He's about one-seventy, one-seventy-five, and strong."

"But wounded. And it was bad."

"Would they both fit in that trunk?"

"Not comfortably."

"Okay, Raymon, I'm callin' in some men and we are searchin' that whole area, tomorrow. Half-mile radius. Maybe a mile. I want to see where this monster went after settin' these scenes up, and they ain't gonna wipe their trail out that far off."

"Desert'll do that for them."

"Usually, but it's been quiet. No storms due till Monday."

"That kills my plans."

"Plans?"

"I was hoping to get Rhonda to join me for a bite."

"She works tomorrow."

"Lunch. Maybe a matinee. Or dinner Monday."

Poor little Reymon; he didn't know what he was up against. Everybody in the world knew Rhonda had a thing for Zeke but was too blind to see it was not at all reciprocated. She was one of those girls who think if they're insistent enough and around enough, then the boy they like will suddenly notice and fall in love with them, like in a romance novel or a music video. She almost wondered if she ought to give Rhonda a push in Reymon's direction. She was only a couple years older than him, and he was sweet.

"I'd aim for Monday, were I you," she said. "I'll make the call, then I'm gonna talk to Dax. Dig more info from him. You hungry?"

"I could eat."

"Then before you go, get me a meatball sub." She pulled a twenty from her wallet. "Whatever you want."

"Thanks. Usual setup?"

"Yeah. Thanks."

He bopped out the door. Yeah, just a bit of a push between him and Rhonda. Might be fun to see what happened.

Eldora wandered out the back door to look around at the horrific beauty of the desert under the setting sun, Reymon's information knocking around in her head. None of this made sense except with Carli Vincenzo in the middle of it, but the lad was right. Grady might have been controllable with roofies, but Nat and Spit? They were too solid and built and — no, actually, Spit was fat as shit. And while Carli had looked strong, was she *that* strong? Like *Wonder Woman* strong? No, she must have had help. And if she'd had help, there was no way she could wipe all traces of it away. So who would be working with her?

Dax's idea didn't sound right, but who else could she have connected with? Winston Deveaux had refused to talk with anyone about his daughter killing herself, except to issue a statement that he didn't believe it. A little research showed he'd become pretty involved with the college since the Vincenzo girl's death. Which all but told her he'd really been working to clear the bitch of any blame in that fiasco. And her confab with the LAPD said they had abandoned the suicide angle. The boyfriend had remembered she was looking past him at someone when he was hit. They had also found another glitch in the building's security system, this time dealing with the garage, so now acknowledged the obvious — the silver Mercedes that drove out was hers and someone had switched the plates for a dealer's.

Like the slip of cardboard stuck to the Mercedes.

This had become a full-fledged murder investigation with overtones of an assassination.

Could Deveaux be dumb enough to believe Dax had something to do with killing his daughter? It wasn't outside the realm of possibility. She'd still owed Dax a lot of money, and you don't screw him over. She'd seen that when she learned from Candy about Chase's ear, and he had flat out refused to explain what happened. She'd had to worm the story out of Dax, then give him another *good talking to*. You just don't do that to college kids over something so minimal, especially those with rich daddies. So the question segued to, was *he* dumb enough to have found some way to shove Stasi off her balcony?

Or some*one* to do it for him?

Oh, stop it, Eldora, she growled to herself. *Timeline's too tight.*

There had to be something else going on. Well, the only way to figure that out was to talk with Dax. Which will probably blow everything out of the water.

Oh, that should be fun.

Pinball Wizarding

Saturday night was surprisingly loud with the college crowd. The pool table worked double-time. There were more requests for super-specialty drinks than usual; fortunately, all were in the bartender's guide. Even Laila was having a hard time choosing which of the rock-jocks to lay her sorrows upon. They started showing up barely ten minutes after the Cantina opened, so Zeke and Rhonda were kept at a run. The only thing missing was a juke box filled with golden oldies, which Zeke had strictly forbidden; instead, he kept the sound system focused on heavy metal through a streaming channel, which the male and female Rock-Jocks seemed to enjoy but drove the Mildreds to pumping up Yanni through their iPhones and earbuds.

About an hour in, Rhonda did manage to sit on Zeke's stool, behind the bar, for a moment, and ask him, "How you doin'?"

He was focused on pulling two glasses of Coors, followed by yet another pitcher of Michelob, so didn't look at her as he said, "I'm fine. Thanks. It's good the joint's popping, tonight. Keep me occupied."

"I could stick around, after we close. Sit and talk and just...I dunno..."

"Thanks, Rho, but I'm fine."

She shrugged, rose and took the pitcher of beer to a couple of Rock-Jocks at the pool table, who were arguing about the true circumference of the cue ball, since one had insisted it was out of round and could just prove it if only the damned table were really flat.

Then who should arrive, pump up the volume on the chaos?

Eldora.

In the middle of a busy night?

In uniform?!

That was never good. She was the type who swapped into comfy fleece by 6pm on a Friday and wore nothing else till Monday morning.

Needless to say, this did not bode well.

She accepted her usual drink, and did her usual inspection of Zeke. But this time without a word. In fact, she was looking at him more closely, insistently, sharply, as if surprised he was wearing jeans instead of shorts. Which finally made him stop to look at her, in askance.

She had simply frowned and coolly strolled over to Dax's booth, where a five-pack of female Rock-Jocks were drinking Mai Tais. She gave them a smile of warning.

Zeke could just hear one actually say to her, "No problem; she's designated."

Another joined in with, "It's a virgin Mai Tai. Taste it."

Eldora still said nothing, just nodded until the group quietly shifted to an open table. Then she had sat there, in the booth's corner, alone, sipping her drink.

And watching Zeke.

Like she was a cat planning to pounce on a blue jay.

Which made him even more self-conscious. He knew she liked him as more than a friend, but there was no way anything was ever going to happen between them. She wasn't ugly or that much older than him; she was just too...well, too close to Dax for comfort.

It wasn't till nearly nine that he heard Loki barking. He started up a pitcher a moment before Dax and JJ came in.

Naturally, Dax snarled, "That fuckin' mutt of yours — "

Zeke cut him off with a quick hand-signal, making him look at his usual booth to see...

Eldora was now watching him.

"Usual," he said, his voice still sharp.

"Already started," Zeke said.

Rhonda came up to the bar to say, "Mimosa, Tequila Sunrise and white wine." Her eyes followed Dax and JJ to their booth, then she sighed. "Oh, shit."

"No shit," Zeke muttered as he put the pitcher, two glasses and a bottle of JD on her tray. "I'm starting up nachos."

"No beans, please."

"Definitely, no shit." Then he forced a chuckle.

JJ slid into the booth, first, then Dax sat across from Eldora, saying, "What's this all about?" in a voice too low to be overheard in the bar's noise.

She sipped her drink as Rhonda brought over Dax's order, then said, "I think I'll try a Brandy Alexander. On Dax."

Rhonda frowned as she set everything on the table. "I'll ask Zeke if he can make one."

"Oh, honey, I think Zeke can do whatever he damn well wants," Eldora purred. "Except maybe run a marathon." Then she chuckled.

"Don't make bet against him," said JJ, trying to grin.

Rhonda left. Eldora helped herself to some of the JD and downed it in one gulp, then sat quietly until Rhonda brought over the drink. Before she set it down, she sniffed at it and said, "That does look good. I'll try one, sometime."

"I know Reymon would love to buy you one," Eldora purred.

"Reymon?"

"One of my deputies?"

"I know, but...Reymon?"

"Yes. Reymon. He's a sweet boy. And very good-lookin'."

"Well, yeah, it's just I never, well, thought...Reymon?"

"Reymon."

Rhonda wandered away, her brain locked on, "Reymon."

Eldora sighed. "Kids these days." She took a ladylike sip of her drink then leaned forward, said, "Okay, listen up," and quietly filled Dax in on everything she knew.

Everything.

Ending with, "A couple other sheriff's offices are sendin' me some men, tomorrow, and we're goin' to scour the countryside around that plateau. I want to know where the bastard who did this went afterwards."

"You think this Carli Vincenzo could have been the woman who picked up Grady?" Dax asked.

Eldora shrugged. "She doesn't fit the description, but I'm still checkin' into that. California DMV's supposed to get me a copy of her license."

"But she's the bitch you were givin' the ticket to," Dax snapped.

"To see if Zeke recognizes her, dumbass. And LAPD's sendin' a man out, on Monday, to compare notes." Her eyes bored into Dax as she added, "Not sure, yet, how much I'll tell him."

Dax just glared back.

She continued with, "I also got a call back from my buddy at Fort Bliss. Vincenzo was assigned to Logistics."

Dax huffed. "Supply chain shit. Not combat readiness."

"True, but she probably knows how to lift heavy items without too much of a strain."

"Like Spit?" JJ asked. "That heavy?"

Eldora rolled her eyes. "Oh, for God's sake, JJ. You drag him. Maneuver him up to the Malibu's trunk. Use leverage. Lift with your legs, in stages."

"What about Chase?" Dax hissed. "He could be helpin' her."

Eldora shrugged an okay. "But why him?"

"He met my guys there. How else could she find the place?"

Eldora nodded. That made sense. "You know where he is?"

"Been lookin' everywhere but can't find him, but when I do..."

Her voice went hard and sharp. "You'll leave him the fuck alone and let me handle this. We're already in too much shit for you to go off half-cocked. You've done enough of that."

"Who the fuck you think you're talkin' to?"

"You, you stupid son-of-a-bitch."

Zeke noticed the anger at the table and called, "Dax, I'm sendin' over some nachos. No beans."

That jolted Dax out of his growing anger, and brought a grin to JJ's face. In fact, the very word nachos got the entire bar interested and suddenly Zeke was being inundated with requests. Rhonda had to do a special dance to get around them and bring the bowl over without it being picked apart by the hungry puppies.

Eldora actually chuckled as they were set on the booth's table. "Got enough chips, cheese and salsa for all?" she asked.

"We buy in bulk," Rhonda said, then added, "Reymon, huh?"

Eldora nodded and helped herself to a chip.

Rhonda wandered away as JJ munched a nacho. Then he added, with a sigh, "They're just not as good without beans."

"But the air quality is," Dax snarled at him then turned to Eldora to continue, "Thinkin' about it, Madrigo's been to that site. Back when his old man was still around. The bastard sold Katty that piece of shit Malibu. I forgot about that sneaky little fuck. Can't find him or Luna, either."

"I know where they are an' they're a possibility, but I'm not facin' that till Monday. As for Chase, I don't think he's the type who'd get involved in murder. But you did cut off his ear, so there *is* revenge."

"Maybe I'll cut off something more important, this time."

Eldora's hands became fists. "Goddammit, Dax, I mean it!"

"You don't tell me what to fuckin' do."

"Christ, how old are you? Twelve? I'm trying to contain a situation and your shit is just going to make things worse, so shut the fuck up and let me handle it."

Dax huffed and snarled but only said, "I...I still think Deveaux's backin' this shit."

Eldora nodded and helped herself to another cheesy chip and jalapeño. "I can't disagree. But I'm still gatherin' my information. Like with Vincenzo..."

"What about her?"

"Well, my source says there's something weird about her file and needs to look into it, more. Won't tell me what, yet, but he's getting back to me, Monday."

"Where's she stayin'?" Dax growled.

"Even if I knew, I wouldn't tell you," Eldora shot back, "so kill any thought of going near her till I've got this sorted out. I know what kind of truck she's got and the tires. If we find any similar tracks anywhere near that plateau, that's probable cause to bring her in. Dig deeper into her background. Connections. That lawsuit she had against the university. But till then, keep away. I don't want anything to fuck this up." Then she sipped at the Brandy Alexander and frowned. "Oh, this does not go well with nachos, at all. It's like drinking dessert at the same time as dinner." She helped herself to more of the JD, instead, then gently asked, "So I hear you've been sending the boys to Loretta's, now. That true?"

"Who the fuck told you that?"

"Is it true?"

Dax eyed her and shrugged. "I bought a subscription."

JJ nodded. "It's a nice place. Just like a spa."

Eldora smirked and nodded. "Go there often?"

"Just once a month. Took Grady a few times, and he took Zeke, a few more. Oh, man, the girls love him."

"I'll bet they do," she all but purred.

"And Loki. Grady says — said they spent a couple days. Got all pampered."

"Thousand bucks each," Dax snapped. "But that still would've been cheaper than all the shit that bitch caused."

"*She* caused?" Eldora huffed. "Dax, your boys raped an innocent girl, and the only reason you didn't get hit with it is because if you'd gone down, daddy's little girl would've, too. Deveaux wasn't going to have that."

"That's the rich," said JJ. "When you deal with them, it's always you that gets fucked."

"No argument there, boys, but you need to keep this in mind — four of the people involved in that girl's rape are now dead. You two are the last men standing."

"Don't you think they'll go after Zeke, too?" JJ asked.

"Don't know. We know he didn't have anything to do with it, but they might not. At least he's got Loki to protect him. You two? Just be careful what you drink and who you fuck, and watch your backs." She had another chip, finished her JD and rose, saying, "If I find out anything, tomorrow, I'll let you know." Then she leaned towards Dax and snarled, "And if I find out you've pulled one of your tricks, I will slaughter your fucking ass."

At which point, she left.

Dax glared after her as JJ let out a long sigh. "Is this it, Dax? Is the ride over?"

"I dunno. Maybe." He took a shot of JD, chased by a sip of beer. "You up for movin' on?"

"Where?"

Dax shrugged. "Texas is pretty wide open."

"I hate fuckin' Texas."

"Yeah. Cali, then?"

"Too fuckin' expensive. What about Utah?"

Dax gave a sad chuckle. "Fuck up some Mormons? That'd be fun. But I got this fuckin' Cantina." He looked around. "Eldora might take it on. She's so hot for Zeke, he'd be safe. Safely *employed*."

They chuckled, JJ saying, "Couldn't be more obvious."

"All those years, I thought she was a dyke." He nibbled at a chip and looked around at the Cantina's crowd. The Rock-Jocks and Mildreds and a few bikers rubbing elbows like they'd always and forever be friends. Laila doing her purring over a lad in a plaid shirt. The rise and fall of voices laughing and chattering and being so alive and wonderful.

It was all completely legitimate. Had taken him years to build it up, some of it due to Zeke taking over and keeping things going smoothly, here. He just plain liked coming to the Cantina. It was comfort. It was home.

"I'll be goddamned if I'm gettin' run off," Dax finally snarled. "Not without a fight."

"What you mean?" JJ was downing the last chip.

"Time to assert ourselves. Let the motherfuckers know who's top dog."

JJ sighed, "Eldora's gonna toss a fit."

Dax shrugged. "What's your buddy say, at the armory?"

"He'll have what we need, tomorrow."

"We'll go, together. Watch each other's back."

"He's on duty at three so we gotta do it 'fore then."

Dax nodded and poured himself another shot. He refilled JJ's glass then lifted his own.

"To Nat and Spit," he said.

"And Grady."

"They shall be avenged."

Then JJ tipped his glass to Dax's and they downed them at the same time.

*****

Carli was in Tucson, dropping a thick FedEx packet into a box at a Walgreen's when she got a call from TF. She glanced at her phone to see it was just past ten.

"What's the noodle, baby-bro?" she asked.

"Movement on the investigation front," he replied. "Just got a tickle. Arizona State Police have started a file on one Dexter Castor. Pro-number's on our site."

"On a Saturday night?"

"Chatter is, they were already looking at him thanks to a certain member of the Legislature *suggesting* they do so. Need any hints as to who it was?"

Carli laughed. "That kind always eats its own."

He continued with, "Today's movement shifted into fifth thanks to a certain young man who appeared at investigator's home. Guy who works for the AG. An address no one is supposed to know about. Which caused a great deal of consternation. He had evidence to *exchange for immunity*, and said the reason he's doing this now is, he saw Mr. Castor had this investigator's address and information on the man's family. *Can't have that.*"

"Jesus, TF, were you drone-spying on them?"

"Carls, they post their crap all over the inter-office message boards. And they think their piss-ant encryption can keep someone like me out? Jesus."

"This is going to be the perfect end to it."

"...It is?"

Cari nodded. "I'm done."

There was a short pause then he said, "Good. So...is Zeke...?"

"No, he wasn't." She let out a long gentle sigh.

"Oh, shit." His voice went sing-song. "You really *li-ike* him. You want to *da-ate* him. You think he's *pre-etty.*"

"Shut up."

He chuckled then gently asked, "Carls, are you happy about it?"

"No. I just remembered an old saying. *When facing down a snake, don't toy with it.*"

"And you pissed off a Cobra?"

"Naw, just a scroungy rattler. But that's mean enough. I'm sending all my info to the AG. Let them handle the rest of it."

"Okay. So now what?"

"How's Seattle, this time of year?"

"Wet. Chilly. I miss the beaches in SoCal. But I love the forests. And the Sound. Hopping the ferry across to downtown. It's like an episode of *Gray's Anatomy.*"

"I'm bringing someone with me. 'Cause once all this hits, he ought to be elsewhere, when it happens."

TF chuckled. "I got room. But careful; I may take him from you."

"You know full well I don't mind sharing. With the right person. Sometimes even at the same time."

"Okay, that was one step too far, for me. Check the site."

"Got it. Thanks."

"Bye."

Carli hopped into the Dodge, drove to an isolated part of the parking lot, and kept it running as she plugged her laptop into the AC outset and pulled up the site on her laptop. From the looks of the emails, there had been discussion about going after Dax, for some time, but not the sheriff. And it did look like Deveaux was the instigator of the investigation, going back about six months. Nothing was dated prior to that. Now it looked as if Stasi's death had shocked them into action, and Chase's sudden appearance had given them enough info to apply for search warrants and file charges, come Monday.

She caressed the urn on the dashboard. So it was happening, anyway. Not over Lara's rape and suicide; just the usual drugs and attendant nonsense. But it was more than they had been doing.

So she figured it was best to leave, tomorrow.

She really did want Zeke out of the way when it went down. Which begged the question — how could she talk him into moving to Seattle with her, now, now, now, without revealing what was about to go happen? His loyalty to Dax was too strong, meaning if she told him about the investigation, he might warn him; that was not acceptable. But there had to be a way to keep him out of the coming arrests.

Maybe she could lead him by his dick, like any other man. *Come with me and you'll cum with me, every night.* That or food, except Carli was only good at nuking that which had already been well-prepared.

She could just destroy his connection with Dax. Emphasize how he had set Lara up to be raped. Appeal to Prince Hot Tatts' sense of responsibility, and drag him out of here by that. It wasn't a nice way to go, but it could work.

That was how she had faced the Army down. She could still get angry over them pushing a Courts Martial for smacking a little shit who'd thought he could use her any way he wanted. So what if she'd been with him once? She should have kicked him off her the second he started humping like a little bunny instead of an adult male. It was damned stupid.

Naturally, he hadn't dared say a word about that previous liaison, it being between a commissioned officer and a non-com.

In the back of a Hummer.

In the middle of the day.

Both fully dressed, except where it counted. Him nuzzling her breasts like some fifteen year old boy. Her slipping her hands inside his boxers to finger his hole when it looked like the little Humper was getting too close to letting go. Oh, had he not liked that, but they had to stay quiet so all he could do is shake his head. She'd had to fight to hold back her giggles in the face of his wounded masculine pride.

But that's how she had kept him going till she was happy. Then a couple of squeezes and he'd fired.

It was at that point, apparently, he had decided she was his and no one else's.

Even though the little fuck was married. With children.

Shit. What was it with men being so goddamned possessive? He had begun appearing wherever she went and calling and just making life difficult, in general. When none of that got her attention, he'd snuck up behind her, stinking of booze, and thought he could drag her into a private office to prove who was boss.

Which is when things didn't quite work out. For him.

Still, his word was better than hers, until she threatened to go straight to Congress and bitch about her treatment. The compromise was, *Just get lost*. Which Carli had agreed to, because in order to find justice for Lara, she needed flexibility, which the Army was not known for.

She'd saved up some money, but it was TF bankrolling her in equipment needed and expenses, so most of the settlement would go to him and the attorneys. All legally arranged, already.

Which meant she'd need to find work, soon, but she had no problem living in Seattle. She could do the ports, with her logistics background. Shipping. Receiving. All of it.

And if Zeke became a part of her life? Well...

Well.

Just the possibility brought a glow to her heart. Yes, that would be nice. She really liked him. Even more than Liam.

She had to laugh at that thought. One night together and she's thinking domestic bliss. That was a first.

But she was going to get Zeke away from here. Even if she had to drug him, bind him and throw him over a shoulder, fireman style. Like she'd considered doing with Mikey. She still had Roofies. Rope. And envisioning it brought a tingle to her heart. And a question.

How do you tie up an amputee so he can't get away? Use Saran Wrap, all around?

Well, let it never be said there was none of her mother in her, at all, because that woman did love her Saran Wrap.

By this point it was well after midnight, so Carli returned to her camp site. Boiled water for a nice shower. Dressed in her most comfortable jeans and blouse. Spritzed a bit of cologne and added a touch of makeup to her face, like she was out on one of her seductions, then she pulled on a slinky jacket and headed over to the Cantina. If her timing was right, she would arrive after the place was closed.

She was only five minutes early.

She stopped in her usual spot to watch the last of the bikers and students depart, waiting for Rhonda to finally come out. That woman had too sharp an eye and might recognize her, despite her disguise on Wednesday.

Wednesday.

And it was only Saturday night. Well, Sunday morning. But still, this time a week ago, Stasi was going over the balcony railing and screaming.

Screaming.

Softer and softer.

Then a gentle thwack. And nothing more.

What had it felt like? Falling and knowing you were going to die? That there was nothing you could do to stop it? It wasn't like the suddenness of a bullet. You're there, one minute, and then you're not. Did you even think? Could it be your brain just shut down in the face of the terror?

She had read, once, about a young man who'd jumped off the Golden Gate Bridge, intending to kill himself. But the second he had let go, he wanted to take it back. And as he had fallen, he'd desperately tried to figure out how to stay alive when he hit the water.

And he *did* live.

Of course, that wasn't the same.

Because Stasi hadn't jumped.

Carli had pushed her.

And hadn't even looked over the railing to watch her fall.

She had just killed someone and was more interested in the pretty picture the unconscious bed partner made.

The image of which still struck her as amazingly lovely. Which made her wonder how Mikey was doing with his soon-to-be-ex? Maybe she could invite him to Seattle and give him to TF. Any man could be turned to any kind of sex, if done in the right way.

Of course, that was if baby-bro was even looking for a daddy.

Mikey, a daddy?

It was hard to believe he had college-age kids, the randy little fuck. Naw, too much of a cub, still. Though she was glad she hadn't sent him over to meet Stasi, by the pool.

Jesus, what a thought. Was this even human of her?

It wasn't like Afghanistan. The men she'd killed hadn't been real. Only targets seen through a sniper scope that gave her an extra couple of layers of separation from the fact she was getting off on ending a life. Even if it was the enemy's, it was still someone who'd had hopes and dreams, once. Who might never have held a rifle or RPG before the day he died.

But she owned it. Loved it. Enjoyed the power of it, and the thrill it sent through her. The need it built in her.

Shit, why was she thinking about this, now?

Why was she thinking about Grady struggling as she raped him in the best way a woman can rape a man? Positioning the vibrator in just the right spot, as detailed by TF.

"Massage his prostate," bro-baby had said, "and he can't control what happens. Really messes 'em up."

"Tested it out, huh?" Carli had asked.

TF had looked at her and said, "Never needed to. But I did some research."

So she'd followed his directions, with Grady. And it had worked. And then she'd castrated him. The fighting and screaming. Suddenly going limp. His eyes open but glazed over. No longer breathing.

And the release she had felt. So overpowering.

Dribbling honey on his body had been anticlimactic.

"Like recycling the garbage," she muttered to herself.

That was a demented thought. Disappointment because you couldn't watch a man scream in agony as ants devoured him. And that was what she had wanted to see.

That was what she had wanted to hear.

So why?

What he did to Lara was hideous. Wrong. Vile. But he hadn't killed her. It was that fucking college that had. It was that fucking bitch who had, by recording that video and uploading it.

It was Lara who killed herself.

She didn't have to. Zeke was right. She'd had options. As vile as momma could be with her beliefs, and her cutting little comments, she would have moved heaven and earth to help Lara during this time. Why didn't she just call her? Why set a path to death when you had other ways you could go? Why act like you've been abandoned?

Because she had been, Carli said to herself.

That was the blunt truth of it. That piss-ant cousin had refused to believe she was his. Refused a DNA test. Not that Carli was pushing for it; she didn't care. Momma had, and she had taken his refusal as proof enough. Caused a lovely rift between her and one of her less-than-endearing sisters that was still open and raw.

Cousins just didn't fuck, don't you know.

Lara'd had no mother, not really. Bottle-fed from birth, momma had taken over as caregiver, but was always Gramma. And always on the watch for any of the same traits in Lara that Carli had shown. Starting out with the same level of distrust that she had developed with Carli, by the age of twelve. With a grandfather who didn't like to show anyone they mattered, unless he was pushed to the wall. And while her five uncles had acted like her brothers, she had never been an integral part of the family.

Like Zeke and his parents...no, his *guardians*.

Was that why Lara had done it? She couldn't face any more of her grandmother's suspicions and wariness about her? She finally felt completely adrift, with no mother or father to anchor her? Someone that one step closer to her than anyone else?

As difficult as she and her mother could be with each other, Carli knew they were always mother and daughter. That might be why Lara was Carli's opposite in every way. Gentle. Caring. Concerned. Wanting to help. Willing to listen. Be part of something. Trying to prove to gramma she should be wanted by people?

An idea that had been circling Carli's mind finally came home to roost. She could see her quest for justice was dishonest. Murder was one thing; torture quite another, which is what she had done. Tortured Grady as he died. She had told herself she was doing this because she felt so fucking responsible for Lara's death. That she was making up for not being there for her. Ever.

But that was only an excuse.

She had loved his pain. Loved his screams. All of it had given her a rush like nothing, before. And she would still love to torture Dax and JJ for hours, if she could. Yes, these men had crushed someone innocent. They deserved punishment. But the thought of them going to prison just wasn't enough. What she was really after was the same sexual thrill she'd had with Grady and wished she'd had with Nat.

Shit...I'm addicted to torturing men to death? Am I that fucking sick? A female Ted Bundy mixed with John Wayne Gacy?

Except, there was Zeke. And him, she would sooner die than let anything happen to him.

Well, at least it's not all men I want to torture to death. Does that mean I'm only a little crazy?

That's when Rhonda started up her bike. Carli slid low in the seat as she rode past her, waiting till she was half a mile down the road before starting the Dodge. She took a moment to compose herself then drove into the parking area and stopped close to the back of the place.

Loki rose at seeing her, watched her exit the Dodge and did not budge as she wandered to the Cantina's back door to knock. He just kept watch on her.

"You're a smart puppy," she said to him. "Trust no one until they prove themself."

Then Zeke opened the door and broke into his glorious smile at seeing her, saying, "Carli," and the look on his face was so happy and his eyes dancing with such joy, she felt a wave of peace wash over her. She looked back at Loki to hide the tears that threatened to trail from her eyes.

"No warning from Loki," she said.

"That's a good sign."

Back in control, she turned to him and asked, "Am I too early?"

"No, c'mon in. You could've come through the front."

"This was closer to where I parked." Which wasn't exactly true. She just didn't want anyone to see her, at the moment. Why? She honestly didn't know, except for a niggling suspicion she was being watched.

Paranoid freak, she thought as she entered.

Except...

Down the road, Rhonda had circled back, her headlight off, and she *was* watching it all. Her bike parked behind a couple of cacti to give her cover. Her face impassive. She waited...then saw Zeke and Carli leave the Cantina and cross to his trailer.

She felt her heart drop as Loki was released and did his running around, like he had accepted that woman.

Then she went cold at seeing them kiss as they slipped inside the trailer.

And grew angry at what she felt was a betrayal.

Rhonda had always come in second, when love was involved. Good friend. Good coworker. Never anything more. And here it was, happening again.

In secret.

What was that bitch hiding, coming here after hours? Why was she sneaking around? Who the fuck was she? From this vantage point, she did not look like the woman who had picked up Grady. But still...

Rhonda quietly walked over to the parking area and wrote the license plate of the Dodge onto her hand. Loki saw her and came over, not close enough to pet but just to sniff and make sure she was okay. She put a finger to her lips and forced a smile.

The dog huffed and went to the porch to lie down.

Then laughter drifted from within the trailer. And the shadows of Zeke and that woman crossed a curtained window.

Heading to the back.

Where the bedroom was.

No, this was not acceptable.

She couldn't do anything tonight without looking like a fool, but she could find out where this bitch was and deal with her, that way.

She calmly walked back to her bike, started it up and rode away, making a mental list of everything she could do in the morning to make that predatory female's life a living hell and protect her Zeke.

Starting with talking to Reymon.

Buzzards Circle for Joy

The next morning, Zeke woke, slowly, to breathe in deep and stretch a little, and find Carli lying on the bed watching him. Fully dressed.

He smiled and murmured, "Morning."

She ran her fingers over his lips. "Good morning."

"Shit, I slept."

"Yes, you did. And it was lovely to watch. Did you know you purr, as you sleep?"

"Purr?"

"Like a kitten. So sweet."

He snorted. "What time is it?"

"Why don't you have a clock in this place?"

"Don't need one. Always know when it's six, and the bar's got one over the main door to tell me it's closing."

"It's after ten."

"Yeah? Shit, I did sleep."

"Have you had a lot of trouble with that? Not sleeping?"

He stretched and nodded. "That's why I don't crash till seven or so. Exhaust myself." He looked down to see his leg was still on. "Oh, crap, I better get this off."

She shifted to beside his leg and said, "Let me."

"Naw, it's okay."

"Please."

He flopped back, looked at the ceiling to give a long, weary sigh then sat up, released the suction holding it in place and let Carli shift the leg down to reveal how the skin was rough, with red splotches visible near the base, despite the tattoos. She caressed him where it was rubbed red then began to massage his thigh, tenderly.

He smirked saying, "I got a massager so you can go hard."

"On what?" she asked oh-so-innocently. "This? Or this?"

She yanked the sheet away from his crotch and chucked a finger under the head of his dick.

He flopped back, laughing. "Careful, you'll get something started."

She giggled and returned to kneading his leg like bread dough.

He grunted but nodded. "Feels nice."

"Your left thigh isn't so much smaller than your right. I'd heard there's a lot of shrinkage in the muscle after...well..."

"I've got a fake one good for exercising. Keeps it a bit pumped up. But gets sore pretty fast, too."

"How many do you have? Legs?"

"Three. The one you took off, that's my work one. Most comfortable. One for riding my Harley. It's easy to flex."

"You're doing so well."

He propped himself up on his elbows to look at her. "Don't do that. Please. Give me a pat on the head just for doing what I gotta do to live."

She did not look back at him. "Is that what you're doing here?"

"Still alive, ain't I?"

"Yes." She smiled and shifted her hands to following the designs in his tattoo. "Uh-oh. I see some motion, down below."

He chuckled. "Been a while since somebody else did this."

"I like the feel of your skin. How lovely your ink looks on it."

"Keep at it long enough, who knows what'll happen?"

"Zeke..." she started, but her trailed off.

"Oh, that doesn't sound good."

"It's just, I'm leaving. For Seattle. I have a brother I can stay with till I get a job."

It took him a moment to say, "Oh. Okay."

"He's got room for two, so I just wondered..."

He sat up to look at her, wary.

"I've got space in my truck for you and Loki," she said, the words spilling out. "And they've got trees and rain and lakes and rivers and mountains up there. Lots of Vikings, too. And a really good music scene and — "

He all but snapped, "Don't kid me like this."

"I'm not kidding. I like you and I...I even think I..."

She could not complete the sentence.

He drew his good leg up to him and wrapped the sheet around himself. "Carli, we barely know each other."

She made herself laugh and say, "Really? After all we've done the last two days?"

"You know what I mean."

"Yeah. Yeah, but...but no, I *do* know you. And I like being around you. I like how you help me find solid ground. How you center me. How you make me feel."

He snorted. "Bullshit. You sound like I'm your therapist."

"A therapist wouldn't fuck their patient, would they?"

"So what is this? You want me for my body?"

She forced a chuckle. "It's a lovely body."

"Oh, yeah, perfect," he said as he slapped his left thigh.

"That doesn't matter." She touched his chest, over his heart. "This does." Then she put a gun-finger to his head. "And this. Will you come with me? Join me?"

He was lost. Completely. Unable to think. Until it hit him. "Shit, I gotta feed Loki. He's gonna be pissed."

"I gave him some kibble, I found."

"Shit, now he's really gonna be upset."

He started to get off the bed. Carli rose to help him but he shook her off. "I can do it. I do it all the time."

He grabbed his crutch and rose to stand up.

"Zeke, wouldn't you like to get away from here? The endless nothing of it?"

He leaned against the wall.

"I'd work for you," she said, her voice soft but filled with meaning. "I'd do anything you want me to. I've never said that to a man, before, but it's just..."

"It's just, you feel sorry for me."

"No! Never. I told you, I like being with you. Being around you."

"Like a pet?"

"Stop it! I know I'm not explaining myself very well because I've never tried to, before. All I can say is, you make me care, again."

He moved around to the door then stopped and leaned against the frame, lost, fighting to find the right words but unable to think. The vulnerability in him tore into her.

Finally, she said, "Don't you want to go?"

"I don't know," he murmured. "It's a lot to think about. I mean, I...yeah, I like the idea, I do, I really do, but I can't just leave Dax in the lurch, like that."

"We could see if the university has someone who could take over, for a while."

"Spring Break."

"Not everyone's going. Not everyone can afford it. I can ask Dean Trevarian, tomorrow."

"I dunno. I just...it's a lot to think about it. It's a big jump and I just don't know, yet."

"You've worked here eight years. Handled that bar for him all that time. And for what? A place to live? Money to feed you and your dog? I think you've more than paid whatever debt you owe him."

"It's not about debt. It's about loyalty."

"Is he loyal to you?"

That made him look at her, sharp and wary. "What do you mean?"

"I...I've talked to people who know him, and he strikes me as an abuser. The type who demands everything for himself but won't give anything back. Who will hurt you if you don't do exactly what he wants. Are you afraid of him? Because you don't need to be."

He almost growled. "I was a marine, Carli. So was Dax. You don't dump on your buddies. It's not the right thing to do. Now I'm gonna feed Loki. And take a shower."

Then he limped away.

Carli flopped back on the bed and sighed.

Well, at least he hadn't said no.

And there were other ways of handling this — like those roofies.

*****

Dax and JJ rode their Hogs to the storage facility, then left them in the unit and called an Uber to take them to the airport, where they rented an SUV. By noon, they were meeting with JJ's buddy outside of Red Rock. He handed them a small carton containing two grenades and accepted a thousand dollars each, for them. Not a word was spoken. Moments later, Dax and JJ were on The 10, headed for Phoenix. They pulled off at Picacho, crossed the tracks, hid the SUV behind a crop of bushes, and changed the license plates to ones from Utah, then pulled back onto The 10 and continued on.

Stasi's service was planned for 2pm, in Scottsdale, so they made it just time. The church was a blinding white faux adobe with a matching bell tower and lots of green grass and space for cars, but no shade. They set up across the street in the lot of an apartment complex, partially hidden by a low wall. Carefully maintained shrubs and skinny trees surrounded them, as did other cars. There, they waited.

News trucks were set up at the intersection next to the church and mourners had begun to arrive. Mercedes after Mercedes after Cadillac after Lincoln after Jaguar after Land Rover after Hummer after Mercedes, and repeat and repeat, all positioning in the church's lot with an extreme precision. It was mostly middle-aged and older couples in dark clothes getting out to go inside; very few people of Stasi's age.

JJ chuckled as he pointed that out. "It appears her peers thought she was a cunt, too."

"No shit," Dax growled.

Then a pair of Ford 15-passenger vans pulled into the lot and parked close to the entry drive.

"Are those meant to ferry everyone to the cemetery?" JJ wondered.

"Naw, there's people already inside 'em."

"This is not comforting. And news hounds make me nervous."

"Yeah. Must be a slow news cycle. But the cars're on the other side of the church from 'em. How long do you need?"

"A few minutes."

"Let's see what happens."

Moments later, a hearse and couple of limos pulled up in front of the church, on the street. Long and black with white detailing. In perfectly respectable harmony.

That is when a group of young men in matching suits and whitewall haircuts flowed out of one of the passenger vans and wandered up to behind the hearse.

"Pallbearers?" JJ asked, in shock.

"Holy fuck, they was hired," said Dax.

A group of young women in matching dresses, all black and gray, bouquets of red roses in hand, exited the other van. More young men in dark suits poured out of the first van to meet them and they and headed into the church, like couples.

JJ nudged Dax. "It's like a wedding?"

The silver coffin slipped out of the hearse and the pallbearers took it then lifted it onto their shoulders and carried it to the church entrance, marching in perfect step.

"Aw, fuck," Dax said. "They're Marines."

"What's he got Marines here for?"

"That motherfucker wasn't in the service. Not that I could find."

"You know any of 'em?"

Dax shook his head. "Naw, these kids're way after my time."

Then Winston Deveaux got out of the first limo and stormed past the coffin to enter the church. Black suit. Long white hair. Prowling gait. The feel of a jackal. A moment later, he was followed by wife number two, who was dressed in shining couture black with lacy white details and six-inch heels. And a flowery hat wrapped in netting. And silver jewelry. And matching bag. And big tortoise-shell sunglasses.

And JJ gasped. "Mother-fucking-son-of-a-bitch."

"What?" Dax asked.

"Jenny fucking Constanza."

"Who? The wife?"

JJ nodded. "I didn't know she landed him. Fuck, she has moved up in the world."

"From Loretta's?"

"Yeah. Shit, look at how he's treating her. Walked straight in the church and made her follow, like a dog."

"Don't even say jack shit to the news."

Then they saw Smythe exit the limo and not move from it, just scan the area like a hawk. He wore a rust-colored suit that didn't fit right, black hair slicked back, aviator sunglasses.

They watched the ex-Mrs. Deveaux stagger out of the second limo, obviously drunk. She was in black ruffles and netting under a pillbox hat. Smythe went to help her, motioning to a group by the church entrance. Another young marine in a neat suit strode over.

"Okay, this ain't gonna work, here," said Dax. "Let's check out his house." He started the SUV and backed away.

"We know what kind of car he's got?" asked JJ.

Dax was about to turn onto the street but hesitated. "You thinkin' the funeral home?"

"Maybe."

"Here." He handed JJ a folder. "Check."

"These are printouts."

"So?"

"It's a waste of paper and — "

"You think I'm puttin' this shit on my phone? No fuckin' way."

"You put it on your desktop."

"An' that's got kick-ass encryption. What the fuck? Can't you read paper?"

"It's just, weird. What if you get raided?"

"I got this thing called a fireplace that's always lit, and did you know paper burns? Fuckin' millennial bullshit. What's it say?"

JJ huffed then read through the pages and said, "Here we go. Aw, man, this is awful. He's got a Maserati sedan. A killer car for an old fuck like that."

"Like daughter, like father."

"I sat in one, once. Really nice, but it was hard to get out of. How the hell does he do it?"

"Forklift?"

JJ laughed. "His wife's got a Porsche Cayenne. Consistent. So what d'you think?"

Dax chuckled and sang, "Oh, we're halfway there."

JJ laughed even harder. "Oh-oh! Livin' on a prayer."

Minutes later, they pulled into a wide parking lot with few cars in it. One of which was a black Cayenne. The Maserati sedan was directly ahead of it.

Dax did a slow drive around the lot as JJ scanned the building for cameras.

"Don't see any, he said."

"Me neither," said Dax. "Okay."

He slowed down while passing the Maserati. JJ showed him the license plate number matched, so Dax swung around and parked next to the driver's door as JJ pulled on tight latex gloves. Then Dax pulled on a cap, exited the SUV and wandered over to the entrance of the funeral home to pick up a brochure, keeping his head down while scanning the area for anyone passing by.

Fortunately for them, the street was quiet.

Using the SUV's passenger door as cover, JJ slipped out and dipped under the Maserati, taped a grenade to the chassis under the driver's seat and taped a wire connected to its pin to the edge of the driver's door. Very quiet and low-key. Then he taped the second grenade to the gas tank and connected that one's wire to the first grenade's. After everything was secure, he slipped back into the SUV.

Dax saw him get in so sauntered back to drive them away. They did not want to be anywhere near Phoenix when those grenades went.

*****

Atop the plateau, Eldora watched a line of two dozen men stretching a thousand feet slowly walk in a circle around it. Reymon was close to her, piloting a drone with a camera feed in a circle, farther out. He had to be careful; a couple of times hawks dove at it, thinking it might be dinner.

He kept finding nothing. And more nothing. And even more nothing, so was about to bring in back when he caught a glimpse of tire tracks that appeared from nowhere. He piloted the drone to follow them to the remains of a fire. He quickly coordinated the location then said, "The foothills over there. Other side. About a mile off."

Eldora used a bullhorn to call, "You boys keep circlin' around. If you find anything that don't look like it should be there, call me on your walkie-talkie."

Then she and Reymon scooted down from the plateau to her SUV. He sat on the passenger window, keeping the drone in hover-mode as they carefully trundled over the desert land. He had to wrap an arm in the seatbelt to keep from tumbling out.

"Okay, around those rocks," he said.

Eldora could see the drone whispering far above. It took a dive as a hawk flew at it then zipped back up. Soon, they were within a hundred feet of the unknown tire tracks so she stopped and they got out.

They walked over a sandy rise and saw the tracks were in a shallow arroyo. They followed them up to the outcropping and found the remains of a fire. As Eldora squatted to check the ashes, Reymon brought the drone down then carefully headed in-between the rocks to look around.

"Looks like somebody camped here," he called to her.

She rose. "Half these ashes are cloth. How far is this?"

"'Bout a mile. Up those rocks, you can see the plateau."

She looked around and watched him pilot the drone up the side, its camera focused on the plateau.

"Go back to the truck," she said. "Call in the coroner. Then let the boys know we got what we want. They'll want to get home."

He headed off as Eldora continued to look around. She noticed naked footprints. Crusted areas where water had splashed into the sand and dirt and dried. Some of the dirt was a dark brown, meaning probably more blood. Fresh scratches on the boulders at just above head-level. And lines of ants were swirling into crevices between the rocks. This was probably where the killer cleaned off so they could head on without suspicion. Nothing much to go on, but if those tire tracks were from the same kind as on Carli's truck, she was hauling that bitch in, to explain.

"Sheriff!" Reymon called from the truck. "They found two sets of car tracks. Both pretty light."

"Tell 'em to secure it!" she called back. "I'll be straight over. I want you to stay here and deal with the coroner."

He ran back to her, carrying a bottle of water, calling, "Should be here in half an hour."

She nodded. "Point 'em to those ants."

"Oh, fun."

"Probably." She gave him a swat on the rear. "When they're done here, I want them over to see if the tire treads match these."

"You got it."

"You ever get a chance to talk to Rhonda?"

"Funny, she got my phone number and called. Haven't had a chance to call her back."

"That is funny. How'd she get it?"

"Dunno."

"She say what she wanted?"

"Nope, just to call her. Maybe I'll drop by the Cantina, tonight."

"Well, good luck with her." Then she headed for the SUV, smiling. Maybe her hint about Reymon had worked.

As regards everything else, she had a pretty damn good idea she was closing in on former Master Sergeant Carli Vincenzo, and boy, would she make her pay for this. Not just because it looked bad for there to be three murders under her watch, but because that bitch had killed Eldora's golden goose.

She had always been smart about taking her share of Dax's proceeds, each week. No fancy living. No flashy anything. Just nicer meals in Tucson. Trips to Vegas to indulge in Blackjack and a lad or two from *The Thunder Down Under*. It was amazing what a thousand bucks would get you in that town.

Of course, she added the rest to a 401K at a bank in Phoenix, under her married name, which no one knew about. The one remnant of her biggest mistake, in life.

Charlie Conner.

He'd been one of those big, broad-shouldered, red-headed lads who rode a horse before he could walk and thought she would be a great breed mare. And that if she objected, a simple pop in the mouth would remind her who's on top.

Instead, he'd lost four teeth the first time he tried that, thanks to her having a skillet close by. They had signed the divorce papers a month later. Six weeks of marriage down the drain. He kept the ranch; she took the 401K and got the hell out of Las Cruces.

Fortunately, she had only taken a leave of absence to get married and see if she wanted to continue in the sheriff's department, so no need to beg for her job back. When asked where she'd been, she'd told everyone, "Went and had some work done. What do you think?"

Not one person had been willing to say they couldn't see any difference, since there wasn't. She could still chuckle over that.

Ten years later, she read about him bolting up one morning as wife number three gelded him then threw it all in a blender. She was sent to prison, despite the long record of abuse the cops had against him, as regards his second wife as well as third, and he sold his ranch and vanished.

It was one of Eldora's happier pieces of information.

Men really did need to learn that women will only put up with so much before they fight back or die. And she was glad number three had taken care of the bastard. He was probably still on his damn horse, somewhere.

Looking more like Dale Evans than Roy Rogers, she had told herself, knowing full well it was politically incorrect to think that. But it still brought a smile to her face.

Now to be honest, he had been a good lay. At first, anyway. Good size. Taking his time. Not much ass, nor was it pretty, like Zeke's obviously was, still it had been enough to enjoy. But the first time she'd grabbed it, he'd damn near jumped off the bed. Only her hands gripping his butt cheeks kept him inside her.

All he'd said was, "Don't like that." Then he'd finished before she was done. That should have been a red flag, but she'd thought she could get around him, eventually. Stupid of her.

Of course, that memory got her to thinking about sweet little Zeke. Maybe it *was* time to make a move. Stay after closing and. well. *bring things to a head?* she thought, with a chuckle.

She didn't know of any particular woman he'd been seeing. Or boy, even. Learning he'd been to the Scottsdale whorehouse had been a real surprise. She'd always thought he was on the ascetic side. Or was the word celibate? She'd have to look that up; see which one to use on him. Maybe tonight. She was in the mood for a man, but Nat was dead and Reymon was off-limits. Dammit.

She checked her watch. It read 4:15. Plenty of time to get finished out here, freshen up and stroll in on Prince Hot Tatts after midnight. Shoo Rhonda off with Reymon. Drink and chat and lead little ol' Zeke into being with her. She knew all the right words to say to get a lovely young man into thinking she'd be a treasure, in bed.

Yes, tonight would be just right.

The mere thought sent a tingle through her.

Unfortunately, there's an old saying about best laid plans, and all that...

The grenades went off at 5:07. Almost simultaneously. First the one under the driver's seat, then the one by the gas tank, which followed with its own explosion and fireball, decimating the Maserati. Winston Deveaux was half behind the wheel; Edward Smythe about to get into the passenger seat. Hideous screaming was heard for a moment, in the midst of the flames. No idea from whom. Then nothing but the crackling of the fire.

Shrapnel cut into wife number two, a couple of cops, a few of the reporters they were keeping away from the car, and some passersby. All of it was caught on glorious video.

Which hit the news feed by 5:14, three minutes after the fire trucks arrived.

The national news networks were broadcasting live by 5:30.

The Scottsdale police, the Maricopa Sheriff's Department, and the Arizona State Police quickly roared in with a massive presence around the smoldering vehicle by 5:51, and the FBI's Phoenix office was calling to offer assistance.

Eldora didn't hear about it until 5:59. She was away from her truck, walking beside two sets of tire tracks leading away from the direction of the plateau down to the arroyo that led to The 14. Both were definitely cars, if the crusted earth in the arroyo's bed was any indication. She also saw the tracks from the two BLM agents roll up to cross over them as they neared the point where it curved around to The 14, so nothing from that point would be much good.

Eldora headed back to her SUV. If Vincenzo was the one who'd killed those men — and Stasi, since it was growing more and more obvious her death was part and parcel of this — then she might not have needed help. Just time and solitude. Of which there is a lot in the desert, at night.

As she drew near to her SUV, she heard her radio crackle and then Reymon's voice. "Sheriff, come in. Eldora, where are you?"

She grabbed her radio and said, "What is it, Reymon?"

"Got an APB from Maricopa County. Bomb went off outside a funeral home."

Eldora froze.

Oh, no, no, no, Dax couldn't be that stupid.

Reymon continued, "They're looking for a white Chevy SUV with Utah plates. Two men inside. Probably armed and dangerous so approach with extreme caution. Might be Proud Boys. You get all that?"

She could not think of what to say. She knew Dax had weaponry but bombs? She'd never thought of him as that sort.

"Sheriff, did you hear me?" His voice was sharp and insistent.

She sighed. "Yes. APB out and everything?"

"Yes. Coroner's still working here, but he's sending a guy over to meet with you. What's your twenty?"

Shit, she had to stay for that. "Uh, you know that arroyo that's between the plateau and The 14?"

"Yes."

"Tell him to follow that to the west and he'll see me, off to its right."

"What about the tire tracks?"

"Just tell him!" she snapped.

"On it."

She could tell from his voice that he was hurt by her tone, but this stupidity, this outright insanity, it threw her. And it killed any thought of Zeke, tonight. This was going to be one hellacious mess, and she had to find a way out of it. A way that could not be traced back to her. Because not only was the golden goose dead, it was damn well cooked. And if she wasn't careful, she'd be the sauce for the gander.

Which did not sit the least bit well, with her.

Coyotes Choose to Dine In

The Cantina was damn near deserted. Just a couple of beefy bikers and a solitary rock-jock of the near-nerd persuasion, who was looking like he would need an Uber home, at the rate he was downing shots of Tequila. Laila had done her wander in then right back out after barely giving him a glance. So it was going to be a long, dead night.

Which Zeke did not look forward to. Too much opportunity to think.

The one good thing was, Rhonda had called right at six to tell him she was running late. On the bar's landline since he never handed out his cellphone number.

Well...almost never.

He'd almost told her not to bother coming in, because she could be a chatter freak to the point of distraction on quiet nights, but then again, that might be good because he did not want to really think.

Instead, he cleaned the bar. Shelves. Bottles. Microwave. Brushed the pool tables. Put the balls in numerical order. Anything and everything he could do to keep from thinking about Carli's proposal.

Without success.

Come away with me, tomorrow, to a land of trees and rain.

The blunt reality of it was scary because, deep down, he really did like the idea. Really did want to. It was freaky how much. Not because he hadn't thought of it, before, but because a woman he liked was making the suggestion, giving it a bit more emphasis than he could, on his own. Going *with* someone. Not just him and his pup, but A woman he enjoyed being with. Side by side. Sharing the journey. That made it painfully appealing.

He had money and his pension, so he wouldn't have to push hard at finding a job. And he figured he did well, tending bar, which would easily translate to anywhere. But it meant making a hard decision and that was what he was fighting.

Because Dax had done right by him. Pretty much. Supported him. Taken him in. Let the gang become his family when he was already drifting too close to being another homeless, alcoholic veteran. Grady had talked him into it while he was in the middle of a serious bender, and it really had been a life-saver. He felt a certain gratitude to Dax, despite his quirks and weirdness and basic psychosis, because he'd been fair and generous.

Until that night.

With Lara.

Jesus, that's when everything had started changing.

Zeke still had a scar under his eye from Dax going off the rails, that night and the following week. And he continued to be confused at how he'd let the man beat him down. Been more concerned Dax might shoot Loki than worried about himself. It was almost as if he felt he deserved the punishment. Which was dumb. All he'd done was...

All he'd done was nothing. But there it was.

That's when Dax had shifted into a paranoid control freak of an asshole. Zeke's focus had been to keep his head down. Get no more involved than necessary. And it had gone okay. Besides, living here away from people, he had actually grown used to the peace and quiet.

Until now.

Because Grady was gone.

His one real friend.

And now he had been offered a lifeline. Like what Grady had given him. A chance to settle and restart his existence.

But still, to just dump Dax with no back-up? That would be too much like what the Lindstroms had done to him, when he got busted. An end to communication. Not one ounce of support. Not one dime in help. He'd had to use an overworked public defender, and that hadn't exactly turned out so well. Then not one word from them in ten years.

He'd always made sure they knew where he was and how to reach him if they needed to, but it was like he no longer existed. So he couldn't do that to anyone he knew. Never.

Besides, Dax had apologized. And hadn't laid another hand on him, since. And he didn't think Dax would really shoot Loki...so long as he was kept chained up during Cantina hours.

But to be around trees and water, again! And cold nights and misty days. Just the thought brought him close to tears. He didn't mind the desert but God, how much he missed snow.

And to be honest, he would love to get away from the growing sense of doom building around this sad Cantina. Made more palpable by how he'd heard nothing from Nat, despite messages he'd left. And the chatter of more bodies found in the desert, those were starting to gnaw at him, as well. Not enough to turn on the news, to verify one way or the other; those reports were always so full of shit and misinformation. It's just, it felt like everything was about to explode.

Now here was a lovely woman who wanted him. A woman he

felt comfortable with. Who was as strong as him — hell, stronger. Not the least bit afraid of life. Who knew what she was doing. Had a plan and, to be honest, had brought him to nirvana more times in the last couple days than in the previous year.

And he was fighting against joining with her?

What the fuck was wrong with him?

She had slipped away while he was in the shower, that morning. Just left him a note saying she had some things to finish up, and asking him to think about it, and that she'd call him, later.

Which she had.

Twice.

He'd let both go to voicemail.

He wanted to talk with Dax, first. See if JJ could take over the bar. He was a sharp guy, and it was mainly beer at this place, so Zeke would leave his cocktail guide for him to use. That could work.

But if Dax said no, then what? Stay?

No. No.

Carli was right. Zeke actually had handled the Cantina for eight years. All on his own. Done right by Dax. He knew it made more money than the man was willing to admit, and he mainly used it as a way to launder his drugs income. Which Zeke honestly did not care about. Can't sell drugs without a market. Besides, whiskey was worse for your body but it was legal while pot wasn't? Made no sense.

Problem was, Dax needed somebody he could trust to handle this place. Somebody who wouldn't get bent out of shape about the cash in the cooler. Or siphon from it. Which would be JJ. Nat was too young and Spit couldn't be trusted with money. And Rhonda, while she knew about everything and might be good, he didn't really know her. Except that she had a thing for him, but that was never going to happen. Especially now. Maybe he could ask, when she came in. Gauge her reaction.

By now, it was nearing nine and the bikers had grown bored with the hard rock playing on the sound system, so left. The drunk Rock-Jock was the only one remaining, half-hidden in a corner booth, face down on the table. After four shots? Wow, that kid couldn't hold his liquor. Well, he was too far gone for an Uber, so give him time to return to his senses. Make some coffee. Get his keys.

Which would be good to take care of, right now, so Zeke limped over to the booth, checked the pockets of his coat then his pants, and pulled the keys out. The guy softly growled, but no chance of him making a getaway.

He was almost back to the bar when Rhonda entered, slowly, lost in a trance.

Zeke noticed and asked, "Rho, you okay?"

She looked at him, confused. "It's awful."

"What is?"

"What do you mean, *what is?*"

"What's awful?" he asked as he dropped the keys in a short whiskey tumbler on a back shelf.

"Haven't you heard?"

Zeke just sighed. Sounded like Rhonda was aiming for her guess *what I'm saying crap,* again. "Heard what?"

"You haven't heard? But it's all over the news."

"C'mon, Rho, you know I don't follow that crap. What is it?"

"It's on the radio. It's all over town. And the news."

"Rhonda..."

"That bomb in Phoenix. They think it had something to do with Nat and Spit and Grady and..."

That stopped Zeke cold. He actually felt himself almost leave his body from the shock. "Bomb? Nat and Spit and...and Grady?"

"Them being found."

Zeke had to grab the edge of the bar to keep from falling over. "What?! What do you mean, Nat and Spit!?"

"You didn't know? But the whole bar was talking about it, last night, and..."

"About more bodies in the desert. But they're always finding bodies in the desert, and half of 'em are drug murders and...and you're saying it's Nat and Spit!? For sure?"

"Oh, thank God, you didn't know."

"What? What d'you mean? Are you sure?"

"They were found, yesterday. Same place as Grady. ID'd today. I found out when I was at the sheriff's office."

"Wait...why're you glad I didn't know!?"

"It means you're not part of it."

"Part of what!? What're you talking about?!"

"That bomb in Phoenix. Killed that girl's father."

"What girl?"

"The one who killed herself."

"Lara?"

"No, um, Deveaux. Her. She died. Grady, next. Nat and Spit. Now her father...and you really don't know?"

Zeke howled. She was just confusing him, so he slammed online to pull up the Tucson news to find...

It was filled with breathless stories about the bomb in Scottsdale, and how Winston Deveaux was dead and Edward Smythe was in very critical condition at the burn unit of a Phoenix hospital. Several were also injured by the shrapnel.

And there were rumors two bodies found in the desert were a

possible motive. They were in the same location where another body had been found. The police were handing out the claim that these two were due to a drug gang war from across the border, but no one was buying it because unnamed sources said Deveaux's daughter's car had been found there, as well.

Now Zeke knew why he'd heard nothing from Nat. He was dead. Both him and Spit.

And suddenly he could not breathe.

He had to sit on the stool. Dax must have known about Nat and Spit last night, but he'd said nothing. Neither had Eldora. They'd stayed in their booth, talking soft and angry in a way Zeke couldn't hear.

Deliberately couldn't hear.

Like they thought he was involved in Nat's and Spit's deaths?

Like Rhonda had?

Shit, she had actually thought he was involved!

For the first time he wondered if his refusal to follow the news might have been a mistake.

*****

At the dilapidated house, Carli was showing Grady's Hog to a cocky young man and a rather solid older gentleman from south of the border. The young man was astride the bike, thrumming the motor. The older gentleman merely watched, smiling in a fatherly kind of way. Her phone was attuned to the receiver, so she was picking up the conversation between Zeke and Rhonda through an earbud.

"Is good sound," the young man said, his accent thick.

"Been taken care of," said Carli.

"The price is very low," said the older gentleman.

"I have to sell it now," Carli said, "or let it stay here and rot. I'm headed to a new job. Leaving, tonight. Truck's packed..."

The young man grinned at the old man, and nodded.

The older gentleman smiled and said, "I will buy it. Cash, you say? And the title?"

Then Carli heard Rhonda say, "Zeke, that woman you're seeing, she's part of this."

Zeke responded with, "What?"

Oh, shit, Carli thought. *She's going to fuck things up.*

She forced herself to tell the gentleman, "I have the title here."

Made special by TF. She had printed it at a FedEx office in Tucson. On cardstock, in color.

She continued with, "Cash; no more bank account."

"The woman you're seeing," Rhonda continued. "After the bar closes. She's Carli Vincenzo. I tried to get hold of Reymon, then I talked to the desk clerk at the sheriff's office. He says they're looking into her as part of it all."

Carli tensed but made herself calmly sign the title over to the gentleman and accept the money for the Hog.

"Rhonda, I don't get it," she heard Zeke say. "Part of what?"

The older gentleman looked at the title. "This will be good to get us to Hermosillo?"

"Yes, all legal, now."

The young man whooped and thrummed off on the Hog.

Carli made herself smile. "You have made your son very happy."

The old man smiled at her, a twinkle in his eye. "My son?"

Carli just shrugged.

At the same time Rhonda was saying, "They think she's the one who killed Grady. And Nat. And Spit. Even that woman in LA. I told him about you and her and he said maybe you're in it, together."

Oh, shit. Carli didn't want to Zeke to know about that. Not until she was ready to tell him. And this bitch was busting all her plans.

She forced herself to remain calm and easy, and waved as the older gentleman drove off, following the young man.

The moment they were out of sight, she bolted into the Dodge as Zeke growled at Rhonda.

"You think I'd help kill Grady!? You think I'd do that to him!?"

"No, no, that's what the desk clerk told me. That's what he says they think."

"Eldora fucking thinks I killed Grady?! And Nat and Spit? Son-of-a-bitch!"

As she started the Dodge, Carli heard him pacing behind the bar, his awkward steps obvious in how the boards creaked.

He continued with, "And Dax and JJ think it, too. That's what they were talking about, last night. Shit!"

Rhonda's voice sounded flustered. "No! No, I think they think maybe she's after you, too. Maybe she's gonna kill you, too. Over what happened."

Oh, this was going to be hard to handle. That woman had to be stopped before she crushed everything. Carli roared down the drive to The 14, hearing Zeke's anguished voice saying, "No, no, they never said a word to me or any warning so they must think — wait? Why would she want to kill *me*?"

"Were you here, that night? The night that girl was raped?"

"No."

"But she might think you were."

"She knows I wasn't."

"How does she know?"

"I told her."

"And you think she believes you?"

"Yes. Why wouldn't she? She told me everything about herself and why she's here and...and..." His voice stopped.

That gave Carli the chills, to it mildly.

Come on, Zeke, she told herself, *if I wanted to kill you I could have done so a dozen times, over the last few days. The first night I came up. Out by your rocks as you slept. Firing the M16. Lying in bed. Clothed or naked. Anytime last night. This morning, with Loki doing his thing, outside. Think about it. THINK about it. Don't let her ruin this. Please.*

*****

In the Cantina, Zeke was frozen in place, wondering if Carli was really a danger to him. He couldn't see it but he didn't really know her and her excuses and reasons for being here had only barely rung true and...wait...

Loki.

He liked her.

Well, liked her well enough to tolerate her. Even some of the girls at Loretta's had to keep their distance because the pup wasn't so sure of them. He hadn't bit, snapped or growled at them; he'd just walked away. The only one he automatically took to was Candy, with her ebony skin and hair like black wool. He'd let her pet him. Wash him. Brush him. Scratch him on his favorite spot. Making him the happiest puppy in the whole wide world. Then he would crash on his special bed so she could minister to Zeke, just as nicely.

Loki would never have let Carli near him if he had sensed any sort of threat. Sure, he wasn't as comfortable with her as he was with Candy, but he was still the best and most certain judge of anyone Zeke knew.

"Zeke," Rhonda continued, "you've got to be careful with her. A woman like that, killing people for no reason."

"Back off, Rho! You don't know what you're talking about."

"She's using you to get to your friends and now she'll stab you in the back."

"What makes you say that? You don't even know her."

"She's the woman who picked up Grady, you idiot!"

"No, she doesn't look like her."

"She was wearing a wig and corset and a ton of makeup, like she was hiding who she was."

"That woman had a driver's license from Nevada and drove a Mercedes!"

"The same Mercedes that was found by Grady's body."

"So how did she get it here? And that Dodge she drives? How'd she get both of 'em here?"

That made Rhonda hesitate, for a moment. "I...I don't know. Maybe one of them was already here and she...she..."

"What? Took an Uber back and forth?"

"She could take one to Tucson. To the airport."

"And leave a trail a mile long. Sounds really smart."

"Zeke," her voice was a near hiss, now. "She might even have set that bomb in Phoenix."

"Shit, Rho, why're you doing this?"

"She's not right for you! She's dangerous and...and..."

He rubbed his eyes then went to the register, his voice cold and under control.

"Rho, I think you should, um, you should take that Rock-Jock back to his place. I've got his keys. Credit card info. I'll set up an Uber for you to come back."

"Zeke!"

"I'll give campus security a call. Ask 'em where he lives."

Rhonda glared at him. "You think I'm lying to you. You think I'm just jealous of that bitch when any idiot could see she's dangerous and out to hurt you when I never would and — "

Zeke almost exploded. "Jesus, Christ, Rhonda! What the fuck?!"

And there is was. She could see it clear, now. He was rejecting her. Backing away from her. Refusing to believe her when she only wanted the best for him.

She was losing, again.

And this time from a guy with only one leg. How dare he refuse to see the truth? How dare he push her away when she was only trying to protect him? Of all the goddamned nerve.

"Take him home yourself, you stupid son-of-a-bitch."

Then she grabbed her purse and stormed out the door. Her bike roared to life, a moment later, and off she went.

Shit.

Well, Zeke told himself, *that took Rhonda out of the running for a replacement bartender.*

He leaned against the bar, shaken, unable to think. This was all too confusing. Too sudden and too much on top of everything else. Finally, he made himself read more of the online news. How the explosion had happened almost immediately after the funeral for Anastasia Deveaux. How the current Mrs. Deveaux was struck by shrapnel, but while she was not seriously injured, her ten-thousand dollar D&G mourning dress was *just ruined.* How the ex-Mrs. Deveaux wasn't there because she had been dropped off at home after the internment, the hint being she was too drunk to drive. How the mayor and governor and senators and speaker of the legislature and a hundred other politicians were chiming in on how awful it was a great man like Winston Deveaux had been assassinated. How they thought it was a grenade that had gone off and blown up the Maserati's gas tank. How Edward Smythe had just died of his injuries. All hushed and rushed and gushed over in *very shocked attitudes* that barely hid the anchors' gleefulness.

Zeke was at a loss. Carli couldn't have had anything to do with this. She was an ex-sniper, and they don't get down and dirty with bombs, when planning to kill someone. A clean shot from a thousand feet would be her method, not endanger dozens of other people.

And yet, he felt like he was really doing nothing more than trying to convince himself of this.

He needed to talk to her, now, now, now.

He grabbed his phone and had just hit her number when, of course, Loki's barking exploded and he noticed the thrum of Dax's bike pulling up.

And the man was laughing.

Shit.

Zeke killed the call, set his phone on the bar and started a pitcher of beer, his hands shaking. He could hold it together till he had a chance to get off alone and contact her.

A moment later, Dax and JJ burst in, jostling each other like a couple of college kids.

"Bar's closed," Dax howled, joyous. He was obviously flying on coke. "Private party! Everybody out!"

They finally noticed the place was already empty, except for the Rock-Jock, who didn't move. JJ exchanged a wary glance with Dax then calmly went over and nudged the guy, who just muttered.

"Shit," said JJ, "he's on planet nowhere. No driver's gonna take him in this condition."

"I want that little fuck outta here! We're havin' a party, tonight, so let Rhonda — wait, where'd Rhonda go?"

"Home," Zeke said as he set out the bottle of JD and a couple of glasses.

JJ noticed Zeke was distracted and headed behind to the bar. He smirked, purring, "Aw, Zekie, did she finally come on to you and you turn her down?"

Zeke tried to laugh as he said, "Something like that."

JJ slapped him on the shoulder. "No big deal, buddy. Women're idiots when it comes to men. Always thinking they can make us over or better or some kind of shit like that. Too bad they're such fun."

Dax chuckled. "That means you'll have to take him, Zeke."

Zeke looked at him, confused. "Take who?"

"That punk in the corner."

"Leave the bar?"

"We're closed! But first, join me in a drink. Lay 'em out. We're celebratin'."

"Dax, if I'm going to drive..."

"One's nowhere near the limit. C'mon!"

More on auto-pilot than anything, Zeke set out three glasses and poured JD into each one. Finally, he asked, "What? What's this about? What's the occasion?"

"Nailed two birds with one stone," Dax laughed.

Zeke felt like he'd been punched in the gut.

The bomb in Phoenix.

Deveaux killed.

And another man.

And Dax was here celebrating.

"What'd you do?" whispered from Zeke.

Dax smirked and chuckled, "To use Nat's way of speakin', we dealt justice to the motherfucker who killed our guys."

"Our *guys*? So Nat and Spit? It's true about them?"

"Shit, Zeke," JJ said, "it was all over the bar, last night."

"Nobody knew who they were."

"Then you should listen to the fuckin' news, now and then," Dax snapped. "But yeah. It's true." Then he took his JD and held it up. "So here's to revenge."

JJ toasted with him and both downed theirs. Dax noticed Zeke was still holding his, shaken.

"C'mon," he said. "Down with it."

Zeke looked at the glass then nodded and drank it.

Dax shook his head. "Didn't know you were so close to 'em."

Zeke could not believe he had said that. "They were friends. Guys I knew. Nat came to Loretta's a couple times, with me and Grady and..."

"Hmph. Sorry."

But he wasn't. Not really. It was obvious. He was giddy from setting off that bomb, and it wasn't right. Three men who'd worked for Dax for years had died, in the last few days, and it suddenly was like that was no big deal to him. He was more exuberant at killing two others, like he had no connection to the men who'd worked for him.

Like he didn't care.

Like Carli had said.

He'd turned off his connection to them like he had turned on

Zeke, twice, over Lara. Then acted like nothing had happened.

"Dax," Zeke said, "I'm...I'm gonna be leaving."

"Yeah," said Dax, "get that little shit out of here. Sooner gone; sooner back. Sooner we're all shitfaced." Then he yanked out a baggie of powder, grinning.

"That's not what I mean," Zeke said. "I'm heading on."

Dax finally noticed his distant tone. "Headin' on?"

"Yeah. It's time I moved on."

"Why?" Dax shot back.

"I want to. I'm not comfortable here and..."

"Why the fuck not? I took care of the problem."

Zeke rested his elbows against the bar and lay his head in his hands, his voice ragged. "Dax, don't tell me any more, please."

"What the fuck's wrong with you? I protected you, you little fuck. And me and JJ, and you're pullin' some shit like you wanna get away from me? Like I did some kind of shit to you?"

They heard a car drive up. Dax growled and snapped, "JJ, tell those motherfuckers we're closed. Little Zeke an' I got shit to discuss, here."

JJ glanced between them then headed to the door. The moment he opened it, he stopped and turned around, saying "Dax, it's Eldora."

"What the fuck?" he muttered and headed to the door to meet her. "I don't want that bitch here, now."

But before he could lock it, she pushed in, still in uniform, dust from the desert on her uniform.

"Gentlemen," she said, with a sickening sweetness. Her eyes focused on Zeke, very quickly aware of his distress, then held up a folder she had in hand as she continued with, "We have a small problem that needs to be addressed."

"Not now," Dax snarled. "I'm closin' the Cantina down for the night."

"Yes, now or never."

"Maybe I choose never."

Eldora tore her eyes away from Zeke to roll them then glare at Dax. "God, you're a stupid son-of-a-bitch."

Dax growled. "Watch what the fuck you're sayin'!"

"You proved it when you killed everything we had."

Dax sneered, turned and strolled down the bar, as cool as butter, saying, "Dunno what you're talkin' about."

"Oh, Dax," she sighed, "you're talkin' to Eldora. Me."

He shrugged. "Then tell me what the fuck you want."

"Zeke, a double, please," she said as she followed Dax. "JJ, have you ever done recon, before?"

JJ sent Dax a wicked grin. "Why would I need to?"

"Well...if you're plannin' an operation at a funeral home in the middle of a major city, it's usually a good idea to get the lay of the land, first."

The cool contempt in her voice made Dax lose his attitude. "I don't go to funeral homes," he snapped.

"Liar," she said. "There's security video showing you at one, stoppin' by Winston Deveaux's car, earlier today.

The man snarled, "What fuckin' camera? I looked around. There's nothin' outside."

Zeke shot a sharp glare at Dax.

Eldora noticed as she said, "Through a window in the office. As you walked past to pick up some brochures. Looking as innocent as a lamb. Granted, it wasn't a great view of you or who's with you." At which she cast a cool glance towards JJ. "But I recognize both your jackets. Can't you idiots even be smart enough to change clothes?"

Now Dax was wary. "You already seen this video?"

She laughed. "Every sheriff's office and police department in the continental United States has seen it, by now. They haven't worked out your name, yet, but it's only a matter of time before they do. Then they'll locate your military records and previous arrests." She gave an exaggerated sigh and shook her head. "Normally, I'd say Mexico's really nice, this time of year, but you are not gettin' across that border. This state's sealed tight."

"They can't prove it was me."

"Oh, Dax, Dax, Dax, they already know you used two grenades of a type that are a bit outdated for our modern forces. But which are still in use by Arizona's National Guard. For *training purposes*. In other words, old Army ordinance. They are now checkin' every armory in the state. You think they won't be able to track that back to you? Really? I'd say, by midnight."

That is when JJ jumped in with, "What about that crazy bitch you were saying killed Grady and Nat?"

Zeke was bringing Eldora her double whiskey when she said, "Nat was shot and bled to death. Bullet's from a long range rifle."

Zeke jolted to a halt.

Eldora noticed. She casually took her drink, deliberately ignoring him, and continued with, "And Spit's windpipe was crushed. You think a woman could do that? To two men? That *bitch* was logistics, remember? You know what that is."

JJ shrunk, a little. "Office work."

"You think the Army trained her as a Ranger then put her behind a desk? Really?" Eldora pulled out a DMV photo of Carli. Showed it to Dax. "Does she look like *Xena, Warrior Princess* to you?"

"Shit." Suddenly Dax was not so sure. He headed for his booth.

"Rhonda, bring the pitcher over."

Zeke picked the pitcher up. "She's not here."

"Where the fuck she go?"

Zeke howled. "I don't know! She left!"

All three of them jolted at his anger, but only Eldora made a real note of it.

"Okay, all right, already," said Dax. "Shit."

"Maybe she'll be back," said JJ, slipping into the booth.

"No. Keep her outta here! We need to think."

"'Bout time you started," Eldora turning back to him.

Dax settled at the booth, after JJ, Eldora across from him. Zeke brought over the pitcher and a bottle of JD. She noticed his hands were shaking as he set everything down. Before he could walk away, she slipped a finger through a belt loop.

"Not so fast, baby," she said. Then she showed him the DMV photo. "Got this, today. Fast for the DMV. Rhonda was in the office. Saw it. Said you might be involved with this lady. Is that so?"

Zeke barely glanced at the photo. "Who is she?" he asked.

Eldora eyed him, then carefully said, "The mother of that girl who was raped on that pool table." She cast a thumb over her shoulder. "She's in town settlin' a lawsuit against the university. She's been seen here."

"...Has she?"

Eldora rose and stood at her full height, looking down at him from just above eye level, saying, "Zeke, I like you. But do not mess with me, right now. Not a good idea. Do you know her?"

Before he could think of a response, his phone chimed with a text. He stiffened. Eldora saw it so kicked his bionic leg out from under him, making him topple to the floor, then strode over to the phone. On the screen was a message from *CarliV*...

ZEKE, GET OUT OF THERE. NOW.

Eldora frowned then calmly brought the phone over to Zeke. She squatted down to show him the text and said, "Ask her where she is."

"No," he said without hesitation.

"Why not?"

"She's got...she's got nothing to do with this."

Eldora sighed. "What makes you say that?" she asked in a soft voice.

"She's just here to finish up a lawsuit," he managed to say. "Against the university. Like you said. She came in, one night, and we just...we hit it off. That's all. She wasn't even in town till Thursday."

"She signed the papers, week ago, Friday."

Zeke hesitated, then shrugged. "Something about money coming through?"

Eldora smiled. "Ah, yes, it's always about money."

Dax shot furious glances between the phone and Zeke. "You sayin' you were fuckin' this bitch?" He jabbed a finger at Carli's photo.

Zeke glared at him. "Back off, Dax." Then he used the table to pull himself back onto his feet.

Eldora slowly rose, sighing, "It's no big deal, Dax. Everybody takes a liking to *Prince Hot Tatts*." And the way she purred his title was almost comical.

Zeke tried to laugh.

But Dax bolted up from the booth to get in Zeke's face, dark and angry. "Motherfuckin' son-of-a-bitch, you weren't just fuckin' her, you were helpin' her, weren't you?"

Zeke shot him a cold glare. "What the fuck's wrong with you? You think I'd help anybody hurt Grady?"

Eldora pushed between them, her business voice in top gear.

"Calm it down! Zeke's right. Whoever killed your boys, it was without his help!"

Dax glared at her like a hyena about to attack. "What the fuck do you know? I told you! She's the bitch who killed our guys! I told you from the start!"

JJ piped in with, "Dax, c'mon, we took care of the guys who did all that."

"Then why the fuck's he sneakin' around with this bitch?"

Zeke shoved him back onto the booth's bench. "'Cause I like her! You got a fuckin' problem with that?!"

"She's comin' after me!" Dax snarled, glaring at him. "An' you're helpin' her, after all I done for you?"

"I still got scars from what you did to me!"

Dax grabbed Zeke's shirt, furious. "You *were* helpin' her! She got you on her side! Against me! You tell me where the fuck she is!"

"Over here, asshole. Jesus."

Everyone jolted and spun around to find...

Carli at the back door, calm, cool, collected...and even more impressive? No visible weapon, though her fingers were caressing the knife hidden in her pants.

"Shit, Carli," Zeke gasped, "get out."

"And leave you to these bastards? I don't think so."

Eldora almost chuckled. "Vincenzo, I resent that implication."

Carli smiled and said, "It was deliberate." Then she wandered to the bar as she continued with, "But I'm kind of confused, Dax. You were claiming Deveaux was behind it all and you were flyin' high at killing him. So when did I get bumped up to prime suspect?"

"Is that what he said?" Eldora asked, her voice careful.

She casually released the strap on her pistol.

Carli noticed so let her hands rise. "As you can see, no gun. And if I had done something like that, would I come in here unarmed? Besides, I'm not dressed for a fight. I really like this shirt. All I want is a drink. Zeke, which one's the best whiskey?"

Zeke started for Carli, saying, "What're you..?"

But Dax gripped the back of his shirt, yanked his pistol out and jammed it to Zeke's neck, saying, "No, you stay here."

Zeke shifted from confusion to irritation. "Shit, Dax, don't go fuckin' crazy."

Carli smiled and asked, "Can he at least answer my question? I don't want to drink the crap you sell the students."

Zeke sighed. "Bottle of JD under the register. Unopened."

"Yes. Here we go," she said. She set out five glasses then opened the bottle. "Why don't you join me? More of a celebration, that way."

"What the fuck you pullin', bitch?" Dax snarled, then he spit at Eldora. "You gonna bust her or not?"

"Put your gun away, Dax," Eldora sighed. "You look silly."

"Yeah," Zeke snapped, "this is dumb."

"I'm tellin' you, she killed Grady, " Dax howled. "She killed Nat and Spit and even that bitch in LA, an' she's after me! And this little fuck — !"

Carli calmly said, "I didn't *kill* anybody," as she poured out the JD. And never mind she was thinking, *I just executed them.*

"You couldn't," Dax snarled. "Not without help. An' ol' Zeke here, he's stronger 'n he looks, an' he loves to pull his innocent shit."

"You are fucking crazy!" Zeke all but howled.

"Dax!" Carli snapped. Then she shifted a couple of glasses down the bar. "Share a little drinkie with me and I'll tell you everything I've done in the last week. Wait, when did Stasi die? Eight days ago, right? Okay, last eight days. Come on. I never drink alone."

Dax glared at her. "I ain't goin' anywhere near you."

Carli sighed. "Then let Zeke pass out the drinks."

"Fuck, no."

Eldora almost sighed then crossed to the bar. "I'll get mine. JJ, you pass out the rest."

"Huh?" was all JJ said.

Eldora put three of the glasses onto a tray then motioned to JJ to come and get them. She took a glass for herself and breathed in the aroma. "Shit, Zeke, this is better'n what you usually foist off on me."

"I pay you too fuckin' much to get the good stuff," Dax snarled at her. "Yours is the sixty/forty kind."

"Cheap-assed bastard," she replied, then took a sip. "Mmmm, I'm going to savor this."

JJ slipped over to the bar and took the tray back to Dax, then stopped to ask him, "How *you* gonna drink one?"

Dax huffed and shoved Zeke away, pistol still at the ready. He took one of the glasses and downed it, whole. Then he frowned. "Wait, Eldora, you had some of this, last night. When we were talkin'."

"Did I?" she asked.

JJ looked around at her. "Yeah, when we were in the booth, before that Brandy Alexander and after it. 'Cause you didn't like it with the nachos."

"That thing must've killed my taste buds," she cooed.

Then Dax blinked and swayed. He glared at Carli, snarling, "You put somethin' in it."

Carli smiled at him. "Did I?" She turned to Eldora. "Is anything in yours, sheriff?"

"No, mine's fine." She smiled at Dax. "Are you being paranoid, again? It's obvious you're flyin' on coke, so..."

Dax rubbed his face. "No. No, this is not — this is — " He staggered back then snarled, "You fuckin' bitch."

He shoved JJ aside.

The last two drinks flew everywhere.

He aimed for Carli but...

Zeke spun and grabbed his arm as...

Eldora cried, "No, Dax!"

Carli slipped the knife from behind her belt as...

The pistol fired!

The bullet tore into Zeke's chest. He cried out and dropped.

Carli screamed and slung her knife as...

Dax aimed at her.

It slammed into his left arm but he still shot at her, twice.

She dropped to hide behind the bar as...

Eldora pulled her pistol and...

Shot Dax square in the head.

He collapsed, his blood and brains staining the booth and...

"Holy shit!"

Eldora spun around.

The Rock-Jock was looking wide-eyed at the carnage...still drunk.

"Stay down," Eldora snarled at Carli, then she slipped over to him. "Hi, son, what's your name?"

He worked his mouth, for a moment, then whispered, "Barry. Barry Lohman."

"It's nice to meet you, son." Then she calmly used her pistol to knock him out before saying, "Okay, you can move, now."

Carli scrambled around the bar to kneel beside Zeke, saying,

"What was that about?"

"Don't want this boy to see you, any more than necessary. Makes things messy. JJ, where the fuck are you?"

Carli motioned to the back door. It was wide open, as was the door to the cooler, and they could hear a Hog starting up.

"I'd say good riddance," Eldora snarled, "but looks like he took somethin' with him that I'd like to have had, the greedy little fuck. "

She crouched beside Zeke. He was unconscious. Carli checked his wound then pulled out her phone and started to dial 911.

"Don't," Eldora snapped.

"He needs a doctor."

"Gunshot wounds have to be reported and investigated. That'll raise nine kinds of hell for us all, includin' Zeke. Tear open his shirt."

Carli did so without a moment's hesitation, saying, "Were you a medic?"

"No, but I've dealt with crap like this, and I know where one is." Eldora raised him, a little, and gently felt along his back. Her hand came away, stained red. "Straight through. Good. And this piddly bit of blood? I'd say it missed his lung and arteries. Get me ice."

Carli bolted behind the bar, grabbed a cloth and scooped ice into it. Then she brought it back, saying, "Slow the bleeding?"

Eldora took it, nodding, then scooped some of it onto Zeke's chest wound. "You in that truck?"

"Yes," Carli said.

"Loretta's has a doctor on call, and she's patched up worse hurts than this. Get some more bar cloths. Tie 'em in a line. We'll use 'em to hold the ice in place."

Carli got to work, but whispered, "Are you doing what I think you're doing?"

Eldora built two compresses of ice, using bar cloths, saying, "*You heard it all, right*? Dax knew Deveaux had Grady, Nat and Spit tortured and killed, hopin' it would scare him into confessin' he'd murdered his daughter. Stupid old man didn't realize how crazy Dax can be. Didn't think Dax would kill him, instead. Now they're all dead, and they can't say otherwise." She slipped one compress under Zeke and wrapped the cloths around his chest and over his shoulder to hold it in place. "JJ's disappearance helps. Okay, let's get sleepin' beauty into your truck."

"What about that one?" Carli asked, motioning to the rock jock.

"Nothin' to worry 'bout, there." Then Eldora cast Carli a cool glare. "So long as *we're* good."

Carli eyed her, wary, then said, "I sent a packet to the AG."

"Of course you did. But I can handle that bastard."

Carli almost smiled, then she slipped her hands under Zeke's arms and as Eldora grabbed his legs. They carried him to the back door, Carli said, "Tell me why you're doing this."

"Does it matter?"

"Does to me."

"Okay," Eldora murmured. "In my honest opinion what you did to Little Miss Deveaux was justice served."

"You helped her get away with it."

Eldora's voice shifted to a growl. "I contained it. Kept it from happenin', again. It was that idiot DA..."

Her voice trailed off, in anger.

Now they were outside. Loki was barking and whimpering as they ferried Zeke to the Dodge.

"In a minute, Loki," Carli said.

"They knew what they were doin'," Eldora said. "The ones you killed. They all deserved what they got."

They carefully laid Zeke in the passenger seat of the Dodge, then Carli lowered it as far back as it could go as she said, "Maybe that's why I didn't kill Mikey..."

"Don't tell me more," Eldora snapped. Then she checked Zeke's wound and carefully put the seatbelt across him as Carli released Loki's chain. The dog scrambled over to jump in and lie at his feet, his eyes on both women.

Eldora eyed him back, then said, "You *have* made inroads. Loki always put himself between me and Zeke."

Carli smirked. "He knows a predator when he sees one."

"Then how'd *you* get around him?" Eldora shot back.

Carli hesitated then had to say, "I fell in love."

Eldora nodded. almost sad. "Never hurts."

"It will if I don't keep him alive. That mutt'll tear me apart." She bolted into the trailer and came out with Zeke's guitar and M16. She tossed them in the back of the truck and covered everything with a tarp. "We'll get him another leg, later."

Eldora chuckled and offered her a slip of paper. "Here's the address. I'll give Loretta's a call."

"Thanks." She scrambled around to the driver's side, jumped in and started the Dodge, then plugged her phone into the truck's AC outlet and input the location. She looked at Eldora. "It says an hour and fifty-five minutes!"

"Do not speed," Eldora replied. "I'm sendin' out an *officer down* call, so State Police'll be everywhere, fast. Don't give 'em an excuse to stop you. He'll be all right."

"...You really like Zeke."

"Not as much as you do. And he sure does like you a hell of a lot more than he ever did me."

Carli hesitated then dug into her wallet. "Here," she said as she pulled out the card with Mikey's information on it. "Your consolation prize. He's pretty and about to be an ex-husband, only he fucks like a bunny rabbit."

Eldora took the card, chuckling. "Y'know, Vincenzo, his could be used as evidence against you."

Carli just looked at her.

The sheriff eyed her back, then cast a glance at the urn on the dashboard, then she slipped the card in her pants pocket. "You better get gone. That ice won't last forever."

Carli smiled, nodded...and she got.

Headed straight out The 14, away from town.

And she did the speed limit all the way to Loretta's.

Re-birthing and Lies Told About It

Sunlight peeked between curtains that were tightly drawn, just not quite tight enough. Bright beams shot into the room at a forty-five degree angle to bounce against a lime green chaise-lounge, reflecting the damn color straight into Zeke's face. He groaned and blinked and tried to roll away from it only to find that even the slightest movement sent the daggers from hell tearing into him. He actually cried out.

An instant later, Carli was between him and the sunbeam, its light giving her a soft halo of rather inappropriate green tints against a very dark background.

"How're you feeling?" she asked.

He let out a sigh of confusion and murmured, "Ache all over. Shit. What'd you do to me?"

Her tone of voice was wickedly fun as she asked, "Do you really want to know?"

That is when he noticed his chest was bandaged and blood stained everything, including the sheets. Bright, blue, cotton sheets. Thread count of twelve-hundred, felt like. And the bed was big and wide and so comfortable.

Then he saw Loki lying next to him, watching him, his judgmental expression on. "Don't look at me like that," he muttered. "You got balls, too, and I let you use 'em."

"Is that a fact?" Carli chuckled.

"Hmm?" He had almost forgotten she was there. He took in a deep breath and tried to shrug, but even that hurt. So he just sighed, "There's a breeder. Up in Phoenix I take him to. Every now and then. He gets his jollies; they get the puppies."

He looked around. The room was too dark to make much out, except he began to recognize bits here and there. The chandelier made of antlers wrapped with tiny white Christmas lights dimmed to barely illuminated. The deep dark drapes that hinted they were a royal blue, thanks to that sunbeam cutting past them. That ugly green chaise. And then it hit him.

"This is Candy's room," he said, trying to sit up, but not doing so well, thanks to his left side.

Carli gently shoved him back onto the bed. "Not so fast,

Superman. You have some healing to do, first."

His eyes were filled with questions, things not quite making sense to him, yet. She ran her hand through the close-cropped hair on his scalp, and over the scruff on his chin and said, "Dax shot you."

"Dax?" He began to remember and shivered. "Aw, he was gonna...was gonna..."

"Yeah," she nodded. "And got damn close to doing it before he was stopped."

"Stopped?"

Her expression told him everything he needed to know. Dax was dead. He looked away from her, not sure what he was feeling. Dax had been good to him, but that night, with Eldora and JJ and...

He looked back at Carli. "JJ?"

"Vanished," she finally said. "No idea where he went. I brought you here to be taken care of, They have an excellent GP. Wait, she refers to herself as a PCP. Personal care physician, not the chemical. Apparently, she's seen worse gunshots than yours and fixed them, as well. Who knew a house of ill-repute could be as well-equipped as an ER? Tells you just how fucked up our healthcare system is."

"You know about Loretta's."

"I'm not the sweet innocent child you think I am."

He snorted. "Never thought that."

"Yeah. Right. I know you've been here many a time. I feel like I should say something to let you feel I'm jealous, but Candy's so sweet, and she and I and her girlfriend had a lovely chat about *Prince Hot Tatts*."

"Oh, shit, that's not something a guy wants to hear."

"Don't worry. Nothing bad was exchanged."

Memories flooded in on him, and Carli could see his eyes growing troubled.

"Carli. They were saying you...Grady."

She put a finger to his lips. "We'll talk about it, later. Just know, Dax killed Deveaux and wanted to shift the blame for everything onto me. Including Stasi's death."

He nodded. "Dax was kind of weird the last week. Wait, what day is it?"

"Tuesday."

"Wow, and Loki been okay with you?"

"He knew we were helping you. And he has been a very well-pampered mutt."

To which Loki huffed.

"Now you rest," she continued. "Got plenty of time to heal."

"Yeah Head's splitting."

"Want something to sleep?"

"Don't need it. Gonna crash. So nice to just sleep."

She caressed his forehead. "Dream of mountains and trees and streams and water and snow in the winter and rain in the spring?"

He almost smiled at her. "Seattle?"

"If you're willing."

He looked at her for a long moment. Ran his hand up her arm. "Gotta be someplace. Still welcome?"

"My brother thinks you're beautiful."

He snorted. "Wait'll he sees me, up close."

"Then he'll just think you're gorgeous."

He snorted, his right hand rested on Loki's back, and he drifted into quiet slumber.

She caressed the smooth loveliness of the tattoos on his arm. Up his neck to his ear. Tickled at his hair and nearly wept. She could not understand it, but felt herself growing stronger merely by touching his gentle beauty. To watch him breathe in and out brought her own breath into synchronization with his as he drew softer and softer until he was quiet and innocent...and sure enough, almost sounded like he was purring.

Now, just to look at him caught her, complete.

What had been great about Loretta's was how all the girls loved Zeke and Loki, so took special care of him. The older doctor, who refused to give her name, was quick and thorough and kept him under to give him a jump on healing. Candy insisted on him being in her room, to wake.

"This way," she had said, "everything will be familiar."

Then she'd had a day bed set up near him, for Carli. It was all so automatic and filled with understanding, she didn't even begin to mind the girls slipping in, between clients, to check on him. Then they would sit and talk a little about him, always wistfully. Always kind. Always tender and loving. Knowing he was Carli's now.

He was hers.

And even Loki finally seemed to accept that.

Dear God, could she be any happier?

*****

A few days later, once Zeke had fully returned to the world of reality, he caught up on the news. Even though he never followed that crap.

The story was, Winston Deveaux had Edward Smythe kill Grady, Nat and Spit, all according to Eldora. It was in retaliation for Dax having Stasi killed, and was given an official stamp of approval by one and all. They hadn't worked out exactly who did what, how, and when, yet, but information discovered on Dax's computer setup, once they cracked the encryption, gave a strong hint that a former lover of Stasi's had been part of a drug cartel. She had ripped him off, too, so he had joined forces with Dax, worked out a way to get into the place and killed the little bitch. True, a couple of anomalies appeared on the mainframe, but the District Attorney now had everything too neatly wrapped up to care about any other outcome. Something Eldora had emphasized in one of her quiet conversations with him.

"Of course, you could wreck it all, quite easily," she had added. "But then you'd have to answer for allowing four rapists and drug dealers to exist under your jurisdiction."

"You were the one tasked with controlling that," he had snapped back.

To which Eldora had simply smiled and said, "I gave everything to you, including a rape kit you *managed to lose*. My ass is covered."

He had seen the light.

Apparently, so had the state's attorney general's office, since Eldora was seen to be above suspicion and remained as sheriff. Carli figured a little blackmail about them helping a member of the legislature protect his low-life daughter probably came into play. But whatever worked was fine.

Chase even helped advance Eldora's chosen narrative, because his story was actually being given the *good guy treatment*. He had *put himself in danger to work with her in eliminating drugs on campus after Lara's death!* The media loved it too much to do any real investigation of his actions, him being very good-looking and his lost ear being seen as proof positive of his trustworthiness. He was carried away to Hollywood to star in a quickie Disney movie about his life, and turned out to be a good actor.

Needless to say, Tulsa wound up on a permanent back burner.

JJ did vanish. Completely. With the duffel bag of money from the cooler. Probably because he had never gone by anything but JJ, so no one actually knew his full name. After six months of trying to figure out *who* he was, let alone where he was, law enforcement shrugged, said they had their killers wrapped up so it was no big deal and moved on to the next really, really serious situation.

The Cantina and trailer burned to the ground, that night, with Dax's body, inside. Eldora was hailed as a hero for pulling a college student named Barry Lohman out of the flames. Then he breathlessly told anyone and everyone about waking up to see Dax try to shoot her before she shot him. Granted, he was rather fuzzy with the details, since he'd still been very drunk, but he knew without question she had saved his life.

Reymon had arrived just as the trailer also caught fire, Rhonda with him. Both were horrified at what happened, and commiserated with each other over ribs at a Chili's in Tucson.

They were now considered a couple.

When anyone asked what happened to Zeke, Eldora shrugged them off by saying he had argued with Dax and then taken off with some woman from Nevada. She suggested they check with one of the male strip shows to see if he'd turned up, there. To her expressed chagrin, no one took her seriously.

He and Carli stayed at Loretta's for ten days. Loki grew to love being petted and pampered by all the girls, even those he'd been unsure of, before. Of course, they had to move to a side room that wasn't as expensive. Much as everyone loved Zeke, Loretta had a business to run. But they were sharing a bed, he got a new leg measured, he was playing his guitar, and his heartbreaking grin never seemed to leave his face, showing everyone how happy he was.

Which was all that mattered to Carli.

Of course, it didn't hurt he had nearly fifty-thousand dollars stashed in a bank from his tips over the years. With Carli's part of the settlement money, after lawyers' fees and TF's repayment, life was good. Soon they'd be heading on, and she would not let anything happen that might change that.

So as she watched the doctor patch Zeke up, that night at Loretta's, Carli swore to herself that she would never tell him the truth about what happened. Because she loved him with a passion that scared her. The wind could stop, the sea grow still and the world whisper into nothingness...but so long as he was next to her, she knew she could face it all.

Which made absolutely no sense, but there it was.

Oh, she wouldn't *lie* about any of it; she'd just let him keep believing what had become the most acceptable story. Further details were superfluous. Because there was no question in her mind, if he knew she had killed Grady, he would back away from her.

Cut her from his life.

Leave her.

And that would destroy her.

But she was adult enough to understand that some secrets were best kept to yourself. Shared with no one. Accepted as yours alone. And some lies were meant to be taken to the grave.

Granted, that was not an easy burden for anyone to bear. But if she could have Zeke till her end of days, she could handle it.

THE END

About the author

Kyle Michel Sullivan is a writer and self-involved artist out to change the world until it changes him, as has already happened in far too many ways.

He has written books ranging from sunshine and light (*David Martin*) to cold and dark (*How To Rape A Straight Guy*, which has actually been banned a couple of times) to flat out crazy (*The Lyons' Den*) to mainstream romantic-comedy (*The Alice '65*). He has ventured into SF-Horror-Suspense with *The Beast in the Nothing Room* and taken Capitalism to its logical extreme in *Hunter*. He has also worked up an adult coloring book, *Demented Dreams (of guys in trouble)*.

He tries to build characters as vivid and real as possible, and has a lot of fun doing it mixed with angst, anger, and amazement ... but that's the lot of a writer.

His paperbacks and hardcovers are available through Amazon, B&N and for order through any independent book shop. Ebook copies are through Smashwords.com.

Links to everything are at http://kmscb.com

Other books by this author

<u>General:</u>
The Alice '65
The Vanishing of Owen Taylor
David Martin
The Lyons' Den
Bobby Carapisi

<u>Adult MM erotic novels:</u>
Hunter
The Beast in the Nothing Room
Underground Guy
Rape in Holding Cell 6
How to Rape a Straight Guy

<u>Adult MM erotic coloring book:</u>
Demented Dreams (of guys in trouble)

<u>Out of Print:</u>
NYPD Blues

www.ingramcontent.com/pod-product-compliance
Lightning Source LLC
Chambersburg PA
CBHW070343200726
48294CB00003B/765